"Another great

—*Urban Fantasy Investigations*

"An incredible read from start to finish."

—*A Book Obsession*

"An action-packed, sometimes-emotional roller coaster with a well-developed world and truly engaging characters."

—*The Qwillery*

BLACK NIGHT

"The Madeline Black series employs a blend of two great common urban fantasy tropes . . . [and] creates a chemistry that adds new zest to familiar concepts, an energy that I thoroughly enjoy." —*All Things Urban Fantasy*

"Madeline Black is back and super badass in her second installment . . . If you're looking for a brilliant urban fantasy with page-turning action, witty dialogue and fun characters—this is your book." —*Rex Robot Reviews*

"Playful and light, yet also adventurous and dark . . . The bottom line is that if you enjoy adventure stories, you will enjoy this book, especially if you're a nonstop-action junky." —*SFRevu*

BLACK WINGS

"A fun, fast ride through the gritty streets of Chicago, *Black Wings* has it all: a gutsy heroine just coming into her power, badass bad guys, a sexy supernatural love interest and a scrappy gargoyle sidekick. Highly recommended."

—Nancy Holzner, author of *Darklands*

"An entertaining urban fantasy starring an intriguing heroine . . . The soul-eater-serial-killer mystery adds to an engaging Chicago joyride as courageous Madeline fears this unknown adversary but goes after the lethal beast."

—*Midwest Book Review*

"Fast action, plenty of demons and a hint of mystery surrounding the afterlife make for an entertaining urban fantasy populated by an assortment of interesting characters."

—*Monsters and Critics*

"Henry shows that she is up to the challenge of debuting in a crowded genre. The extensive background of her imaginative world is well integrated with the action-packed plot, and the satisfying conclusion leaves the reader primed for the next installment."

—*Publishers Weekly*

"Readers will enjoy a fast-paced adventure with an interesting cast, especially Beezle, the gargoyle, and be ready and waiting for a future still yet unwritten. Pick up your copy of *Black Wings* today, and stay tuned for *Black Night*."

—*Romance Reviews Today*

"A fast-paced first novel . . . *Black Wings* is a lot of fun."

—*Fresh Fiction*

"Henry does an excellent job of unveiling the first layers of her unique world and its fascinating inhabitants. There's plenty of kick-butt action and intriguing twists to ensure that this story grabs you from the very first page. One to watch!" —*RT Book Reviews* (4 stars)

"The story was a nonstop action blast full of smart-alecky gargoyle guardians, devilishly handsome (and enigmatic) love interests, arrogant demons, wicked witches and more jaw-dropping revelations than a Jerry Springer show. I barely had time to catch my breath between chapters."

—*All Things Urban Fantasy*

"Fast-paced, action-packed and hard-core—breathing new life into the vast genre of urban fantasy . . . *Black Wings* is intense, dark and full of surprises." —*Rex Robot Reviews*

"Amazing . . . Henry's pacing is incredible and keeps you absorbed, plus the characterization is fantastic . . . I strongly urge all you [urban fantasy] fans to get this book!"

—*Read All Over Reviews*

"I recommend Christina Henry to readers who enjoy the dark humor of Ilona Andrews's Kate Daniels series and the demon politics of Stacia Kane's Megan Chase series."

—*Fantasy Literature*

Ace Books by Christina Henry

BLACK WINGS
BLACK NIGHT
BLACK HOWL
BLACK LAMENT

BLACK LAMENT

CHRISTINA HENRY

ACE BOOKS, NEW YORK

THE BERKLEY PUBLISHING GROUP
Published by the Penguin Group
Penguin Group (USA) Inc.
375 Hudson Street, New York, New York 10014, USA
Penguin Group (Canada), 90 Eglinton Avenue East, Suite 700, Toronto, Ontario M4P 2Y3, Canada (a division of Pearson Penguin Canada Inc.) • Penguin Books Ltd., 80 Strand, London WC2R 0RL, England • Penguin Group Ireland, 25 St. Stephen's Green, Dublin 2, Ireland (a division of Penguin Books Ltd.) • Penguin Group (Australia), 250 Camberwell Road, Camberwell, Victoria 3124, Australia (a division of Pearson Australia Group Pty. Ltd.) • Penguin Books India Pvt. Ltd., 11 Community Centre, Panchsheel Park, New Delhi—110 017, India • Penguin Group (NZ), 67 Apollo Drive, Rosedale, Auckland 0632, New Zealand (a division of Pearson New Zealand Ltd.) • Penguin Books (South Africa) (Pty.) Ltd., 24 Sturdee Avenue, Rosebank, Johannesburg 2196, South Africa

Penguin Books Ltd., Registered Offices: 80 Strand, London WC2R 0RL, England

BLACK LAMENT

An Ace Book / published by arrangement with the author

PUBLISHING HISTORY
Ace mass-market edition / November 2012

Cover art by Kris Keller.

ISBN: 978-0-425-25657-2

ACE
Ace Books are published by The Berkley Publishing Group,
a division of Penguin Group (USA) Inc.,
375 Hudson Street, New York, New York 10014.
ACE and the "A" design are trademarks of Penguin Group (USA) Inc.

PRINTED IN THE UNITED STATES OF AMERICA

10 9 8 7 6 5 4 3 2 1

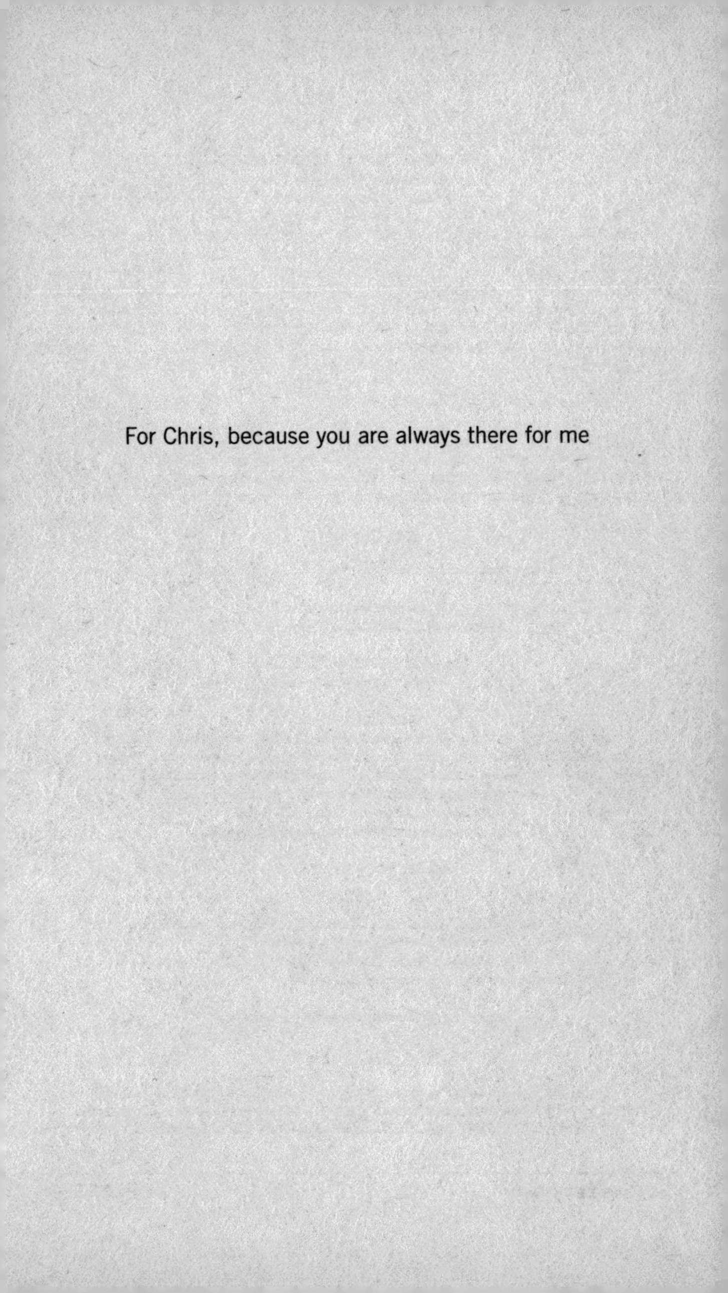

For Chris, because you are always there for me

ACKNOWLEDGMENTS

As always, much thanks is due to my gracious and ever-patient editor, Danielle Stockley, who makes my books better than they would be without her.

Thanks to my awesome and incredibly hardworking publicity team, Brady McReynolds and Rosanne Romanello.

So many thanks to my emotional support team—Sarah, Faith, Anne and Pam—for always listening when I need it.

Much gratitude to the hardworking Einstein Bros. crew—Cynthia, BJ, Pedro, Jessie, Michael and everyone else—who let me drink their coffee all day and make my bagels just the way I like them.

Special thanks to Krista McNamara for all that you do for me and Maddy, and to Chloe Neill for assorted kindnesses.

Thanks to Nancy Holzner for her always-wise counsel.

Thanks to all the awesome authors who let me sit up onstage

with them at panels this year, especially Chloe Neill, Laurell K. Hamilton, Patricia Briggs, Anton Strout, Edward Lazellari, Rachel Caine and Kim Harrison.

Love to Mom and Dad.

As always, all the love in the world to Chris and Henry.

1

LUCIFER PUT HIS ARM AROUND ME. IT FELT COMFORTing, like the act of a parent, a parent I'd always wanted—a father. The air filled with the scent of cinnamon. It reminded me so strongly of Gabriel that the tears that always hovered beneath the surface spilled over.

Lucifer said nothing, only held me as I wept. After a long while, it felt like there were no more tears to be cried. I lifted my head and saw Lucifer watching me with great compassion in his eyes.

"If there is one human emotion I truly comprehend, it is grief," Lucifer said. "I lost Evangeline and my children so long ago, and I never stopped grieving for them."

"So it doesn't stop hurting, then," I said dully.

"The pain becomes, perhaps, not quite so sharp. In the future, you may find that days may pass when you do not think of him at all, but when you do there will be a tenderness there, like a bruise that has never healed."

I didn't need Lucifer to tell me that. A piece of me had been taken forever when Gabriel died. You can't replace the missing parts of your heart.

Lucifer released me. I felt lost again, empty, except for the flame that burned bright with anger at the thought of Azazel. He would not be able to run far enough.

"Still, all is not lost. Gabriel lives on inside you," Lucifer said.

"Yes, I've heard all the clichés." I sighed. Beezle and Samiel had been repeating them ad nauseam.

"No, I mean Gabriel really does live on inside you," Lucifer said. "Here."

He put his hand on my abdomen, and I looked up in shock.

Far below, deep inside, I felt it.

The beating of tiny wings.

A child. Gabriel's child. Wonder smothered the grief, just for a moment.

"My grandchild," Lucifer said.

There was such possessiveness in his voice, in his face, that I pulled away from his touch, covering my stomach with my hands.

"So that's why you wanted me to marry Gabriel," I said angrily. "So I can be a part of your supernatural breeding program?"

"That sounds so . . . indelicate," Lucifer said.

"And yet still true," I said.

Lucifer didn't bother to acknowledge this. Instead, he said, "You and Gabriel are powerful beings born of my line. Your child, no doubt, will be magnificent."

"You can't have him," I said fiercely. "He's mine."

Mine and Gabriel's.

Lucifer took me by the shoulders and kissed me on the forehead. I stayed perfectly still, my hands fisted at my sides, until he released me.

"Careful, my dear. Every time you try to cross me you just get pulled further into my orbit."

He climbed down the steps of my front porch and walked away down the snow-covered sidewalk. I watched him until he was out of sight, his words echoing inside my head.

Every time you try to cross me you just get pulled further into my orbit.

It was true that I hadn't managed to beat Lucifer at his game yet. It was also true that when I tried, something horrible would happen, like my being named the Hound of the Hunt.

But I was not going to let Lucifer use my child as part of his plan for total world domination. I was not going to let Lucifer take my last piece of Gabriel away.

Gabriel.

I felt my shoulders sagging, the familiar weariness settling on me. I wanted to go to sleep, which was pretty much all I'd wanted to do since Azazel had killed Gabriel right in front of me.

I went back inside, locked the front door and climbed the steps up to my apartment. Beezle and Samiel were nowhere to be seen, which meant that they were probably in Samiel's apartment downstairs watching a movie.

I took off the coat that Lucifer had given me. For half a second I contemplated folding it up and tossing it in the trash, but practicality won. Both of my coats had been ruined in various battles with monsters, and I was too broke to afford a new one. On my best day I couldn't have bought a coat as nice as this.

I hung the coat up carefully by the back door and

wandered down the hall to the kitchen. The idea of a nap suddenly had less appeal. I didn't want to climb in bed and find myself lying awake thinking about Gabriel or about ways to keep Lucifer from taking my baby.

My baby.

How was I supposed to raise a baby? I was surrounded by enemies who tried to kill me on a regular basis. The only reason I was still alive and hadn't died of my injuries yet was because Gabriel had been around to heal me.

And now he wasn't. And I was back to where I'd started, the place I was always trying to escape but found that I circled back to, endlessly.

Azazel's sword in Gabriel's chest. Gabriel falling to the ground.

I was on my knees, my arms wrapped around my body, trying to stop the pain that never left me, the grief that hung over me like a cloud.

I put my cheek on the cold tile floor and closed my eyes, hoping I would not dream of Gabriel's blood in the snow.

I woke to the insistent tapping of a little gargoyle hand on my cheek.

"Maddy, wake up," Beezle said.

My eyes felt glued shut. My chest hurt, like I'd run a long way taking gasping breaths of air.

I didn't open my eyes or sit up. "Go away, Beezle."

"You need to eat something," Beezle said.

"It won't hurt me to lose a few pounds," I mumbled.

"No, but it will hurt your baby."

I opened my eyes. It was dark in the kitchen. Light streamed in the back window from the streetlamp in the alley behind my building. Beezle sat frowning on the floor in front of my face.

"How do you know about the baby?" I asked. My voice sounded rusty and unused.

"Gargoyles can see the true nature of things," he said gently. "I've known since the morning after your wedding night."

"Why didn't you say anything?" I said, sitting up slowly. I was tired right into my bones.

Beezle shrugged. "You had enough on your plate. Besides, I figured you'd find out soon enough from . . ."

He trailed off.

"Gabriel," I finished. "Yes, I suppose he would have known."

It was hard to know how to feel about that. Gabriel had probably figured out immediately that I was pregnant, just as Lucifer had. But he hadn't told me.

"Will all the fallen know as soon as they see me?" I asked.

Beezle shook his head. "They can sense children of their own line. Lucifer, especially, is sensitive to the presence of children of his blood. Evangeline would never have been able to disguise Lucifer's children from him without Michael's help."

Evangeline, my crazy ancestor who'd started everything by falling in love with Lucifer millennia ago. She'd been kidnapped by Lucifer's enemies while pregnant with his children. The archangel Michael had found Evangeline and convinced her that he could keep the twins safe from her lover's enemies. Michael had covered Lucifer's presence so thoroughly that the Morningstar never found the children of Evangeline, or the descendants of those children. Until he found me, daughter of Katherine Black, last direct descendant of Evangeline's line.

He had other offspring, of course. I didn't know how many. Two of his sons had been insane monsters, and they'd both tried to kill me. I wasn't in a big hurry to meet any more of Lucifer's progeny.

"Wouldn't Azazel have known I was pregnant?" I asked. "I am of his line, too."

"If he knew, it would only have made him angrier than he already was about your marriage," Beezle said. "He was never happy with your inability to fall in line."

"I wasn't very interested in being a good little soldier for a father who never acted like one," I snapped.

"And you don't need to get angry with me about it," Beezle said mildly. "I'm on your side."

I rubbed my forehead in the place where a headache was starting to form. "I'm sorry, Beezle. I just . . . I don't know what to do."

"About what?"

"About anything," I said. "I just want to go to sleep and never wake up. I don't want to face the day. I don't want to get up in the morning knowing that Gabriel's not here."

I was crying again. I couldn't seem to stop.

"And the baby?" Beezle looked very grave.

"There is a part of me that's happy," I said, wiping my face. "A small part. But the bigger part of me is scared, because I know that if I live long enough to deliver this child, he will have a target on his back for the rest of his life. Every enemy that Lucifer has will be after this baby."

When I thought about it that way, my future looked overwhelming. Was I ever to have a normal relationship with this child, or would I always be on the run, always fending off new threats?

"You've got to secure a future for the baby now," Beezle said. "You can't wait until the demons are at your door. You have to find a way to make sure he is protected."

I stared at him. "Are you suggesting what I think you're suggesting?"

"Make a pact with Lucifer," he said. "Now, while you can still dictate your own terms."

"I can't believe you're telling me this," I said. "You know that I don't want to be another one of Lucifer's pawns. Besides, he wants the baby for himself. I can't trust him."

"No, you can't trust him," Beezle said. "But if you wait until you have no other option for the child's safety, then Lucifer will make you pay more dearly than you can imagine."

"Did you have to tell me this today?" I said tiredly. "Don't I have enough to worry about already?"

"Your problems won't go away just because you want to put a pillow over your head and pretend they're not there," Beezle said.

"You don't have to tell me that," I said grimly. "My problems never seem to go away no matter what I do. They just grow and multiply like gremlins."

We both sat in silence for a few moments, contemplating the sad truth of this statement. Every time I attempted to extricate myself from the fallen, I found that I'd gained more enemies and more entanglements than I had before.

Subtlety is not my best thing. Politics requires a delicate hand. Those qualities are stock-in-trade for the fallen. I'm more of a hack-and-slash-and-then-burn-it-all-to-the-ground kind of girl.

I pushed to my feet, and Beezle fluttered up to the kitchen counter. I stood there for a moment, feeling lost.

"Food," Beezle reminded me.

"Yes, food," I said.

I opened the refrigerator door and looked in. There was absolutely nothing in it—not even a jar of mayonnaise.

"When was the last time I went shopping?" I wondered.

"The day that you and Gabriel followed Amarantha's ghost to the park," Beezle said.

"Well, that was . . . a while ago," I said, trying to count backward and failing. "I guess I have to go to the store."

"And I'll come with you," Beezle said.

"Okay," I mumbled.

"What? No protest? No smart remark about my being a home guardian?" Beezle asked.

"You can come if you want," I said tiredly. I couldn't think of any smart remarks. I just wanted to get through this task so that I could eat something and go back to sleep.

I shuffled down the hall, pulled on my boots and coat, stuffed some cash in my pocket.

"Are you coming?" I asked, turning to Beezle.

He hovered in the hallway, watching me with an indefinable expression on his face.

"You can't wander around in a fog like this forever," he said.

"I know," I said softly.

I did know. Sooner or later, the world would come knocking at my door. Sooner or later, some enemy would appear, some new threat would manifest, and I'd have to wake the hell up and deal with it. But not now. Not yet.

"Let's go," I said.

Beezle landed on my shoulder, and we went out the door without another word.

Beezle took advantage of my total lack of energy and convinced me that we needed a lot of junk food that neither one of us should be eating. I was too tired to argue so I just bought whatever he pointed at, paid for it and trudged home.

I had my head down, watching my boots pushing through the snow, and wasn't thinking of anything in particular except more sleep.

We were almost to the front porch when Beezle tapped me on the shoulder.

"Maddy," he said. His voice was urgent.

I looked up. There was a figure standing in the shadows on the front porch. Someone tall, wearing an overcoat . . .

"Gabriel?" I said, my heart thundering in my chest.

"No," the person said, and stepped into the light.

It was Nathaniel.

"You," I snarled.

I dropped the grocery bags in the snow and charged up the steps. Nathaniel put his arms up in the air, stepped backward, but he was too slow and I was too angry.

I put my shoulder into his stomach, heard his hard exhalation as the breath went out of him. I tackled him down to the porch, kneeling with my legs on either side of his chest, and punched him in the face.

"You," I repeated. All I could see was Nathaniel's face under a haze of red.

I felt him struggle, try to push me off, but his arms were locked tight against the side of his body. He should have been able to move me. He was an angel, and I was only a half-blood. But I had a strength I'd never had before, a strength fueled by rage and betrayal.

My hands closed around his throat, squeezing tight. I pushed at the fragile accordion of his trachea, wanting to crush it to a pulp, wanting to kill him once and for all.

"Maddy!" Beezle shouted, but his voice sounded far away.

"Maddy, you're going to kill him!"

"Yes," I whispered, and when I looked at Nathaniel's purpling face I saw Azazel's malicious grin as he pushed his sword into Gabriel's heart.

Nathaniel bucked hard, trying to throw me off again, his eyes wide and desperate.

Another pair of hands covered mine, peeled my fingers off Nathaniel's throat with unnatural strength.

"No!" I said, clawing at Nathaniel's neck, drawing blood, trying to renew my grip.

Those same arms surrounded me, pulled me from Nathaniel, carried me backward as I kicked and screamed like a madwoman.

"Samiel, no!" I shouted. "Put me down! Let me be!"

I felt Samiel shaking his head behind me. His arms tightened. Beezle fluttered in front of me. Nathaniel coughed, gasping for air.

"Maddy, you have to calm down," Beezle said.

"I will *not* calm down!" I screamed. "I want him dead!"

"He didn't kill Gabriel," Beezle said. "He's not Azazel."

"No," I spat. "He's Azazel's lackey. He sold people's memories to vampires. He sold *children's* memories. He knew Azazel was planning to rebel against Lucifer. And he tried to kill me the last time we saw him; do you remember?"

"He's a cockroach, I agree. But if you kill him like this, you'll never forgive yourself," he said.

"I've killed plenty before," I said bitterly.

Ramuell. Baraqiel. Amarantha.

"To defend yourself, or someone else," Beezle said. "Not like this. You're not a cold-blooded murderer."

I thought of Azazel again, and said, "Yes, I am."

I could—I *would*—kill Azazel without a shred of pity or remorse.

Nathaniel got to his feet, rubbing his throat. The sight of him made me furious all over again.

"You'd better run," I said, struggling against Samiel's grip. "Because when I get down I'm going to finish what I started."

"I will not run," he said. "I came to speak with you."

"I'm not sure this is the best time," Beezle said to Nathaniel. "She seems a little . . . unreasonable right now."

"Don't talk about me like I'm not here," I said. "I'm not a child."

"Then cease behaving like one," Nathaniel said.

I narrowed my eyes at him. "You're not doing yourself any favors here, pal. What did you come here for?"

"I told you, to speak with you."

His calm demeanor was making me angrier, which hardly seemed possible. There was a well of rage inside me that I had barely tapped. I'd been so foggy with grief that I'd forgotten how furious I was until I saw Nathaniel.

"How can you stand there like that, arrogant as ever? How can you stand there and pretend that you've done nothing wrong?" I said.

"Because I have spoken with Lord Lucifer and atoned."

I froze, blank with shock. "You . . . what? You spoke to Lucifer and he didn't strike you down on the spot? You participated in Azazel's rebellion!"

"I had no other choice," Nathaniel said icily. "Azazel was my master, the lord of my court. I must do as I am bid."

"That's a really convenient load of bullshit," I said. "You had choices. You could have chosen to go to Lucifer when you had foreknowledge of the rebellion. You could have saved the lives of the people that were killed before you sucked their memories from them. You could have done a hundred things differently and in the end you chose to do exactly what you were told even if you knew that it was wrong."

"If I had defied Azazel, I would have paid for it with my life," Nathaniel said. His voice had an undercurrent of anger.

"So you chose your own worthless skin over the lives of innocents," I said, letting my contempt show on my face.

"Regardless of my past actions—" he began.

"Your past actions are very relevant," I said.

"Will you allow me to complete a sentence?" Nathaniel said angrily.

I'd finally cracked his icy façade. Yay for me.

"No," I spat. "You deserve no courtesy from me."

"Last time you saw her you did call her 'hell's own bitch,'" Beezle pointed out.

"Lord Lucifer has heard my plea and accepted me as a part of his court," Nathaniel said.

"What you mean is that Azazel's plan didn't go the way he intended, and he abandoned you, so you were forced to crawl to someone else," I said.

"You have never respected me," Nathaniel said, his eyes sparking furiously in the light from the streetlamps.

"No, I haven't," I said. "I don't see why I should have to."

"You were my betrothed."

"Do not bring up that farce of an engagement again," I said through my teeth.

"It was not a farce to *me*," he said. "When Azazel told me that you had married the thrall . . ."

He looked lost suddenly, vulnerable in a way that I had never seen him before. But his reference to my husband as "the thrall" set me off again.

"That's why I could never respect you. Because you cleave to this ridiculous notion that you were better than Gabriel."

"I was," Nathaniel said. "You were the only one who could not comprehend what an insult it was for you to marry one such as him."

I thought I'd reached maximum rage, but apparently I was wrong.

"Get off my porch. Leave this city and never come back."

"That will be extremely difficult," Nathaniel said, icicles dripping from every word, "as Lord Lucifer has bid me protect you as my penance."

"No," I said, pushing at Samiel's arms so he would release me. "No."

Samiel tightened his grip, and I turned to look up at him. He cocked his head, asking me with eyes, *Can I trust you?*

"I won't attack him," I said. "I promise."

Samiel looked like he wasn't sure.

"I won't," I said again, and he let me go.

I marched up to Nathaniel, who took a half step back. Good. He'd better be afraid of me.

"Now, hear this," I said softly. "I don't care what Lucifer says. I will never submit to this."

"Lord Lucifer has said that I am to protect you," Nathaniel said tightly. "That, I will do."

"And the first time your life might be threatened you'll run away with your tail between your legs. I can take care of myself, and that ought to be abundantly clear by now," I said with a pointed glance at his still-bruised throat. Angels heal fast, so I must have really damaged him for the marks to still show.

"You cannot refuse Lord Lucifer," Nathaniel said, and there was a touch of desperation in his voice.

I had a feeling a lot was riding on his ability to get me to cooperate. Too bad.

"Watch me," I said, and walked into the house.

2

"MADELINE!" NATHANIEL CRIED.

I slammed the foyer door behind me and unlocked the door to my apartment. Beezle and Samiel hadn't followed me in. I wondered what they were doing.

I wondered what Lucifer had planned now.

I hung up my coat, took off my boots and realized I'd left the groceries out in the snow. A second later Samiel and Beezle came in. Samiel carried the grocery bags into the kitchen, patting me on the shoulder as he went by.

I looked at Beezle. "What's Lucifer up to?"

Beezle shrugged. "It is not for me to comprehend the ways of the Morningstar."

"He had to know that I wouldn't accept Nathaniel," I said. "Why send him here?"

"Lucifer has to be thinking of the child," Beezle said. "He wants the baby protected."

I looked at Beezle incredulously. "And you think that Lucifer thought *Nathaniel* was the best choice to protect a child he will no doubt despise because of its parentage?"

Beezle shook his head slowly as the smells of something cooking came from the kitchen. Samiel was getting pretty good at turning a small amount of ingredients into something delicious.

"No. I think that Lucifer presented an unappealing option that he knows you'll refuse out of hand so that he can then send you the person that he really wants here."

I nodded. It made sense. It was exactly the way Lucifer operated.

"And his leniency toward Nathaniel is no doubt dependent on Nathaniel's ability to get me to cooperate," I said.

"Which is why Nathaniel is still on the porch," Beezle said. "He said he'll sleep there if he has to."

I thought about calling the cops to remove him, but Nathaniel would just return over and over again until he got what he wanted. I didn't believe that he cared about me one whit. I knew for sure that he cared about keeping all his body parts in their proper places, and that meant that he would go to any lengths to please Lucifer.

Fine. He could stay on the porch if he wanted. I hoped he froze to death.

"Maybe you should think about accepting Nathaniel," Beezle said thoughtfully.

I stared at him. "That's the second insane thing you've told me to do tonight. First I'm to make a pact with Lucifer; now I'm supposed to accept Nathaniel?"

"Think about it," Beezle said urgently. "You'd have leverage with Nathaniel. You could use him to find out what Lucifer is up to. Plus, you'd definitely throw the Morningstar for a loop if you accept a bodyguard he was certain you'd reject."

"Nathaniel is a killer," I said heatedly.

"So are you."

"I didn't kill innocents. And I don't try to justify anything I did saying I was under orders from someone else."

"Nathaniel can't help that," Beezle said, shaking his head. "It's something you never understood about Gabriel either. You've never submitted to anyone's authority in your life—not your mother, not me, not your Agency supervisors, not your teachers at school. You were born contrary."

"You say that like it's a bad thing. I'm an independent thinker."

"Or, depending on one's perspective, you're a stubborn mule, but that's not the point. The point is that you've never understood why angels don't contradict their master, why they follow orders that would seem unreasonable to you. It's because they've had respect for the hierarchy drilled into them from birth. They've been taught to be unquestioning, to do what they're told even if it's something a human would consider morally wrong."

"So they've been brainwashed?" I said skeptically.

Beezle sighed. "No. Think of them as soldiers in an army. A soldier might doubt the validity of a commander's order, but that soldier would still do as his commander said. Because that's the way he's made. That's the way he's been taught to behave, because an army is not made up of one person. Its strength comes from the sum of its parts."

"So all the angels are taught to do as they're told because it's so important for each court to preserve its base of power."

"Yes," Beezle replied. "It's also why rebellion is never initiated from the bottom. Most of the lower hierarchy could never conceive of going against Lucifer. But Azazel and Focalor are both Grigori. They have their own courts. They are used to answering only to Lucifer, and in recent years it seems he has given them more leeway."

"But why?" I asked. "You told me once that Lucifer would do anything to maintain his base of power. And Gabriel once said that he thought Lucifer had enough power to have dominion over all things."

"I'm pretty sure he does," Beezle replied.

"Then why loosen his grip?" I wondered.

"To see what would happen," Beezle said. "To see who is truly loyal to him."

I scowled. I really disliked the idea that Lucifer would allow a rebellion to fester just so he could watch the game play out. I was also disturbed by the idea that Nathaniel might not be entirely at fault for his part in the memory-selling enterprise. He wasn't completely blameless, not by a long shot, but it seemed it would have been difficult for Nathaniel to refuse Azazel.

He had tried to kill me in Azazel's court. But he had also helped us save Wade's cubs.

I shook my head. I didn't know what to do about Nathaniel right now. It seemed too complicated to sort out what was right and what was wrong, and that worried me. Those shades of gray were Lucifer's provenance.

Samiel came into the dining room carrying a tray full of food. He set three bowls on the table.

"Yum, chili!" Beezle said, diving toward his portion.

"Use a spoon," I said before he went headfirst into the bowl. "You're not a pig at the trough."

Beezle muttered crossly to himself, but he perched on the edge of the bowl with a spoon held in his fist. He scooped chili into his beak with the rapidity and care of a toddler just beginning to use utensils. Food dribbled from his mouth to his stomach.

Don't look at him, Samiel signed. *You'll lose your appetite.*

I try not to look at him generally, I replied.

Samiel went back into the kitchen and returned with a plate of corn bread and three glasses of milk. He indicated I should sit down across from him, looking inordinately pleased with himself.

"This looks great," I said.

I wondered where he had found all the ingredients in my very bare kitchen. I was pretty certain I hadn't bought all of this stuff with Beezle, so I asked Samiel.

I had most of the stuff downstairs, he signed, pausing between bites.

His bowl was almost empty already, and I'd had only a small taste. Samiel eats like a teenage boy who's not sure where his next meal is going to come from.

"But where did you get the money for the groceries?" I wondered aloud.

Lucifer gave it to me.

I raised my eyebrow at that.

He knows that I don't work, and he was worried about you because he knows you depend on the rent from the apartment.

"Yeah, I'll just bet he was worried," I muttered into my chili so that Samiel couldn't read my lips.

Everywhere I looked Lucifer was there, entangling me in his spider's web. I knew Samiel was loyal to me, but I also knew that Lucifer was very good at making simple things look confusing.

If Samiel continued to accept an allowance from Lucifer, then one day in the future the Morningstar might come to Samiel asking for a favor. And Samiel might think that one little favor was small repayment to the angel who had given him so much. Then Lucifer would ask for one more thing, and another, and another, until Samiel was well and truly trapped.

"Aren't you eating?" Beezle asked, breaking my reverie.

I glanced over at him and wished I hadn't. He was covered in chili from horn to claw and was presently stuffing corn bread in his beak. The bread crumbs sprayed everywhere as he chewed. I covered my eyes.

"I don't know why, but I seem to have lost my appetite," I said loudly.

"More for me," Beezle said gleefully.

Samiel pried my hands from my face so I could look at him.

You have to eat, he signed.

Do you know about the baby, too?

He nodded, looking rueful. *Beezle told me.*

Listen, Samiel, I signed. *Do you want to work?*

He looked uncertain. *Yes, but Lucifer said I wouldn't be able to get a regular job, because I can't hide my wings like you can.*

"It's nice that he's thought of everything," I mumbled to myself, then looked at Samiel and spoke. "You could work at the Agency. There are a lot of supernatural creatures working for us that aren't Agents."

But I thought you didn't get paid?

"*I* don't. Agents don't because collecting souls is a 'sacred duty,' " I said, making air quotes with my fingers. "But the support staff and the management collect regular paychecks. Don't ask me where the Agency gets its funding from, though. That's apparently need-to-know only."

Do you really think I could work there? Samiel looked doubtful.

"Sure. I'll talk to J.B. about it." As I said this, it occurred to me that I hadn't picked up any souls for a couple of days, and I wondered if I had been neglecting my sacred duty while wandering around in a depressed fog.

"Before you start panicking," Beezle said, reading my thoughts, "you should know that J.B. called a few days ago and said he was reassigning all of your pickups for the next week."

"Do you think you could actually deliver my messages in a timely manner?" I said. "Or, better yet, don't pick up the phone *at all* and let the answering machine fulfill the purpose for which it was created."

"What?" Beezle said. "You're getting the message now."

"That's not the point," I began, and trailed off. The snake tattoo on my right palm tingled. I stood up. I'd learned not to ignore Lucifer's mark.

What's wrong? Samiel signed.

"Danger approaching. Stay in the house," I said to Beezle.

I yanked on my boots, grabbed my sword and pounded downstairs in just my jeans and sweater. Samiel followed.

I threw open the door at the bottom of the stairs. Through the glass of the outer door I saw Nathaniel silhouetted in the light of the streetlamp. I stepped out on the porch beside him, Lucifer's sword in my right hand.

He appeared alert and wary. Samiel stood on my other side, his hands fisted.

"There's something wrong," I said.

"I sense it as well," Nathaniel replied.

There was no movement on the street. I wasn't sure of the time since the winter dark came so early, but it seemed like most people were inside and buttoned up for the night.

That was good. It diminished the possibility of collateral damage.

I smelled woodsmoke and the faint traces of car exhaust. The cold air bit into my skin. My hand grasped the sword tighter.

It suddenly seemed as if the night had gone blacker, like the stars were extinguished. I gasped for breath through air that felt thick and heavy as tar. The night was smothering me, suffocating me. All around us the lights in my neighbors' houses winked out, as if the normal humans felt the presence of this creeping darkness and wanted to avoid drawing its attention.

I staggered, struggling for breath, and Nathaniel caught my shoulders, holding me upright.

"Gods above and below," he whispered, and in his voice was a mixture of awe and fear. "It's a Grimm."

"A what?" I said, trying to find air in the omnipresent blackness. I shrugged out of his hold, standing as tall as I could with the air pressing down on me.

"A creature of Faerie. No one has seen a Grimm for hundreds of years. I thought they were legends."

Faerie? I thought, and then the tentacle came flying out of the cloak of darkness. It wrapped around Samiel's ankle. He grunted as he fell to the ground, clawing at the porch. The creature yanked hard at its prey as I cried, "Samiel!"

I dropped the sword and dove for his hands. The tips of his fingers brushed mine. I saw his panicked face, and then he disappeared into the night.

"No!" I cried.

Nathaniel pulled me roughly to my feet, pressing the sword in my hand.

"Do not let go of your weapon," he hissed. "Do you want to live?"

"Samiel," I said. I couldn't lose Samiel, too.

"Focus," Nathaniel said. "If you want Samiel back, you must defeat this creature."

If Samiel's still alive, I thought. He could be dead already.

The night seemed to be watching us, taking our measure. Nathaniel was right. I couldn't afford to fall apart now. Nathaniel murmured something beside me, and a glowing ball of orange flame appeared. He threw it into the darkness, where it was swallowed whole. Nothing was illuminated by the course of the flame. The creature did not seem to have been harmed in any way. Nathaniel's spell had been smothered by the dark.

I held the sword in front of me, my heart thundering. The tension stretched out unbearably as the night closed in around us. Nothing happened. My palms were slippery on the hilt of the sword, and cold sweat trickled in the small of my back.

I was afraid. No, I wasn't afraid. I was terrified. It seemed like all my childhood fears of the dark, fears I had long forgotten, returned to me in a paralyzing rush.

I remembered lying in my bed, small and afraid, desperately needing to use the bathroom but being unable to move, unable to throw off the covers and walk down the hall because once I left the safety of my bed the Bad Man would be able to get me, and he waited just outside my door.

The Bad Man was a composite of horror-movie killers and urban legend maniacs whose escapades I'd overheard from other students at school. His face was burned. He walked with a limp. His left hand had been replaced by a hook that he used to catch you, snag you so that he could slice open your belly with the knife he held in his right hand.

I was always sure he waited for me, that I could hear the harsh anticipation in his breath, the thump-drag of his limping walk that preceded his arrival. I would lie in the darkness, eyes wide-open, weeping in silent terror, too scared to run to the bathroom because if I went into that hallway, I would die.

"Madeline," Nathaniel whispered, and he put his hand on my shoulder.

I swung the sword at him without thinking, locked in the memory I'd long since buried. Only his preternatural speed kept him from losing his head, but I managed to nick him just below his left ear. I stared, panting with terror, as the blood welled and dripped onto the porch.

I noticed then that it was not completely dark, that I could see Nathaniel. I could see the blood that ran over his neck. It was as if he were lit faintly from within, and he was surrounded by a gently glowing halo of light.

I looked at my own hand. No halo, but I could barely make out the shape of my fingers in the light he cast. Must be a pureblood-angel thing. My own lineage was far too muddied by humans for me to have a halo.

"Madeline," he repeated, stepping close to me. I automatically took a half step backward, the way I always did when he crowded into my space.

"The Grimm is a creature that thrives on fear," he said in a low and urgent voice. "You must not give it any fuel. The more terrified you become, the more you open yourself to its power."

I realized that while I was contemplating the mysteries of Nathaniel's internal light, the pressing, suffocating fear had receded. Now that I was conscious of it again, it roared back.

My hands trembled. My heart pounded. I struggled through the fear that choked me.

"Can we fight it?" I asked Nathaniel.

"I do not know if we can fight it in the traditional sense."

His face was white and strained. I wondered briefly what Nathaniel feared, what bogeyman stalked his sleep.

"It took Samiel. I saw its arm."

"An arm that may not exist anymore. The Grimm is nebulous, formless. It is fear that gives it shape."

"Are you telling me that a marshmallow man is going to come stomping down the street?"

Nathaniel frowned at me. "I do not understand."

"Of course you don't."

Again it seemed that while we spoke, the fear had rolled back. I took a firmer grip on my sword and went down the steps.

"Madeline, where are you going?" Nathaniel hissed.

"Nothing's going to happen if we stand on the porch wringing our hands," I said.

I could feel the dark blanketing me, trying to squeeze. I raised the sword in front of me with two hands and called out.

"I am *not* afraid of you. Give Samiel back and return to wherever you came from."

Sweat dripped into my eyes and I swiped at it with my sleeve. It seemed the blackness all around became more complete, more smothering.

"I am not afraid of you," I repeated, and I didn't know if I was trying to convince the monster or myself.

LIAR.

The voice came from everywhere and nowhere. It seemed like it was inside my ears, inside my blood and brain, permeating to the very heart of me, the small, secret place where my primal self was hidden.

And then I heard it.

Thump-drag. Thump-drag.

He loomed out of the dark, the Bad Man of my nightmares. I was paralyzed for a moment, and he slashed at me with his butcher's blade. I stumbled backward at the last moment, the tip of the knife just catching the collar of my sweater, skimming over flesh and drawing blood.

"Madeline!" Nathaniel cried. I heard him coming down the steps, coming to help me.

NO, said the darkness.

A tentacle flew out of the shadows again and seized Nathaniel. I heard his cry of rage, but I couldn't focus on him. I could see only the Bad Man coming for me. He swung out his hook, trying to snag me with one hand while slashing with the other. His burned face was set in a contorted grimace of delight, his small blue eyes cruel under the hood of ruined flesh.

I swiped at his legs with the sword but he leapt aside with surprising agility for a man with a limp. I stumbled backward, caught my heel on the edge of the steps and fell to the ground. My sword flew from my hand.

He was on me in an instant, his knife coming for my throat. I caught his wrists as he fell on top of me, the stink of his blood-scented breath making me gag. He was strong, much stronger than an ordinary human, but so was I. The angelic blood that ran inside me made me just a little stronger, a littler faster. I held him off me, though I was blinded by tears, certain the fate I had always feared as a child had come for me.

For a second, for just the tiniest moment, I thought, *If he kills me, I can be with Gabriel.* At that thought, the child that was so small inside of me that it was barely a speck of light beat its little wings in distress.

And suddenly my fear was gone. It wasn't bravado for the Grimm, but the true disappearance of terror.

"No," I said, and fire ignited in my blood.

The place where I held the Bad Man's wrists smoked. His eyes widened, uncertain. Then he screamed in pain as I pushed magic through my hands and into his skin.

He fell off me, rolling onto the sidewalk, his body lit from within by fire. Smoke poured in a dark cloud as he howled.

I stood on legs that trembled no more and faced the dark.

"I am not afraid of you."

The night seemed to pause, to take my measure one last time. Then it released me.

ANOTHER TIME, AGENT.

And the cloak of darkness suddenly lifted.

3

NATHANIEL AND SAMIEL TUMBLED OUT OF THE SHADows, almost as if they had been thrown by gigantic tentacles.

"Samiel. Thank the Morningstar," I said, rushing to him. I patted him all over, looking for injuries.

He shook his head, signed, *Nothing hurt but my pride.*

"What did it do to you?" I asked.

"Simply held us immobile so that we could not assist you," Nathaniel said. He seemed to be gathering the ragged remains of his dignity around him. It probably stung his pride to be dispatched so easily, and so soon after he'd declared he would protect me.

The regular sights and sounds of nighttime seeped back in. I heard cars driving too fast on Addison, the hydraulic lift and lower of a bus pulling to the curb, the jangle of a dog on a leash farther down the block.

I looked at the smoking husk of the Bad Man in alarm.

"We've got to move that thing before somebody sees. I don't even want to think about what J.B. will say if he intercepts a nine-one-one call about another dead body on my property."

I'll do it, Samiel signed. He lifted the body by its shoulders, wrinkling his nose.

"I know. It smells horrible," I said apologetically. My own nose was kind of overloaded with the stench and had reached a state of shock.

He looked at me questioningly and I understood what he was asking.

"The shed?" I said helplessly.

"Kind of an obvious place to hide a body," Beezle said, flying down to my shoulder.

"I see you've cleaned up since dinner," I replied. "Last time, we put the body in the basement and covered it with a tarp and you didn't approve of that, either."

"One of these days J.B. isn't going to intercept a call in time and the cops are going to come sniffing around here," Beezle said.

"You act like I'm a serial killer trying to hide evidence of my crimes. May I remind you that these monsters that show up at the door are trying to kill me and that I am just defending my life?"

"And is that what you plan on telling the nice detective before he drags you off to the sanitarium?"

"You've been watching too many old movies. Besides, do you really think that Lucifer is going to let me get captured by the human authorities?"

"Then why so concerned about the body?" Beezle asked.

"Can't we just try to act normal for the sake of the neighbors? I already get enough weird looks as it is."

"Perhaps the two of you would stop bickering long enough to address the problem at hand," Nathaniel said loudly.

I gave him a bland stare. "This *is* how we address problems around here, angel-boy."

He visibly bristled at the "angel-boy," but his voice was clipped and controlled when he spoke.

"Then why is it neither of you have bothered to ask why the Grimm was here, and why it appeared to be targeting Madeline?"

"You said it's a creature of Faerie, right? So I'll just ask J.B. what he knows," I said, shrugging.

"Duh," Beezle added.

"And since I get targeted by something new and freaky every other day, it's hardly notable." I sighed. It was really sad that the appearance of a creature that had apparently not been seen for hundreds of years was just another footnote in my life.

"Are you going to call J.B. now?" Beezle asked as Samiel rejoined us.

"I don't think it's a good idea to wake him up. He's grumpy when he's tired," I said.

I wasn't sure of the exact time, since I'd fallen asleep on the kitchen floor and woken up in the darkness, but the city had that settling-down feeling. It seemed most people were either in bed or behind locked doors for the night. Anyone who was still out at this time was either young, stupid or dangerous. I felt a trace of uneasiness, but put it down to the lingering effects of the Grimm's influence. The tattoo on my right palm gave me a nudge, like the comforting touch of a dog's muzzle.

I was abruptly aware of the deep cold and the fact that I was underdressed, as usual.

"Let's go in," I said.

Samiel and Beezle headed for the door. Nathaniel looked at me with a raised eyebrow.

I blew out a breath. I still had to deal with Nathaniel.

Samiel stopped at the top step and turned back to look at me expectantly.

"It's all right; you guys go ahead," I said, waving them inside.

Beezle landed on Samiel's shoulder. "Get me inside before my wings fall off."

"Let's stand in the foyer," I said to Nathaniel. "I'm cold."

Samiel and Beezle disappeared into Samiel's apartment. Nathaniel silently followed me into the small space between the outer door and the two inner apartment doors, which he could enter only because I'd invited him to do so.

A small safety light burned over the mailboxes built into the wall. In its glare I could see the dark circles under Nathaniel's eyes, the blond stubble on his cheeks. The ends of his hair looked choppy, and his white button-down shirt, normally pristine, was actually dirty. All in all, he looked uncharacteristically raggedy.

But I guess that's what happens when you help foment a rebellion against your highest lord. I imagined Nathaniel hadn't had much time for manicures or trips to the dry cleaner's while he was groveling to Lucifer.

"Listen," I said to him without preamble. "You can't stay here. You can't sleep on the porch like a homeless person."

"Lord Lucifer has charged me—" Nathaniel began, but I cut him off.

"Do we really have to have this conversation all over again?" I said, annoyed. "I *know* what Lucifer told you to do. *I'm* telling you that I don't need a freaking bodyguard."

"With all of the attacks you say you have suffered, would not it be wise to at least have someone around who can assist you?"

"No offense, but I can think of half a dozen people I'd

rather have back me up," I said frankly. "You haven't exactly demonstrated your strength in a crisis situation."

Nathaniel drew himself up haughtily. "I will have you know that Azazel considered me one of his finest warriors."

"You got captured by Amarantha's guardians in her forest. And you fell under the influence of her spell."

"I hardly think that should be held against me. She cast a spell on the whole party," Nathaniel said angrily.

"Which did not have any effect on me," I pointed out.

"Yes, well, no one seems to be certain why you were immune, so I would not brag about it."

"You were also captured by the Grimm."

"As was Samiel," he said.

"And every time you and I have fought, *I* have won," I continued relentlessly. "When you tried to rape me in Amarantha's castle. When you tried to kill me in Azazel's ballroom. It seems more likely that I would end up protecting you from the Big Bad Wolf than the other way around."

"This is why you have always had contempt for me? Because you are stronger, more competent than I?" Nathaniel asked. "If so, then you should lower your standards. I have never known any creature to match you in strength of will save Lord Lucifer himself. You are so much more his child than Azazel's."

That gave me pause for a moment, but I couldn't contemplate my and Lucifer's shared traits just now.

"Nathaniel," I began. "I have had contempt for you, yes. It's an ugly trait, and I'm not thrilled to admit it. But I have felt that way, and it has nothing to do with your strength or weakness."

"Then why?"

"Because you valued appearance and status above everything else. Because from the moment we met you treated me like a trophy you'd been awarded without having done anything to earn it. Because I believe that you would not choose to do the right thing unless it was also the most useful to your purpose. I believe you value yourself above anything else."

Nathaniel's face had gone bloodless during my litany.

"And these are not the traits of a husband—is that it?" he said through his teeth. "These were not the traits of your precious thrall."

"Don't call him that," I spat. "And Gabriel doesn't come into this."

"Yes, he does. His shadow has stood between us from the very first, and now his shade will linger there forevermore. How can I compete with a ghost?" he said bitterly.

I looked at him uncertainly. "The way you're talking, it's almost like you wanted me as something other than a prize."

"You never gave me a chance," he said. "How could I prove that I wanted to be a better man?"

"*Do* you want that?"

"Does it matter?"

It kind of did matter, because I was starting to wonder if I had horribly misjudged him. And if I had, I had lost the chance to gain at the very least an ally. The Morningstar knows I needed as many allies as I could get.

And yet . . . Beezle and J.B. had warned me before that I was too trusting. Nathaniel might legitimately want to be my friend. Or he might see me as the clearest path to fulfilling some agenda of his own. This was a time when a little of Lucifer's foresight would come in handy.

"Did Lucifer strike a deal with you?" I asked. "Did he promise you something in exchange for acting as my bodyguard?"

"He said he would allow me to live," Nathaniel said. "Although Lord Lucifer understands that I only acted as instructed by the lord of my court, rebellion is still a serious matter."

"I'm surprised he gave you as much leniency as he did," I said.

"As was I," Nathaniel replied. "I asked for mercy, but I did not expect to receive it."

"Why didn't you go to ground like Azazel?" I asked.

"I will not live my life like a hunted animal. Either I would die honorably by the sword before Lucifer's court or I would benefit from his mercy. I would not run."

There was a kind of strength in that, a nobility I hadn't expected from Nathaniel.

"But if you fail in protecting me, Lucifer will kill you," I said. I was very uncomfortable with the idea that Nathaniel's life was dependent upon my benevolence.

"I truly believe that Lucifer expects I will die in defense of you," Nathaniel said.

"You seem awfully calm about it," I said, searching his face for any sign of fear.

He shrugged, and the gesture seemed so out of character for him that I smiled. The smile faded when he spoke again.

"It is not such a bad thing to die in battle. Perhaps I could regain some of the honor I lost. Perhaps you would then think better of me."

I felt that the longer he spoke, the more confused I became. It was easier to think of his actions as black-and-white, to think of Nathaniel as the enemy. I didn't want to credit him with humanity.

We stood in the little foyer, staring at each other. And then I jumped about six feet in the air when someone knocked on the outside door. It was J.B., standing on the other side of the glass with a grim expression on his face.

I opened the door, scowling. "Give me a heart attack, why don't you?"

"What's he doing here?" J.B. asked, jerking his thumb at Nathaniel.

I looked at my raggedy ex-fiancé and sighed. "It's complicated."

"It always is," J.B. said. "Can I have a word?"

"Come on up," I said. "Nathaniel . . ."

"I will remain outside," he said.

He and J.B. slipped past each other in the doorway. I swear I could see their hackles rising as they passed.

I silently led J.B. upstairs and waved him into the apartment, closing the door behind us.

"I'm assuming you're here because of the body," I said.

"What body?" he asked sharply.

"Um, never mind," I said, backpedaling.

"Black . . ." he said menacingly.

"Oh, fine," I said, and explained about the Grimm's attack.

J.B. listened intently until I was finished "Well, I guess I'm a little late in warning you."

"Warning me about what?" I asked warily.

"The blood price on your head."

I rubbed my forehead. "Whoever wants to kill me now had just better take a number."

"Certain factions of my kingdom are demanding your life in exchange for killing the queen."

It took me a second to remember what J.B. meant by "kingdom." It was hard for me to recall sometimes that he was now king of Amarantha's court.

"How can there be factions demanding anything?" I

asked. "I thought they all fled when Lucifer punished Amarantha."

"Now that the stigma of a monstrous ruler has been lifted, the court has returned."

"So none of them would openly support Amarantha while she was disfigured and lived, but now that she's dead they're demanding vengeance?" I said skeptically.

"Don't ask me to explain how faeries think," J.B. said. "At any rate, there are some very vocal groups asking me to take action."

"And one of them sent the Grimm."

"Very likely."

"Can't you keep control over the court?" I said, thinking of what Beezle had told me earlier about the rigid caste system in the fallen courts. "Don't faeries love order?"

"They also love playing politics. I have not had many opportunities to establish authority and gather allies. The Agency management is pressuring me to clean up the mess from the memory-stealing incident."

I realized then how tired J.B. looked, and how thin. "You're getting it from all sides, aren't you? You shouldn't be here worrying about threats against my life. I'm small potatoes."

"Like I would stand by and let some discontented faeries take a swipe at you? You should think better of me."

"I didn't mean that," I said, irritated now. "I just meant that I can take care of myself. You don't have to worry about me."

"But I do," he said, brooding.

"Faerie magic can't take me down," I said lightly. "At least, it hasn't managed to yet."

"You haven't seen the worst the faeries have to offer," J.B. said.

"What can be worse than the Grimm? The Maze? Giant spiders and tentacled monsters?" I asked.

"There's worse."

"Oh." I tried not to imagine what might be worse than what I'd already faced. I had enough trouble sleeping as it was.

"At any rate, I'm doing my best to ferret out the fractious individuals. Until I find them, watch your back. Do you want me to arrange for protection?"

It wouldn't do me any good to feel irritated that yet another male in my life seemed to think I needed a human shield to get through the day. I knew J.B. was asking because he cared, not because he had a secret agenda.

"I'm cool," I said. "I can always call Jude for backup if I need it."

"What's Nathaniel doing here? Weren't we trying to get rid of him?"

I explained about Lucifer's deal with my former betrothed.

"I don't like it," J.B. said. "He could be double-dealing again. Who's to say he's not a plant from Azazel come to stab you in the back when the time is right?"

"I don't disagree," I said. "I'm not sure I can trust him, which is why I'm not officially accepting him yet. But I don't think I can send him back to Lucifer knowing the Morningstar will kill him for failing."

"You seemed perfectly happy to stab him to death a week or so ago in Azazel's court," J.B. said.

It annoyed me that J.B. was presenting the same argument I'd given Beezle only a short time before.

"That was different," I said crossly. "He was the enemy then."

"And now he's not?" J.B. pressed.

"I don't know!" I said angrily. "Call it the privilege of a pregnant woman. My hormones are confusing me . . ."

I trailed off, because J.B.'s face had gone white.

"I forgot that you didn't know," I said in small voice.

"When did you find out?" he asked, sounding strained.

"Today," I said. "Lucifer told me."

"He must be thrilled," J.B. said flatly.

"Oh, believe me, he is," I said grimly, thinking of the possessive look on Lucifer's face.

"And you?" he asked carefully.

"I . . . I don't know," I said honestly. "It's a little piece of Gabriel inside me, and part of me is thrilled to have that."

"But?"

"But once my pregnancy becomes widely known, the target on my back is going to get even bigger."

"Does Nathaniel know?" J.B. asked.

"I don't think so. I'm sure he would have acted like I had an infectious disease if he knew I was carrying the 'thrall's' baby."

"Don't tell him until you have to," J.B. advised. "It might push him over the edge."

"Yeah."

We looked at each other.

"We're a pair, aren't we?" J.B. said. "Things would have been a lot easier if you'd fallen in love with me instead."

"I don't know about that," I said sadly. "Your baggage is about as heavy as mine."

"Well," he said, clearing his throat. "Be careful."

"And you," I said.

He left without another word, and I was left alone, as always.

* * *

I tried to sleep, but was dogged by nightmares of blanketing darkness and monsters worse than anything I'd imagined before. At dawn I gave up the pretense and stumbled into the kitchen to find Beezle eating Nutella from the jar with a spoon.

"You look like garbage," he observed.

"Don't speak," I said shortly, feeling my way toward the coffeemaker.

"No coffee for you," he said with way too much cheer in his voice. "You might harm the little biscuit."

Right. Pregnant women aren't supposed to drink coffee. I slumped over with my head on the counter. "Can I have anything that makes life worth living?"

"Herbal tea," Beezle said.

"I said something that makes life worth living."

"Sorry," he replied, and he didn't sound sorry at all.

"Where's Samiel?" I asked.

Beezle rolled his eyes. "Entertaining Chloe."

"Entertaining . . . Chloe?" I asked.

"You heard me right, so there's no need to stand there blinking those big brown eyes at me," Beezle said.

"Chloe who works at the Agency?" I asked.

"Do we know any other Chloe?"

"How long has this been going on?" I wondered how this could be happening right under my nose.

Beezle shrugged. "She's been sniffing around here pretty much since the first time she saw him at the Agency."

"How could I have missed this?"

"Easily, since you've spent most of the last week in a depressive funk."

"My *husband* died," I said. "How else am I supposed to behave?"

"I'm not saying you shouldn't mourn him," Beezle said hastily. "But you can't lay around the house in a daze anymore, especially not if the faeries have put a blood price on your head."

"Been listening at windows again?" I said nastily.

"You don't have time to cover your head with a pillow."

"I'll thank you not to tell me how to deal with my own grief," I said, storming out of the kitchen and into the bathroom.

I turned on the water for the shower, fuming. It didn't matter that part of me knew Beezle was right. I didn't want to be told that my behavior was unacceptable, that it wasn't okay to feel so sad, so sick with loss that I couldn't get out of bed. Because if losing your first and only love wasn't justification for that, then what was?

By the time I'd gotten out of the shower, I'd cooled down. I'd also realized a few things.

One, Beezle was right. (I'd never tell him, though.)

Two, I needed to do something about Nathaniel before Lucifer popped by for a family visit and made the decision for me.

Three, my husband's killer was still out there and I'd done nothing about it.

I got dressed, combed my hair and wound it into a braid. My face was white and my eyes were rimmed with dark circles. I looked about as sickly as Nathaniel did.

I made a quick phone call to Jude, then marched out of the bedroom loaded for bear. Beezle was nowhere to be seen, which meant that either Samiel was done "entertaining" Chloe and he'd fled downstairs, or the gargoyle was hiding from me so that he wouldn't have to deal with my wrath. I shoved a granola bar in my mouth and hoped it would suffice for breakfast.

The fancy coat Lucifer had given me hung by the front door. I pulled it on, collected my sword, keys and cell phone and headed downstairs. I peeked through the outside door.

Nathaniel was asleep on the front porch. His back rested against the railing, his eyes were closed and his very long legs stuck out in front of him. His breath rose and fell in an even rhythm. He looked wiped out, and I had to remind myself not to feel sorry for him. Whatever condition he was in now was his own fault. And I still wasn't sure I could trust him.

I stepped out the front door and kicked him in the ankle to wake him. His eyes opened immediately and he came swiftly to his feet without a sound.

"Some bodyguard," I said.

He looked chagrined. "I . . . I have not been sleeping well, or often, of late. I assure you this is not a regular habit."

I gave him an assessing look. "I'm going to Azazel's court to see if I can find any clues about where he might have gone and what he's up to now. You can come with me, and if you don't annoy me, I'll let you stay here so that Lucifer doesn't kill you."

"Madeline . . ." he began.

"But you are *not* my bodyguard. Number one, I don't need one. Number two, you'll probably just get in my way. And you're not sleeping in my apartment."

"Shall I remain on the porch, then?" he asked coolly.

"No," I said, thinking fast. "You can sleep in the basement."

The basement wasn't in the best of shape, but it was finished and there was an old sofa with a pullout bed down there. It got a little cold in the winter, but since Nathaniel had spent the night on my porch in January in Chicago, he could probably deal with a little chill.

"The basement is quite far from you in the event you need me," Nathaniel said tentatively. It was a little unnerving to see that expression on his face.

"You'll be close enough," I said. Too close, actually, if Nathaniel wanted to sneak up on me in the middle of the night and slit my throat.

He hesitated for a moment, as if he were considering arguing some more, but I'm sure he realized he wasn't going to get a better offer from me.

"Very well. I look forward to proving my worth to you," he said, some of his old arrogance returning. "How shall we travel to L . . . Azazel's mansion?"

I pretended not to notice that he'd nearly said "Lord Azazel." I imagined some habits were very difficult to break.

"Portal is fastest, but I don't want to arrive inside the property."

He nodded. "That is wise. Even if Azazel has abandoned his home, there may yet be soldiers loyal to him that were left behind."

"I don't know why you would bother staying loyal to someone who would ditch you, but whatever. Can you get us close to the house without putting us directly in it?"

"There is a little-used road that runs along the front of Azazel's property," he said slowly. "The disadvantage of arriving there is that we will be easily seen by anyone looking out the front of the mansion."

"Yeah, but that will be a problem no matter which direction we approach from. The house is surrounded by open lawn. There's no tree cover close to the mansion," I said, picturing Azazel's estate in my head. "The road is probably the closest we can get without actually being on the property."

"The portal will be less conspicuous if we leave from your backyard," Nathaniel said.

"I'm not sure I should even bother trying to be inconspicuous at this point," I said, but I followed Nathaniel into the back.

"Hold on a sec," I said, crossing to the small shed that I used to store gardening supplies.

It was one of those home-supply-store do-it-yourself jobs, and several Chicago winters had taken their toll on it. The doors didn't quite shut all the way, and the metal sides and roof were dented and rusted. I yanked one of the doors open and gagged at the smell that billowed out.

I covered my nose with my sleeve and peeked inside. The corpse of the Bad Man was propped in the corner. It was decomposing far too rapidly for the frigid temperatures. Chunks of burned flesh and skin had already fallen off bone, and it seemed as though the body had shrunk.

"You may not have to worry about disposing of the corpse," Nathaniel said. "It will likely be completely gone by tomorrow."

I shut the door. "Let's just hope the police don't show up in the meantime. J.B.'s got enough to deal with already."

4

NATHANIEL RAISED AN EYEBROW AT ME.

"Don't worry about it," I said. "It's an Agency thing."

He conjured a portal in the center of the yard. Litter from the alley behind us skittered across the ground and into the swirling tunnel. The branches of trees bent toward the portal.

"My lady," Nathaniel said, indicating I should enter.

"Uh-uh," I said, shaking my head. "While I'd normally be thrilled at this demonstration of respect for my skills, I think *you* can go first."

"You believe I would deliberately send you into harm," Nathaniel said flatly.

I just looked at him, my arms crossed.

"Someday you will realize you can trust me," he said angrily, and stepped into the portal.

"That day is not today," I muttered, and followed him. I

hoped there wasn't an assassin waiting for me on the other side.

My head felt like it might collapse under the pressure of traveling through the portal. This kind of travel was a lot harder on me than it was on Nathaniel. The strain of mortality in me made negotiating the supernatural world several degrees more difficult than it was for all the immortals that hung around.

I tumbled out the opening, expecting to fall flat on my face as usual (somehow I still haven't mastered the knack of landing on my feet). Instead, Nathaniel caught me easily around the waist, holding me just at his eye level.

His hands were hot. I could feel their warmth through the layers of clothing I wore. There was an unwelcome flare of something I didn't want to name inside me, and I was reminded of all the times Gabriel had caught me just this way when I'd come through a portal behind him.

"Put me down," I said. I didn't need to feel any more confused about Nathaniel than I already was.

He lowered me to the ground, but didn't release me, his eyes searching mine. I pushed his hands off and stepped back.

"Keep your hands to yourself," I said, now embarrassed beyond measure because I'd revealed something to him that I'd have preferred he'd never seen.

"Of course," he said coolly, and moved away from me.

Then a gigantic wolf slammed into him.

A second later Nathaniel was flat on his back with a red-and-silver wolf snapping at his throat.

"Jude!" I shouted.

The wolf growled, glancing back at me.

"Don't kill him," I said.

Jude growled again, turning to Nathaniel and showing the angel his teeth.

"Don't," I repeated.

He gave one last menacing grumble close to Nathaniel's face. The angel had lain very still while Jude stood on top of him, correctly interpreting that the wolf would kill him without blinking if he moved an inch.

Jude stepped off Nathaniel's chest. He went blurry for a moment, and then there was a man standing before me. A six-foot-four, 220-pound *naked* man.

I covered my eyes. It was like seeing my brother naked. "Where did you put your clothes?"

"Why is *he* here?" Jude said angrily. "I thought the ceiling fell on him in Azazel's court and he was dead."

"Please get dressed and I'll explain," I said, getting tired of staring at the backs of my fingers.

Jude blew out a breath; then I heard him move noisily through the grass. I knew it was deliberate because Jude can be more silent than air when he wants to.

"The wolf has gone into the woods," Nathaniel said.

I uncovered my eyes and took a look around for the first time. We stood on the edge of a forest that ran along the road across from Azazel's mansion. The house itself was directly opposite us, perched on top of a small rise. It was surrounded by a long, open slope of snow-covered grass on three sides.

I knew from my last visit that the back of the house had a similar open expanse, filled only by flower beds and topiary animals. The remainder of the property stretched away into the woods.

Gabriel had once told me that Azazel's estate covered dozens of miles. There were certainly no sounds of humanity anywhere—no cars on the road, no people hiking through the trees. There weren't even any planes flying overhead. It was almost as if they wouldn't dare to cross Azazel's airspace, or perhaps he had arranged for them not to.

Jude emerged from the trees wearing what I thought of as his tailgating outfit—gray sweatshirt topped with a down vest, jeans, work boots and a knit hat. Since he was from Wisconsin, his hat was dark green with a Packers logo.

"Remind me to buy you a Bears hat," I said.

"Tell me why this traitor is here with you," Jude said, giving Nathaniel the evil eye.

I sighed. Jude was never one for levity. I quickly explained about the deal Lucifer had made with Nathaniel, and my subsequent agreement to allow him to stay.

"I don't like it," Jude said flatly.

"Yeah, well, big surprise that you don't like anything to do with Lucifer," I muttered. "I don't love it, either, and I'm not entirely sure I trust him."

"I don't trust him at all," Jude replied, his ice-blue eyes burning daggers at Nathaniel over my head.

"But he's sworn his intentions are good, so I've decided to give him a chance," I said firmly. "If he proves otherwise, then you can kill him."

"Have you forgotten I am standing right here?" Nathaniel said angrily.

Jude and I both looked at him and replied, "No," simultaneously. It was better if Nathaniel was aware of what was in store for him if he tried to betray me again.

I looked at Jude. "I don't trust him, but I trust you."

Jude nodded. He had my back. Nathaniel would be less likely to try anything funny with both of us there.

"What is the wolf doing here in the first place?" Nathaniel demanded. "Do you not think his behavior is suspicious?"

"She called me," Jude said blandly.

"Before I left the house," I said, nodding.

"Werewolves run very fast," Jude said, and Nathaniel had to be content with that.

The mansion loomed, white and silent, on the hill before us. The hair on the back of my neck prickled.

"Something's watching," I said quietly.

"I know," Jude replied. "But I can't tell where it's coming from."

"It feels . . ." Nathaniel began.

"Like it's everywhere," I finished, and the other two nodded. "Well, we can't just stand here. We can deal with whatever it is when it decides to reveal itself."

The three of us crossed the road and started up the rise toward the front door. The sensation of being watched and pursued intensified.

"It's behind us," I breathed. My body broke out in goose bumps.

Jude started to glance behind us, but I laid a restraining hand on his arm.

"Don't. Don't look back," I said.

"Why?"

"Just a feeling," I said. "I think we should get inside as quickly as possible. But don't run."

We all picked up the pace a little. Sweat poured off my brow, but it was from fear, not exertion. The muscles in my legs trembled. The front door looked like it was a hundred miles away.

Just for a second, I thought I felt the pointed tip of a claw drag down my spine.

"Don't look," I said again, and then my boot heels were clattering on the porch. My hand closed over the door handle and I hoped that it wasn't locked.

It wasn't.

We all tumbled through the door and slammed it shut. I looked at Nathaniel and Jude. They were both chalk white and covered in sweat. I leaned back against the door.

"What was that?" Jude asked.

"Something faerie," I said, glancing at Nathaniel. "It felt like the Maze, or the Grimm. The same kind of magic."

"I am not certain of the identity of the creature. But I believe you were right in telling us not to look back. That kind of acknowledgment can give a child of faerie more power."

Three hard knocks pounded on the door behind me. I stumbled away from it, spinning around to stare at the knob. It didn't move.

"Don't open it. And don't look out the window, either," I warned Jude, who was moving to do that very thing. "I don't think we want to know what's out there."

Three knocks sounded again, and a whisper floated under the door.

"Madeline."

I deliberately turned my back to the door. Several deep breaths did nothing to slow my pounding heart. The thing whispered my name again.

"Come on," I said to the other two.

We were in a foyer that was wider than my apartment. Entryways stood in front and to the side. I realized I'd never even been in this part of the mansion.

"Where do these go?" I asked Nathaniel.

"To the left is the receiving parlor. To the right are servants' quarters and the kitchens. Straight ahead is the passage to the ballroom."

"And on the second floor are Azazel's labs, right?"

Nathaniel nodded. "I was never permitted inside them. Azazel's experiments were under strict lock and key."

"He's probably taken everything of importance with him," I said. "Were you still here when Azazel took off for parts unknown?"

"No. After the battle I went immediately to Lord Lucifer."

"Making sure your own ass was secure," Jude said contemptuously.

"I do not have to explain my actions to you, wolf," Nathaniel said.

"Don't start arguing," I said with a quelling look at Jude. "Let's take a look around upstairs anyway. If Azazel was in a hurry to skip town before Lucifer heard about the uprising, then he may have left something useful behind."

"Follow me," Nathaniel said, and led Jude and me through the doorway before us.

There was a thump behind us, almost as if something had slammed its fist against the front door in frustration.

We entered a long hallway with several doors leading off it. The air had the staleness of an abandoned place. Here and there were signs of a hasty retreat. Doors had been thrown open, objects scattered. In one room I saw a trail of blood from the hallway crisscrossing around the space as someone had collected items. A large cabinet stood open and empty.

"This was Antares' room," I said. The cabinet was exactly like the one where Greenwitch had stored her spells. "I guess that means the cockroach is still alive."

"Looks like he was bleeding pretty badly," Jude said. "How do you know he made it out of here?"

"It'll take more than a little blood loss to get rid of him," I said. "I've never known any other creature to have such an immense capacity for tolerating physical pain."

"I have," Jude said. "You. It must come from Azazel."

"Please don't remind me that I share DNA with those two."

"Still, the wolf is correct," Nathaniel said thoughtfully. "I never fully considered your ability to survive situations that would kill an ordinary mortal. Lord Azazel is not only one of the most magically powerful of the Grigori, but one of the most physically powerful as well."

"So I got something from Daddy besides the color of my eyes," I said impatiently. "So what?"

"A blood connection has power. You, of all people, should understand this. It is why Lucifer pursues you so doggedly."

I understood the strength and importance of bloodlines all right, but I failed to see why this particular trait was so meaningful to Nathaniel.

"Let's keep moving," I said, continuing down the hall.

I thought about the little one growing inside me, wondering what traits it would get from me, and which ones it would get from its daddy. For the first time since I'd found out about the baby, I felt a little chill of fear. There were monsters in this child's bloodline. Would my baby be another horror unleashed upon the world?

We crossed through several more rooms and hallways until I was hopelessly lost. Everywhere we went were signs of damage and destruction. Strangely, there were no bodies. I knew for a fact that we'd taken out dozens of Azazel's soldiers as well as a ton of charcarion demons. We reached the ballroom, and I pushed open the doors.

The room was smashed to pieces. Chunks of the ceiling were missing, and the floor-to-ceiling windows that bordered the back lawn were shattered, letting in the cold Minnesota air. Outside, the sky was gray and still. A whisper of menace drifted through the open window.

"Madeline."

"Can we move to another part of the mansion?" I said, shutting the doors hastily and moving down the hall to a set of steps that I thought would lead to the labs.

The stairs were stained with blood and other sticky gunk from the nephilim we'd battled, but again, no bodies.

"What happened to everyone?" I asked as we climbed the stairs. "Did Azazel actually take the time to have all the corpses carted away?"

"Doesn't make sense," Jude said.

We reached the upper hallway. Four doors stood on the left side before the hall terminated in another short flight of stairs. All four doors were padlocked.

"Interesting," I said, looking at Jude.

He nodded. "What's the point of locking doors if there's nothing behind them?"

I approached one of the doors to inspect the lock.

"Be careful," Nathaniel warned. "Azazel surely protected those rooms with something stronger than just a human's lock."

I hovered my right hand above the lock. The snake tattoo on my palm shifted, warning me that Nathaniel was correct.

"There's some kind of spell on the door," I said, thinking. "But there has to be a limit to how much damage it will do."

"Why would you say that?" Jude asked.

"Because Azazel would want to deter the curious without potentially destroying whatever he was trying to protect. So I think it's safe to assume the door won't blow up or anything like that."

I stepped back, searching my pockets. All I came up with was some lint.

"Have either of you got a coin?" I asked.

Nathaniel silently produced a quarter and handed it to me.

"You know, the two of you need some help in the playful banter department. The quality of the conversation really goes down when Beezle's not around."

"We should argue with you for no productive reason in order to make you more comfortable?" Nathaniel asked.

Jude looked at me impassively. No help there.

"It's like being with two stone sentinels," I muttered.

I tossed the coin at the door. It hit the spell that covered the entrance. For a second I thought the magic was just a warning, or that it wasn't working properly. The coin dropped toward the floor, and then suddenly it crumbled into ash.

"That's not good," I said.

"Kicking the door in isn't an option, then," Jude said.

"That was almost a joke," I said. "Your delivery needs some work, though."

We all stared at the door as if a solution would suddenly present itself. And then one did.

"Why do I keep forgetting about that?" I murmured.

I stepped forward and put my hand on the wall beside the door.

"What are you doing?" Jude asked.

"I am the Hound of the Hunt," I said quietly, "and no walls can hide my quarry."

The wall became fluid beneath my touch, and my hand passed through it.

"I'll see if I can get the door open from the other side," I said, and disappeared into the wall.

I emerged in a clean, bright room that could have been a chem lab at a university. Beakers and tubes filled with various mixtures sat on shelves. There was a long counter with a microscope at one end. On the opposite wall were several black three-ring binders.

I checked the impulse to immediately start going through the binders and instead turned back to the door. There was no obvious sign of a spell on this side—no handy "off" switch, and I didn't think I'd be able to turn the knob with the padlock on the other side, anyway.

I stuck my head back through the wall. Jude and Nathaniel stood with their arms crossed, scowling at each other.

They turned to me simultaneously, starting to speak.

"I don't want to know," I said, cutting them off. "There are some binders in here that I want to go through, and I can't see any obvious way to open the door. I'll look through them and be out shortly."

I ducked back into the room before either of them tried to speak again. I was pretty sure I knew what they were arguing about. Jude had probably questioned Nathaniel's loyalty/bravery/masculinity and Nathaniel had gotten angry. Cue downward spiral of civility from there.

I grabbed one of the binders off the shelf at random and opened it. The pages were filled with equations and chemical notations. Well, it wouldn't do me any good to look these over. I'd barely gotten through high school. Chloe might know what it was all about, though. She seemed scientifically minded.

I put the binder on the floor next to me and flipped through another one. More chemical jibber-jabber. This time I noticed that the sections were dated, and the binder I held was from two years ago. That was unhelpful. I wanted to know what Azazel was up to now, and I didn't want to carry every single binder with me. Besides, I could always come back and get the others if I needed them later.

I flipped as quickly as I could through the binders, trying to find the most recent information. After several minutes I had compiled a stack of four binders that represented the last six months.

Whatever Azazel was experimenting on, he'd spent a lot of time on it recently. Several of the notations were followed by cryptic comments like "Poor tolerance" and "Donors ill." I wondered who the "donors" were, what they were donating, and whether the donation was voluntary. Somehow I doubted it.

I carried the binders out into the hall. Jude and Nathaniel's relationship had degraded further. Nathaniel's right eye was bruising and his lip was bloody. He was sitting on the floor, sulking, near the entrance to the hallway. Jude stood by the door to the lab with a self-satisfied smile on his face despite the fact that the front of his vest was covered in nightfire burns.

I raised an eyebrow at him.

"You said you didn't want to know," he said, shrugging.

I thrust the stack of binders at him. "Find some convenient way to carry these while I look in the next lab."

"Are we just going to stand around in the hallway while you explore?"

"Yes, unless you can find a way to get into the labs without disintegrating," I retorted.

"The spell may not be on every door," Jude pointed out.

I held out my hand. "Give me some pocket change, then."

Jude fished out a couple of pennies and tossed one at the next door. The coin fell to the floor in one piece. The wolf gave me a pointed look.

"Okay, okay," I said. "So we just need to get through the padlock, then. Although whatever's in there is probably not that important if Azazel didn't bother to enspell the door."

Jude unceremoniously dropped the binders on the floor and waved me out of the way. I scooted away from the door as Jude turned his shoulder to one side and ran toward it.

There was the sound of splintering wood as the door cracked and came off its hinges. An ordinary human would never have the strength to do that. I grinned at Jude.

My smile faded almost immediately as we were hit by the smell. I gagged, bile rising in my throat. I tried to take deep breaths to calm down. If I puked in front of Jude and Nathaniel, they might suspect about the baby. I didn't mind Jude knowing, but I wanted to keep it from Nathaniel for as long as possible.

I covered my mouth and nose with my sleeve and went to stand behind Jude. Nathaniel had gotten up during the ruckus and joined us.

The door hung lopsided, blocking most of the view but allowing that horrible rotting smell to leak into the hallway. Jude looked at me questioningly.

"We've got to see," I said, my voice muffled by my coat.

He pushed the door and it fell through the opening and to the floor with a tremendous crash. And then I saw, and I wished I hadn't.

5

THE THREE OF US FILED RELUCTANTLY INTO THE ROOM.

"I guess these are the 'donors,'" I said bitterly.

The room stretched away before us, three times the length of the lab, and the remaining two doors that emptied into the hall were visible farther down along the wall.

The rest of the room was filled with cages. The cages were stacked floor to ceiling, and each one had a person inside it. A dead person.

"He treated them like lab monkeys," Jude said, and I could hear the undercurrent of fury in his voice.

I walked slowly down the aisle between the cages. Azazel hadn't discriminated in his choice of donors. There were men and women, boys and girls. Some of them were very old, some middle-aged, some of them so young that I had to turn away, sick at heart.

He'd left them here to die, slowly and painfully, while

he'd fled. This was the work of the angel who had fathered me. This was the monster I had come from.

I whirled on Nathaniel, tears blurring my eyes. "Did you know about this?"

"No, I did not," he said, his face troubled.

"How could you not know?" I asked. "You lived here. Whatever Azazel was doing, he could hardly have hidden the presence of dozens of prisoners from his right-hand man."

"On my honor, I swear to you that I did not know," Nathaniel insisted. "Whatever faults I may have, I would not have condoned this."

"Your honor doesn't mean a whole lot," Jude growled.

"And you didn't seem to mind when Azazel was capturing people to steal their memories," I said. "How is this any different?"

I turned away from him, not wanting to hear any more excuses. Even if he didn't know what was in the lab, I wasn't certain Nathaniel would have objected. No matter how morally repugnant Azazel's actions, Nathaniel's favorite person was Nathaniel. Defying Azazel would have put his favorite person at risk.

I stared into the cage in front of me, automatically cataloging what I saw. The woman was in her mid-twenties, dressed for a night out at the clubs. Her makeup was smeared on her face and her once-neat manicure was torn. She had probably clawed at the bars of the cage, screaming until her voice was gone.

She lay on her stomach, head turned to the side, and I noticed a large bruise at her neck. I stepped closer, heedless of the stink and the rot, to look more carefully. There were two little puncture wounds inside the bruise.

"Vampires," I breathed. "Check the others. See if they have bite marks."

Jude and Nathaniel moved closer to the cages. I walked down the row, searching the bodies for evidence of vampires. Almost every corpse had at least one bite mark.

"They've all got them," Jude said.

"So whatever Azazel was experimenting with, it involved some kind of chemical mixture, human blood and vampires," I said. I thought about the cryptic notes in the binder. "Maybe he was concocting something that the prisoners ingested and it was then passed to the vampires in human blood."

"Why?" Jude said. "And what?"

"I don't know," I said helplessly. "I hope Chloe can figure out what Azazel was making from the notebooks."

Jude frowned. "That fruitcake who works at the Agency?"

"She's a little eccentric," I admitted. "But she *was* the one who figured out how to restore the stolen memories."

Jude grunted, which was probably the highest praise Chloe would ever get from him. Jude was a man of few words.

"I do not understand," Nathaniel said.

We both turned to look at him. He frowned at the body in the cage in front of him.

"What's not to understand?" I asked.

"In order for these people to be so damaged, a vampire would have to be living on the premises. Lo . . . Azazel may have been able to explain away the presence of humans, but not vampires. Most angels cannot tolerate the presence of vampires."

"Is there someplace in the mansion that was off-limits to everyone? Besides the labs?" I asked.

"The basement has long been guarded by Azazel's soldiers," Nathaniel said slowly. "But there are prisons down there, for Azazel's enemies."

"And wouldn't the soldiers have blabbed if Azazel was hiding vampires in the basement?"

"Azazel's special guard cannot speak. They have had their tongues cut out."

He said this very matter-of-factly, as if the soldiers' disfigurement was of no note whatsoever.

I sighed. "I guess we have to check the basement, then."

"To what end?" Jude said. "Surely the vampire will have moved on with Azazel."

"But if it hasn't, we might be able to find out what Azazel was trying to accomplish. Wherever he's gone, Azazel is going to try to finish what he started, and that can't mean anything good."

"Madeline is correct. We should at least investigate before we leave this place," Nathaniel said.

Jude grumbled something under his breath but he went into the hall. Nathaniel and I followed. Jude collected the notebooks on the floor and slung them under his arm.

"Which way?" he asked Nathaniel.

"The best way is to return to the ballroom and then enter the basement stairs at the rear, behind Azazel's throne."

We backtracked down the stairs toward the ballroom. Jude kept sneezing and blowing air out of his nose.

"What's the problem?" I asked.

"There's too much death in that room. I can still smell it. And if I can still smell the corpses, then I can't smell anything else that might sneak up on us," he said, exhaling air through his nose again.

My own sense of smell had been almost completely deadened by the stench in that room, and my nose wasn't even a fraction as sensitive as Jude's. It must feel like being blind for a werewolf to be unable to smell.

Jude and I walked side by side, Nathaniel trailing

behind. We reached the ballroom, and the snake on my palm twitched just as I pushed the doors open.

For the second time that day, I wished I had left a door closed.

The room was filled with vampires.

Not a few to help Azazel with his vile project. Hundreds.

"Gods above and below," Nathaniel said. "Where did they all come from?"

The vampires had turned as one silent entity to face us when we'd opened the door. The majority of the creatures stood in shadow, but a few were touched by the weak beams of winter sun that came through the windows. Their dead flesh smoldered where the sun touched, but instead of fleeing from the solar rays, the creatures stood and burned.

The vampires watched us, but made no move to approach. It was as if they waited for an order.

Beside me Jude transformed into a wolf. The binders clattered to the floor.

"We can't fight them all," I hissed. "So don't do anything foolish."

Jude barked at me, but I couldn't tell if his reply was agreement or argument. I hoped he would restrain his natural impulse toward aggression until we got free of this mess.

The vampires stood silent and still. They were acting so weird, so un-vampire-like. I took a step backward, and Nathaniel mirrored me. I would have felt safer with my sword in my hand, but I didn't want the vamps to construe that as aggression and attack us. Jude reluctantly followed Nathaniel and me while growling low in his throat.

We had gone about five paces when the vampires suddenly surged forward as one body.

"Run!" I said, but Jude leapt at the first vampire to approach him, tearing at its throat.

The vamp fell to the ground, wounded but not terminated, and I cursed as I ran to help the stubborn wolf.

"Get out of the way!" I shouted, and swung the sword to separate the fallen vamp's head from its neck. It started flaking into dust immediately.

Nathaniel blasted a vamp with nightfire and it burst into flame.

There are three ways to kill a vampire—stake it, decapitate it or burn it. Anything else will slow the monster down but won't kill it.

Jude attacked another vampire and I swung the sword at any creature that came near me. I dusted quite a few of them, but they kept coming, endlessly, relentlessly, unconcerned about the possibility of damage or death. They weren't behaving like vampires at all, but zombies.

I don't know how long we stood in front of those doors, hacking and burning, but there was suddenly a lull in the never-ending tide. My eyes were tearing from all the dust in the air, and it was hard to breathe without coughing. I wiped my eyes with my sleeve and saw several of the vampires were bottlenecked in the door.

"Now's our chance," I shouted, backing down the hallway. Nathaniel threw one last ball of nightfire at the nearest vamp and joined me.

"Jude!" I shouted. The wolf had taken down another vamp and was in the process of ripping its throat out. "Come on!"

The vampires were stopped up in the doorway like a cork, but the pressure of the advancing horde behind would have them through in a moment. I wanted to get out before that happened.

The wolf ignored me, ravaging the struggling vampire.

"Jude!" I shouted again.

He turned toward me, blood on his muzzle, just as the mindless vampires broke through.

"Let's get out of here!" I shouted, and ran toward the doorway at the end of the hall.

I glanced back to see if Jude followed and saw he was a few feet behind me. Nathaniel brought up the rear, which was strange, as he'd been right beside me a moment before. There were a lot of vampires following but they were moving slowly, so we were able to outrun them to the foyer.

I threw open the front door, Jude on my heels, and pounded out to the lawn. Nathaniel pulled the door closed behind him and joined us. We turned in unison to face the mansion, backing away slowly, our eyes on the door.

"They can't possibly come outside," I said. "They'd burn up as soon as they stepped into the sun."

"They were not behaving like typical vampires," Nathaniel pointed out.

I was so focused on the possibility that the door might burst open at any moment that I'd forgotten about the thing that had chased us into the house. So when the whisper of breath brushed across my ear I was too strung out with tension to think properly.

"Madeline," it whispered.

I turned, and in turning acknowledged the monster at my shoulder. And I saw it in all of its terror and glory, and knew that if I survived this, every I time I closed my eyes from now until the end of my life I would see this horror in my sleep.

It wasn't the biggest creature I'd ever seen—just about Nathaniel's height—and it was vaguely humanoid in shape. Its hands and feet had elongated digits, twice as long as a normal person's, and something about them put me in mind of tree branches.

The eyes were oversized for its face, protruding like a

frog's, and its few long and wispy hairs trailed greasily from the top of its head.

The worst of it, though, was that the skin looked like it had been turned inside out, and it oozed with reddish brown fluid that might have been blood.

Then the creature smiled at me, and every one of its teeth was a tiny, sharp triangle, like the gaping maw of a shark. It looked like a distorted goblin, a thing from a fairy tale with a bad ending.

Jude barked in warning, and I glanced back at the front door. The vampires were pouring forth into the day despite the fact that they began to smolder almost immediately.

"Madeline," the goblin said again, and I turned in time to see its claws slashing at my throat.

I jumped backward, but the tips of its fingers grazed my cheek. I felt the skin tear open, the hot blood run down my face. I smelled the ozone of nightfire, the burning undead flesh of the vampires, heard Jude's growls as he attacked once more.

But I couldn't look, couldn't help, for my death had come for me. I swung out blindly with the sword in my right hand, trying to keep the thing from me as I conjured nightfire with my left hand. The creature laughed, a horrible high-pitched cackle that chilled my blood, and then it disappeared just as I threw the spell at it.

I stared dumbly at the spot where the goblin had stood, and then I felt its finger slide down my spine for the second time that day.

Spinning around, I slashed with the sword. The monster laughed and disappeared again.

It was playing with me. It was *playing* with me, and I was in no freaking mood for games.

As seemed to happen to me so often, the rush of anger

cleared my head, steadied my nerves. The blaze of Lucifer's power lit in my blood, poured down my hand and into my sword. It didn't burst mindlessly from the blade but lay charged and waiting for my call.

The creature reappeared on my right, just in the corner of my eyesight. It stabbed at me with its claws again, tearing through the shoulder of my coat and drawing blood. Instead of darting away or spinning around to face it, I allowed the creature to injure me and then disappear again. I wasn't going to jump around for this monster's amusement.

I felt the goblin's fingers curl around the end of my braid and pull, hard enough to hurt but not enough to knock me from my feet. The goblin giggled, but its laugh sounded confused. I wasn't reacting the way it thought I should.

Soon, I thought. The sounds of battle behind me receded as my head filled with the buzz of magic, an unnatural calm coming over me.

The creature winked in and out of sight, slashing at my jeans, tearing through my right thigh. For a second I saw its hideous face twisted in malice, heard a growl instead of a laugh, and knew it was time.

When the goblin appeared before me once more, I pushed the sword into its chest and let loose the magic I had stored there.

The creature's eyes widened for a moment, and then it just exploded in a confetti of flesh and flying droplets of blood. I was too close to avoid getting splashed, and I looked sadly at the new coat Lucifer had given me, now shredded and covered in gore.

The sword still hummed with stored power. I turned to help Jude and Nathaniel. Both of them stood a few feet away, their backs to me, and I realized they'd kept the vampires from me while I fought the freaky thing from Faerie. Most of the vamps were blazing from the touch of the sun even as they staggered determinedly forward to destroy us.

There wasn't much point in expending more energy when the sun would eventually finish the vampires off for us, so I whistled to attract the attention of the other two. Jude glanced over his shoulder and I waved at him to join me. He barked at Nathaniel and the three of us ran down the hill in front of the mansion, crossed the road and stopped at the edge of the woods.

Nathaniel murmured a few words, a portal appeared before us and I dove into it, the other two following close behind. A moment later I crashed face-first into the hard-packed snow of my backyard.

Jude leapt lightly to his feet beside me and nudged me with his nose. I lifted my stinging face from the snow and gave him a weak smile. I heard Nathaniel's uncertain footsteps crunching in the ice behind me.

"Well, that was fun," I said, pushing up to my knees.

The back door burst open and Samiel clattered onto the wooden porch, followed by Beezle. Samiel's face went white when he saw me. Beezle looked furious, and his face was covered in popcorn kernels, a sure sign that he'd been eating under stress. My gargoyle landed on the railing, his little hand balled in a fist on his chest.

"Don't you dare do that again," he said. "I'm an old gargoyle. You could have given me a heart attack."

"Do what?" I asked, still on my knees in the snow.

Samiel charged me, hauling me to my feet with his arms under my shoulders. His eyes scanned me anxiously, frowning at the claw marks at my cheek and shoulder and thigh.

How could you go out without telling one of us? he signed angrily. *You were gone; Nathaniel was gone. We didn't know what to think.*

"We called J.B.," Beezle said.

"What did you do that for?" I asked, annoyed. J.B. had probably raised the alarm. There would be Agents looking for me all over the place. "Why didn't you try to call *me*?"

"We did. You didn't answer your phone," Beezle replied.

I patted my pockets for my cell, pulled it out. There were three missed calls from my house phone, and two from J.B. There was also an alert indicating that I had several voice mail messages. I was sure I didn't want to listen to those. They probably involved yelling.

I called J.B. while Samiel glared at me.

"Black," J.B. barked.

"Hello to you, too," I said. "I'm not dead or in mortal peril, so you can call off the search party."

"Where were you?"

"I'll explain later. By the way, what do you know about a creepy goblin thing that looks like its skin is turned inside out?"

"Can this creature appear and disappear at will?" J.B. asked.

"Yes. And it has kind of popping frog's eyes?"

"The Hob," J.B. said, his tone alarmed. "Did it come after you?"

"Don't worry. I killed it."

There was a long silence at J.B.'s end.

"What?" I asked. "What now?

"I'm coming by the house later," he said, and hung up.

I gave my phone a dirty look since I couldn't give one to J.B., and then stuck it in my pocket.

"Let's go inside," I said to Samiel. "You can yell at me at your leisure while I drink something warm."

We filed into the house, Nathaniel bringing up the rear. I was too tired to argue with him about staying outside so I let him join the throng trooping upstairs to my apartment.

Beezle landed on my unwounded shoulder. “I see you’ve managed to ruin another coat.”

“I see you’ve been in the popcorn stash while I was gone,” I said.

“I don’t know what you’re talking about,” he said, wiping popcorn crumbs from his belly.

“You’re hardly surreptitious,” I said.

“What do you expect? It’s your fault if I’m bingeing. You shouldn’t have disappeared without a word.”

“I’m sorry I worried you,” I said.

“You should be,” he replied.

I pushed open the door and entered the kitchen. “This is your cue to apologize to me for being rude before I left.”

“For what?” Beezle asked. “Telling the truth?”

I shook my head. Beezle would never see that there was such a thing as being too blunt. And apologizing for hurting my feelings had never been very high on his priority list.

I looked at Jude, still in wolf form. “We need to get you a stash of clothes you can keep here.”

I can get something for him, Samiel signed.

“I don’t think your clothes will fit,” I said.

Samiel was a few inches shorter and stockier than Jude, who was about as tall as Nathaniel but a lot more heavily muscled.

“Some of Gabriel’s things might fit,” I said reluctantly. “Come with me.”

Jude trotted after me. I could feel Samiel, Nathaniel and Beezle staring.

“Wait here,” I told Jude, and went into my bedroom.

I opened the closet. There was a row of neatly pressed

white shirts. Beside it were several pairs of black dress pants. Gabriel never wore anything else.

I reached for a shirt, my hand trembling, and realized suddenly that I couldn't see. My eyes were blurred by tears. I couldn't breathe. I was choking on my grief. I couldn't do this. I couldn't go on without him.

I was on the floor, sobbing like I'd never stop.

"Come on," Jude said gently, pulling me to my feet. I hadn't even heard him enter the room. He'd wrapped a bath towel around his waist in deference to my modesty. "If you stay here too long, the others will come looking. You don't want Nathaniel to see you like this."

He was right. I didn't want Nathaniel to see me broken, even if I was. I didn't want him to think I was weak. Because if he thought that, he might try to take advantage of my weakness.

Jude put his hands on my shoulders. "This won't be the last time you break down. But you have to get up again, every time. Your life is not your own anymore."

He gave me an intent look, and I understood that he knew about the baby.

"How did you find out?" I asked.

"I can hear its heartbeat," Jude said.

"Really?"

"Not always. Only in quiet rooms, like now."

"At this rate I won't be able to keep it a secret," I said.

Jude nodded. "Your enemies will come for the child. I will speak to Wade about staying here for a time."

I knew that what Jude offered was an extraordinary sacrifice for him. He was Wade's second-in-command, and he had important responsibilities in the pack. It would also be hard for him to be away from the other wolves' physical proximity. Wolves slept in wolf form and in large community piles. It strengthened the bond within the pack.

I shook my head. I couldn't let him do this. "Though I appreciate the offer, I can take care of myself."

"You can," Jude acknowledged. "But why should you have to? Why will you not accept help when it is offered freely?"

"I guess I'm just used to being on my own," I said slowly.

"I will stay," Jude said. "At least until you find Azazel."

Jude unfolded my fingers from the shirt I was clutching. I handed it to him. "See if this will fit you. At least until we get you something else."

I wiped my cheeks and went back out to the kitchen to face the others. Nathaniel leaned against the back door, arms crossed, body tense.

Samiel stood against the counter, his body in the same posture, eyes locked on Nathaniel.

Beezle sat in the breakfast nook on the table, his eyes shifting back and forth between the two of them.

"Stand down," I said to Samiel. "He can stay. For now."

I explained to Samiel and Beezle what we found at Azazel's. Jude came out in the middle of my monologue wearing Gabriel's clothes. The pants seemed to fit okay, but Jude was too barrel-chested to get the shirt buttoned. I ignored the little pang in the region of my heart and continued the story.

Jude carried my first-aid kit in his hand. He indicated I should sit down and take off my coat; then he started cleaning and dressing the wounds on my shoulder and face.

Beezle looked thoughtful when I was done recounting the events of the day.

"It sounds like Azazel had the vampires under some kind of compulsion," Beezle said. "I can't believe they would have voluntarily gone into the sun."

"It was like they had been triggered by something, an early-warning system," I said. "But I don't think they would have agreed to be Azazel's automatons."

"Who said they agreed?" Jude growled.

"I wish we knew what Azazel was doing with those experiments," I said, frustrated. "But I'm pretty sure the binders are buried under a pile of vampire ash."

Nathaniel moved suddenly, and it was like he'd set off an automatic alarm. Samiel pushed away from the counter, hands curled and ready to punch. Jude stood and bared his teeth.

My former fiancé gave my two overzealous defenders a scathing glance, then pulled something out of his coat and tossed it on the table.

It was a binder.

6

"HOW DID YOU . . . ?" I ASKED IN WONDER, PICKING IT up and opening it.

"I managed to collect it before we escaped."

I remembered that Nathaniel had been beside me in the hallway, but when we started running he'd ended up behind Jude. A tiny seed of hope blossomed inside me. The binder he'd grabbed had been the most recent one, so it was probably our best chance of figuring out Azazel's foul intentions. At the very least, we weren't completely in the dark.

I looked up at Nathaniel, who watched me intently.

"Thank you," I said. "You risked your life to go back for this."

"I knew it was important to you," he said softly.

Samiel slammed a fist on the table so that we would look at him.

You're not helping yourself by trying to come on to my sister, he signed angrily. *I don't trust you.*

Beezle translated this rather gleefully for Nathaniel, who looked puzzled.

"There is no need to remind me every second of the day that none of you trust me," Nathaniel said icily. "I am well aware of your feelings on the matter."

"And if we want to remind you of them, then you will just have to deal with it," Jude said.

"You're the one who came here seeking asylum," I said.

"I came to protect you, as per Lord Lucifer's orders," Nathaniel said.

"Because it was the only option to save your life. If your own skin hadn't been on the line, you never would have come back here," I said.

"How can you be sure?" he asked.

My temper flared. "Look, you want consideration from the rest of us? Then stop playing games. Maybe if you stopped pretending to be enthralled with me and put your agenda on the table, everyone would stop threatening you every second of the day."

"You give me no credit at all, do you?" Nathaniel said angrily.

"What's it going to be?" I asked. I felt the flare of magic under my skin, but pushed it down. I was getting better at controlling my power, at keeping my abilities at bay when my emotions were unsteady.

Nathaniel stared at me from the other side of the table. I matched his stare beat for beat. Jude and Samiel flanked me, ready to lunge at my say-so.

After several moments he turned his head aside. "Have it your way."

"That doesn't really sound like a concession," Beezle said, landing on my shoulder.

"Very well. I will admit to being interested in saving my own life. But I hardly think that is an unreasonable desire."

I acknowledged this with a nod. "And?"

"And what?" Nathaniel challenged.

"And what else were you planning when you came here?"

"I intended you no harm, if that is what you are asking."

"What do you intend?" Jude asked.

"To regain Lord Lucifer's favor by protecting the most beloved child of his line," Nathaniel replied.

"So you just want your status back," Beezle said.

"If I admitted to anything further, I would be accused of falsely manipulating Madeline's emotions," Nathaniel said. "So, yes."

The four of us exchanged silent glances. I could tell we'd all come to the same conclusion. He *probably* really was interested in regaining power, and as long as I didn't interfere with that, I was *probably* safe. But if I ever got in his way . . . Well, let's just say I didn't buy Nathaniel's protestations of affection.

"I guess I have bigger things to worry about than you stabbing me in the back, especially since every freaking faerie thing that ever was seems to be crawling out of the storybooks to kill me."

"Does that mean you will permit me to stay?" Nathaniel asked.

"Yes," I said.

He's not sleeping up here, Samiel signed.

"I was going to put him in the basement."

Samiel shook his head. *He can stay with me. That way I can keep an eye on him.*

"Won't that cramp your style with Chloe?" I asked.

To my surprise, Samiel blushed. *We're not . . . I don't know what Beezle told you . . .*

"Ah," I said. "She comes on pretty strong, huh?"

Yes, he replied, nodding fervently.

I tried and failed to smother a grin. It was so cute to see Samiel disconcerted by a punk-rock scientist half his size.

Don't laugh or I'll sic her on you next time she comes over, Samiel warned. *She's dying to see where the famous Madeline Black lives.*

"Who's laughing?" I said, attempting to school my face in lines of sobriety.

"So the angel will stay," Jude said. "And so will I."

"It's going to be interesting trying to feed everyone around here on your non-salary," Beezle said.

"Some of us might have to do without second helpings occasionally," I replied.

"Some of us need to keep up our strength in order to fulfill our duties as home guardian," Beezle replied loftily.

"The only thing I've seen you guarding lately is the popcorn bowl," I said.

"Even the hardest-working gargoyle needs a break occasionally."

"Or forever."

Jude laid a hand on my shoulder. "I will return to the pack this night and speak with Wade. I will arrive back here tomorrow. With my own clothing."

"Okay," I said. I didn't want to admit that I would be relieved that he wouldn't be using Gabriel's things.

"Bring food," Beezle added.

"How dire is your situation?" Jude frowned.

"Very," Beezle said at the same time that I said, "Not bad."

He looked from Beezle to me. "Which is it?"

"It's okay if it's just me and Samiel eating," I said. "But two more mouths would be a stretch."

"What about me?" Beezle said.

"If you didn't eat for the next year, you still wouldn't be back at fighting weight," I said.

"She's trying to kill me," Beezle said to the room at large. "An old gargoyle, one that has devoted the best years of his life to raising and protecting an ungrateful child . . ."

"I can pay my own way," Jude said.

"As can I," Nathaniel said.

"Thanks," I said, and meant it. It would be a huge relief to not have to worry about stretching my meager food budget.

Jude clapped me on the shoulder. "I will return soon, Madeline Black. Your husband's clothes will be outside when you're ready to collect them."

Jude disappeared through the back door.

I pressed my hand to my cheek. The claw marks hurt, and I was extremely tired all of a sudden.

"I can heal you," Nathaniel offered. "Those marks will scar you permanently otherwise."

"That's okay," I said. "I don't want them to be healed."

I didn't want to have the pain taken away by an angel's magic, an angel other than Gabriel. More than that, I wanted those marks to stay, to remind me every time I looked in the mirror I was still human. No matter how many monsters chased me, no matter what politics I was expected to play, I was still a human being. And my child would be part human, too, even if it would be the smallest part of him.

Nathaniel looked like he wanted to speak again, then changed his mind.

Come on, Samiel signed, pointed him to the door. *Let's get your sleeping arrangements sorted.*

I translated, and Nathaniel followed Samiel without another word.

Beezle stayed behind a moment when the others left. "You should let Nathaniel heal you. Your strength is being sapped enough by the baby. If you run yourself down on top of being pregnant, you'll make yourself sick."

"I don't want to be indebted to Nathaniel," I said.

"You may not have a choice."

"I lived fine for plenty of years without magical emergency care," I pointed out.

"You also lived plenty of years without knowing who you were and without dozens of enemies waiting outside to kill you."

"I know what I'm doing," I said.

"Just don't let your pride get in the way of doing what's necessary," Beezle said.

Then he flew out the back door, slamming it shut behind him.

And I was alone. The tick of the analog clock that hung over the stove sounded like the beat of a drum. It was the middle of the afternoon, but I felt like I could go sleep for twelve hours. I needed to get some pregnancy books or something so I could find out if it was normal to be this tired.

"Yeah, I can probably squeeze that in between hunting Azazel and fending off faerie assassins," I said to myself.

I doubted the pregnancy books would cover supernatural births, in any case. Somehow I didn't think there would be a chapter on what to do if the father of your baby was part nephilim.

I dragged my heavy feet into the bedroom, pulled off all my clothes and went to shower off the blood from the wounds the Hob had given me.

The marks on my right thigh were not deep but they were raised and swollen. Jude hadn't disinfected them while we sat in the kitchen with the others.

I scrubbed the wound until the scabs came off; then when I was out of the shower I poured hydrogen peroxide into it. I hissed as it stung and the peroxide bubbled.

The heavy, wet mass of my hair kept falling in the way as I bandaged my leg. Irritated, I threw it over my shoulder but it kept falling back. It had been months since I'd gotten it cut and it was well past the middle of my back now. Gabriel had loved my hair.

I straightened, the bandaging complete, and caught a glimpse of myself in the mirror. The humidity from the shower made my curls coil with wild energy around my head. The slash marks from the Hob's claws stood out in bright relief against my white skin. The dark circles under my eyes added nothing positive to the overall impression.

I looked like a mad Medusa, the kind of woman people crossed the street to avoid.

The impulse was there, so I didn't stop to think about it. I opened the medicine cabinet and pulled out a pair of scissors. Then I started to cut.

Some time later I was surrounded by a pile of hair. What was left on top of my head was a shapeless mess, but it was short. I rubbed my hand over the nape of my neck, which felt bare and exposed. I looked down at the remains of my crowning glory, remembered Gabriel with his hands in my hair.

Tears welled up again, but I suppressed them ruthlessly. I had made this choice, and it was too late for regrets.

I dusted the hair off me with a towel, then swept up the rest of it and dumped it in the trash. I went into the bedroom without looking in the mirror again. I pulled on a tank top and pajama pants and fell into bed.

My dreams were filled with blood and ash and snow.

Someone was touching my hair, a featherlight hand brushing over my head.

"Gabriel?" I asked, my mind still muffled by sleep.

The hand stilled, drew away. I opened my eyes.

It was dark out, but in the winter it was dark by four thirty in the afternoon. There was a glint of streetlight on the metal frames of glasses.

"J.B.," I said, sitting up. My head felt strangely light. I reached up unconsciously and felt the shorn ends.

"That's a different look for you," he said.

"How did you get in the house?" I asked, swinging my legs out and shivering when my bare feet touched the cold floor.

"Beezle let me in."

"What time is it?"

"A little past seven."

My stomach grumbled. I honestly couldn't remember the last time I'd eaten.

"Can we move this discussion to the kitchen?" I asked, getting up and pulling a sweatshirt and heavy socks from my dresser.

I followed J.B. into the hall and down to the kitchen, flipping on lights as I went. The refrigerator revealed its usual sad lack of nourishment, but there were some eggs that appeared fresh and a couple of tomatoes. I couldn't remember whether I'd bought them or Samiel had brought them upstairs, but it was fortuitous all the same.

"Want an omelet?" I asked, checking the bread box. There were two pieces of mold-free bread left in the bag. I popped them in the toaster.

"I ate," he said shortly.

Something in his tone made me pause. He stood in the

middle of the kitchen, watching me bustle around, his hands fisted at his sides.

His eyes flickered from my hacked-off hair to the claw marks on my right cheek.

"I know," I said resignedly, putting the carton of eggs on the counter. "I've looked better."

"When are you going to stop taking stupid risks?" he said, his voice low and angry. "When you're dead?"

"I didn't think I was taking a stupid risk," I said, stung. "I need to find Azazel."

"Why?" J.B. asked. "Why is it your job to find him? Let Lucifer do his own damn dirty work."

"He killed Gabriel."

"And when you hunt down Azazel and kill *him*, that will make everything better? Gabriel won't be dead anymore?" His face was taut with emotion.

"No," I said, my temper rising to match his. "But he has to pay for what he did."

"A blood price? Retribution? That's the reason the faeries are after you. Why are you right and they're wrong?" J.B. said, his voice getting louder.

"Azazel killed the innocent. I killed Amarantha because she was helping him, because the two of them were willing to run over anyone who got in their way. Don't you *dare* try to compare me to them, or to the faeries who want me dead because of some breach of etiquette," I shouted.

"You never take politics seriously," J.B. said, crossing the room to put his hands on my shoulders. He gave me a little shake. I slapped his hands away.

"I don't have time for politics," I said. "I don't have time to play games with posing monsters of any variety."

"You call it a game, but to everyone else it's deadly serious. You make more enemies because you refuse to play by the rules. And every time you make another enemy, the sand in your hourglass runs a little faster."

My blood went cold. "Do you know something? Has the Agency seen my end?"

"No!" J.B. shouted. "But how do you think I goddamn feel every time that list comes across my desk? Every time I read it I can feel my heart pounding, just praying to every god there ever was that I won't see the name 'Madeline Black.'

"And while I might feel a moment of relief, it's immediately replaced by the anxiety of knowing that at that very moment you're either out there fighting for your life or pissing off someone or something that's going to try to kill you for the insult later."

My temper faded. "J.B., I . . ."

"Don't apologize," he said furiously. "You won't change, so don't tell me you're sorry."

"Something else has happened," I guessed. "That's why you're so angry."

The fight seemed to go out of him in a rush. He ran his hands through his short black hair. "You killed the Hob."

"Which was trying to kill me at the time," I said, pointing to my cheek.

"Well, to the faeries that's a lot like killing Lucifer's Hound of the Hunt," J.B. said.

"Oh, no," I said. "I'm not taking over the Hob's position in your court. I already have enough to do."

"You misunderstand. The Hob was the creature of the highest lord and lady of all the faeries—Titania and Oberon."

I blinked. "You mean they're real?"

"Yes." J.B. smiled briefly. "But they aren't figures of comedy. They are creatures of the deepest cruelty, and they rule over all the minor courts of Faerie with fists of iron."

"So, from a social-status point of view, they're on the same level as Lucifer," I said.

"Yes."

"And they were the ones that sent the Hob after me?" I asked, narrowing my eyes.

"Yes, because I 'refused to address the problem,'" J.B. said.

"Meaning you refused to have me dragged before your court and massacred for the amusement of the nobles as retribution for killing Amarantha," I said. "So you've earned the ire of Titania and Oberon as well."

"I don't care about that," J.B. said. "I care about the fact that they are going to come after you with everything they have in response to the insult you have done them by destroying their assassin."

"Why can't these immortals play fair?" I complained. "I defeated their guy. That should be the end of it. Why do they get to keep throwing monsters at me until I'm crushed?"

"Because they're immortals," J.B. said. "Because they have all the time in the world to grind you under their heel."

I felt small suddenly, disturbingly mortal despite all the power in my blood. I'd never wanted power or politics. I'd never wanted anything more than to be plain Madeline Black, and to spend the rest of my ordinary mortal life with Gabriel.

Now Gabriel was gone, and every step I took put me in further danger because of someone else's game. I felt the little flutter of butterfly wings deep down, and covered my stomach with my hands.

"I'm afraid."

I didn't realize I'd said it aloud until J.B. put his arms around me and pulled me close. His lips touched the spiky strands on top of my head before he rested his chin there.

"I don't know how to keep you safe," he said.

"I don't think you can." I sighed. "And it's not your job, anyway."

"I can't stay here. I have too many duties," he said. "You need more help than just Beezle and Samiel."

"Jude's coming back for a while. And . . . Nathaniel's staying with Samiel."

"What? Why the hell are you letting him stay instead of sending him back to Lucifer?"

I pushed lightly on his arms so he would release me. Then I explained what happened that day while I put an omelet together. I split the omelet in half and plated one for each of us along with buttered toast. Despite his earlier protestations, J.B. seemed happy to eat once the food was in front of him.

After a while he spoke.

"Whatever Azazel's doing, it sounds like it's a lot bigger than rebelling against Lucifer. Does he have some kind of agreement with the vampires? What could he possibly be making that they want?"

"Those better be rhetorical questions, because I definitely do not have the answers. I was hoping Chloe would look at the notes in the binder and see if they made any sense to her."

"Good idea," J.B. said. "I'll send her over here tomorrow."

"You don't want to take the binder with you?" I asked, surprised.

"There is some flak coming down from upper management about using Agency resources for non-Agency problems."

"When have you ever abused your authority?" I asked. "You're the straightest arrow I've ever met."

"The official decision on the memory-stealing episode

is that it was a fallen matter and I should not have gotten the Agency involved."

"That's stupid," I said. "The presence of the lost souls should have automatically made it the provenance of the Agency."

"I'm getting the impression that the higher-ups want to avoid entangling the Agency any further with outside courts. Especially after the attack in November."

"More politics," I said disgustedly.

"Like I said, you can be as contemptuous as you want, but it affects you, too," J.B. said. "They can't avoid the fact that you're the child of a fallen angel, but they can punish you if you step out of line."

"What are they going to do? Fire me?" I asked. "I've been looking for a way out of this crappy gig ever since I was fourteen."

"If you push them hard enough, they'll send the Retrievers after you," J.B. said.

"Don't tell me you believe that fairy tale about Agency bogeymen," I scoffed.

"It's not a fairy tale," J.B. said.

I stared at him. "Are you trying to tell me there really is a superspecial team of assassins for Agents gone bad?"

J.B. nodded. "And since you've already got plenty of enemies after you, let's not give the CEO an excuse to sic the Retrievers on you.

"So, the first thing is that you've got to pick up your workload again. I could get away with giving you a week off because you were grieving, but I can't keep passing your soul pickups to other Agents. A few of them are already grumbling, and if the grumbles get too loud, it will attract attention."

"Okay," I said. The last thing I felt like doing was

escorting the souls of the dead, but I didn't want J.B. to get any more grief than he was already getting.

"And if you want Chloe to help you, it's going to have to be on her off-hours."

"I think she's been spending a lot of her off-hours time here, anyway," I said, smiling.

J.B. gave me a questioning look.

"Apparently she's been pursuing Samiel," I said.

J.B. blinked. "Really?"

"Yes, very aggressively."

He smiled, and that smile transformed his face. He was under so much stress that I hardly ever saw him without knit brows and downward mouth.

I was reminded of how handsome he was, and hard on the heels of that thought was the memory of Amarantha's servant Violet pursuing J.B.

He was king of the court now, and he probably had faeries throwing themselves at him to be the next queen. I felt a little jealous, and then I reminded myself that I was in no position to feel that way. I'd never considered J.B. as a lover, and even if I did, it would be impossible to avoid feeling like I was betraying Gabriel.

My life was complicated enough.

J.B. watched me very soberly, and I wondered how much of what I was thinking was evident on my face.

Quite a bit, it seemed.

"You know," J.B. said carefully. "Someday you will stop missing him quite so much."

"I'll never stop missing him no matter how much time has passed," I said.

"Okay," he conceded. "But one day you might realize you don't want to spend the rest of your life alone, or that maybe you'd like your baby to have a father."

"I don't . . ." I started.

J.B. held up his hands. "All I'm saying is when that day comes, whenever that day may be, please consider me."

I shook my head. "J.B. You can't wait forever for the possibility that I might choose you."

"I'm hoping I won't have to wait forever," he said steadily.

"I don't deserve you," I said.

"Probably not," he replied, and he put his hand over mine.

Which was how Nathaniel found us when he knocked on the back door and walked in without waiting for an answer.

7

"EXCUSE ME," NATHANIEL SAID TIGHTLY, TURNING BACK to the door.

I felt guilty, and I didn't know why, which made me angry. I pushed away from the table and stood.

"What did you want?" I asked.

Nathaniel paused at the door, not looking at me. "Only to see if you were well."

"I'm well," I said. "And in the future, please wait for me to answer the door before coming in."

"I apologize. Everyone else is permitted to come and go. I presumed it would be acceptable for me to do as well."

"It's not."

"I understand," he said, and went out again.

I slumped back into my chair, my adrenaline crashing.

"Never mind the stress of being hunted by all and sundry.

I may not survive the stress of having Nathaniel in the house," I muttered.

Beezle pushed the back door open and flew in. He gave an exaggerated double take when he saw my hair.

"Speak and you die," I said.

"What?" Beezle said. "I was going to ask if you made an omelet for me."

"Really?" I said skeptically.

"Well, no, I was going to say it looks like you took a hacksaw to your head, but I suspect such comments would be frowned upon in your current condition."

"You suspect correctly," I said.

J.B. stood up. "I'll send Chloe to you tomorrow."

"Let me know if you overhear of any further plots on my life, will you?"

J.B. nodded and left.

I looked at Beezle. "I'm thinking we shouldn't wait around to see what shows up at the door next."

"You want to confront Titania and Oberon?"

"Good, you were eavesdropping so I don't have to trouble myself to explain the situation," I said.

"Maddy," Beezle said, and his little face was very grave. "I'll admit that you've defied some pretty powerful beings in the past, and you've even managed to defeat most of them. But Titania and Oberon are on Lucifer's level, and you haven't managed to get the best of him yet."

"What do you know about them?" I said.

"Nobody knows how old they are. They might be as old as Lucifer."

"Very ancient beings. Check," I said.

"They adore children but have only managed to have one of their own in all these millennia, so they are not above stealing someone else's child."

"So I should avoid revealing my pregnancy to them for as long as possible."

"Oh, yeah. To steal a child of Lucifer's line would be quite a coup for them."

"Have they been trying?" I asked.

"Well, the difficulty comes from not knowing just who Lucifer's been bonking," Beezle said. "Remember what a surprise Baraqiel was?"

"I wonder why the faerie king and queen have so much trouble conceiving while Lucifer seems able to father a child on pretty much anything."

"For some reason, faeries don't seem to reproduce easily. But rumor has it that the only child of Titania and Oberon isn't Oberon's, if you know what I mean."

"The faerie king is shooting blanks?"

"So some say."

"Where do you get these rumors from, anyway?" I asked. "It's not like you leave the house unless you're with me."

"I have a Facebook account, as you well know."

"You're discussing the paternity of the faerie kingdom's heir on Facebook?"

"Just because you don't know the value of social media doesn't mean everyone is like that," he said.

"Then I want you to put your pastime to good use. See what else you can find out about Titania and Oberon."

"Are you looking for some specific information?" Beezle asked.

"Yeah. I want to know their weaknesses."

"Besides the usual immortal flaws of vanity, jealousy and self-righteousness?"

"Yes. Although those give me something to start with," I said, thinking. "If there is any truth to the rumors about Oberon, then there's some leverage there."

"Careful where you tread," Beezle said.

"I know. They would crush me just for implying their heir is not legitimate."

"It definitely hits Oberon's pride. And Titania will apparently do anything to keep him happy."

"So they love each other, then?"

"Not in the way you would think of love, probably, but yes, they do."

"And that's something to work with, too," I said. "Love is a weakness. If you care about someone, then you can be hurt."

Beezle looked at me. "Aren't we ruthless?"

"I know better than anyone how love can cut you to pieces."

"But love isn't just pain," he said, his eyes troubled. "Isn't there happiness, too?"

"Just enough to make the cut deeper when it comes," I said.

We both stared at the table, lost in our thoughts.

"Let's not brood," I said, after a while. "Want to watch a movie with me? Something funny?"

"Yeah, *Night of the Living Dead*."

"It's funny to watch people get their guts eaten by zombies?"

"It is if they're too stupid to get away. Zombies *shamble*. You could escape them with a brisk walk and yet these idiots are getting overtaken all the time."

"It's the number of zombies that's the problem," I said, "not the speed at which you attempt to escape."

Beezle waved a hand at me. "This is starting to sound disturbingly like a nerd argument, and I am not a nerd. You make the popcorn; I'll get the DVD."

I laughed as he flew out of the room. For just a moment,

everything felt normal. And I wanted to keep it that way. At least for a little while.

I woke the next morning on the couch. Bright sunshine streamed through the picture window. The scent of bacon filled the air. I rubbed my eyes, rolled over and saw Chloe sitting on my coffee table, staring at me.

She wore a leather vest that revealed the sleeve of tattoos on each arm and a pair of faded jeans. Sparkly purple polish on her fingers and toes matched the shocking violet of her hair.

"What did you do to your head?" she asked.

"Who let you in here?" I asked. Did nobody respect my privacy anymore? The house was starting to feel like a dorm.

"I came up with Samiel," she said. "I can fix that, you know."

I rubbed my hand over my hair. The thought of Chloe near my head with scissors was quite terrifying.

"Really, I can't stand to look at you like that," she said. "It'll put me off my breakfast. Come on."

She grabbed my hand and yanked me to my feet. I thought *I* was brusque.

"Are you staying for whatever Samiel's cooking, then?" I asked.

She pulled me into the bathroom and lowered the toilet seat lid. "Sit."

I didn't have the energy to argue with her. Besides, it didn't seem that arguing would do any good. Chloe was like a force of nature. I could see why Samiel was so disconcerted by her.

She took the scissors from the cabinet and began to snip here and there. Every once in a while she would tell me to move my head this way or that. I closed my eyes and hoped I wouldn't end up looking like G.I. Jane.

"There," she said with a satisfied tone in her voice. "Look."

I stood, a little afraid, and looked in the mirror. And was pleasantly surprised.

She'd shaped the hacked-off mess into a neat pixie cut that framed my face.

"It suits you," she said.

"Thanks," I replied.

She nodded and walked out. I brushed my teeth, washed my face and took a moment to admire the new me in the mirror before something bad happened to me again. Of course, the new me came with a set of slash marks across my face courtesy of the Hob. The cuts plus the hair made me look a lot like an anime character.

Chloe and Beezle sat at the table in the kitchen. Both of them were shoveling pancakes and bacon in their mouths as fast as Samiel could make them.

"Are you preparing for an appearance on *Man v. Food*?" I asked.

Chloe and Beezle both grunted at me and kept eating.

"Where's Nathaniel?" I asked Samiel.

He said he wasn't certain he would be welcome so he would eat downstairs, Samiel signed, shrugging.

"Well, if he thinks I'm going downstairs to soothe him out of his sulk, he's got another think coming," I said.

Samiel plated some pancakes and handed them to me. *You'd better take this before it hits the table; otherwise one of them will devour it.*

I sat down with my pile of pancakes and started eating. After a while, Beezle came up for air.

"I went online last night after you fell asleep."

"And?"

"And it seems that all is not quiet on the faerie front.

Certain factions in Titania and Oberon's court believe they should not have sent the Hob after you."

"Really? I'd have thought all the faeries were on the vengeance-for-Amarantha team."

"There are some who believe that Amarantha brought her troubles on herself by involving the court in the affairs of angels. And now that the Hob is dead, those folks are saying that to pressure you further is an unnecessary risk."

"It seems your reputation for complete and total destruction precedes you," Chloe said.

"And they think it would be stupid to pick a fight with a child of Lucifer," Beezle added.

"Why? Lucifer's never bothered assisting me before."

"But just because he hasn't yet doesn't mean that he won't in the future. And nobody wants Lucifer angry with them. They know what he did to Amarantha."

"Yet Titania and Oberon don't share their trepidation," I said thoughtfully. "Why?"

"They must think whatever power they've got can stand up to Lucifer," Beezle said.

"Can it?"

"They are probably more or less as powerful as they seem, but I think it's been millennia since Lucifer really bothered to exert himself."

"So if he wanted to, he could squash them like bugs."

"I think so. But it would be more like squashing a nuclear power plant."

"If you kill something that old and that magical, there will be aftershocks," I guessed.

"Right."

"So what these factions are really worried about is being in the way when the explosion happens."

"You can't credit most faeries with concern for the greater good," Beezle said.

"J.B. is pretty noble-minded," I said.

"He's only half-faerie, and he spent most of his childhood with his father. He's more human than you are."

"Thanks," I said, chewing slowly and thinking about what Beezle said.

Titania and Oberon's actions didn't make sense. Even if they believed I owed them for Amarantha's death, the matter should have been settled after I killed the Hob. They had to know that if the Morningstar got involved, it would be bad for everyone. It was almost as if they were . . .

"They're picking a fight with Lucifer," I said aloud. "But *why*?"

"Remember what Jude told us when Wade was missing? All the courts are choosing sides for a future war."

"Yeah, but Titania and Oberon are not just lining up on one side of the battlefield or the other. They're actually trying to start the war."

"What's in it for them?" Chloe asked.

"I don't know. They must think they'll get the spoils. But this brings us back to what we were just talking about. Lucifer is more powerful than anyone knows, so there's no way they could win."

"Except maybe he's not," Chloe said.

"You think Lucifer is not as powerful as he's perceived to be?" Beezle asked.

I thought about the strain of magic that ran in me from Lucifer's line, diluted by hundreds of generations and yet infinitely stronger than any other power I carried.

"He *is* that strong," I said. "But the faeries must think they've got something stronger."

Beezle looked at me. "Or that they've found his weakness."

"I am not Lucifer's weakness. He would happily throw me on a bonfire if he thought he could get something out of it."

"Maybe before, but not now," Beezle said pointedly.

"But they don't know about . . ." I said, trailing off. I didn't want to talk about the baby in front of Chloe.

"If that meaningful silence is for me, don't bother. I can totally tell that you're pregnant."

"Really? How?"

"You've got that puffy look that pregnant women get."

"I'm maybe two weeks pregnant. I do not look puffy."

Chloe's eyebrows winged up to her hairline. "Whoa. So you look like this all the time?"

"Moving on," I said. "There's no way the faeries could know. And even if they did, I don't think killing me is the best way to weaken Lucifer. I don't think he would sit at home crying over me; do you?"

"No. He would probably blast the entire kingdom of Faerie into oblivion," Beezle said.

"Exactly. So it doesn't make sense. Nothing they've done makes sense."

A headache was brewing between my eyes. There were too many plots, too many loose strands to collect. Azazel and the vampires on one side, Titania and Oberon and their obsession with vengeance on another. A common desire to overthrow Lucifer linked them both. Were the two plots connected, or was it just coincidence that they both decided now was the time? Why had Lucifer suddenly been perceived as vulnerable?

I didn't have enough information to try to decipher the

ways and means of Lucifer's enemies. So I had to focus on what I did have—Azazel's notebook.

While Chloe and Beezle demolished the rest of the pancakes, I explained what had happened the day before.

"So we need to find out what Azazel's experiments are all about," I said, presenting her the binder that Nathaniel had found.

She took it from me with a look of gleeful curiosity on her face, scanning the pages quickly.

"He's definitely using some known chemicals, but some of the other symbols seem to be unique," Chloe said, frowning over Azazel's equations.

"Maybe they're shorthand for magic?" I asked.

"Possibly, but there's no sure way to establish what magic he might have invoked for each symbol," she said.

My face fell. "So we have no way of breaking down these formulas?"

"I didn't say that," Chloe said with a touch of asperity. "I just need a little time."

"I don't know how much time we have," I said grimly.

"Then I guess I'll have to get to work," she said, pushing away from the table and tucking the binder under her arm.

"J.B. said there's been some flak about outside projects at the Agency," I said.

"Don't worry. I know how to avoid getting caught," she said.

Samiel was standing at the sink washing the prep dishes. She approached him like a big cat stalking its prey. A second before Chloe reached him, Samiel turned, almost as if he sensed her approach. His eyes widened as she flattened herself against him and pressed her lips against his.

I turned my head away, hiding my smile under my hand. When I looked back Chloe was marching toward the front door with a satisfied look on her face, and Samiel appeared stunned.

Beezle opened his mouth, like he was going to make a smart remark, and I shook my head at him.

"What?" he asked.

"Leave Samiel alone. He has enough to handle without you giving him a hard time," I said.

"What's with the new touchy-feely policy in this house?" Beezle complained. "I hope you aren't going to turn into a wuss just because you're having a baby."

"Don't worry. I'm sure I can drum up enough smart remarks about your personality flaws to keep you happy," I said.

"What personality flaws?" Beezle asked indignantly.

I pushed away from the table. "I've got a soul pickup this morning. Since I doubt that you'll return to your regularly scheduled job—"

"What's the point of guarding this house? Everything that shows up to attack either gets you while you're on the front lawn anyway or it rings the doorbell."

"Since you're not doing much these days besides driving Samiel up the wall, you can go back to your online buddies and collect some more information for me. Find out who's leading the opposition in Titania and Oberon's court."

"Why? You think they'll cut a deal with you?" Beezle asked.

"It doesn't hurt to find out who might be receptive to me if I decide to approach them," I said.

"Just be careful . . ." Beezle began.

"I know. Faeries are deceptive. Don't worry. You be careful, too. You never know who you're talking to online."

"Yes, I do," Beezle said.

"You can't possibly think that everyone is truthful about their identity."

"Of course I don't think that. But gargoyles can see the true nature of things, and that means that I know when someone is lying to me about their identity, even online," Beezle said.

"That's . . . really weird," I said. "But useful."

Beezle shrugged. "Magic is often weird but useful."

I went to dress and check the time and place of my soul pickup. It was on Southport in an hour, just under the Brown Line stop. There was an asterisk next to the name, and the footnote at the bottom of the page said, "Possibility of collateral damage."

That didn't sound like a routine soul collection. I was surprised that I was the only one assigned if there was the possibility of other deaths. It was annoying that the Agency seers hadn't bothered to give me any further information. They knew how the person was going to die. Didn't they think it would help me to know that, too?

The thing about the Agency seers is that they like to keep Agents in the dark. There's always a possibility that an Agent might try to prevent a death if he or she knew how the death would occur. That is absolutely, positively not allowed. Once a death is foreseen, that's it. It's in the books, and no matter how unfair or gruesome that death may be, we are not allowed to stop it.

I slung my sword over my shoulder. "Possibility of collateral damage" meant that only one death was certain; the others could be prevented. It was best to be prepared for anything.

I pulled on a coat, hat and gloves, and made sure Beezle and Samiel knew where I was going—no sense in having them raise the alarm again. Then I flew out the back window toward Southport, which was east of my house.

The winter sun shone so bright I regretted not bringing sunglasses, but it was still close to zero degrees with the wind chill. The snow on the streets and sidewalks was getting that grungy look, gray from dirt and pollution. The cars on the street were coated in a thin film of salt.

Cloaked by my Agent's magic, I landed near the corner of Roscoe and Southport, in front of a liquor shop that was connected to the El station. On the other side of the station was a two-story building under construction that would eventually hold a fitness center and some more shops.

I checked the clock on my cell phone and saw that it was a few minutes until showtime. I hadn't identified the soul yet, so I settled in to wait.

A minute or two later a college-age girl stepped out of the El stop. She was bundled up so thoroughly I could see only her eyes peeking above her scarf and the long strands of her ponytail emerging from under her hat. Her backpack looked like it was laden with textbooks. She turned north when she left the station, away from me, and I pushed away from the wall. This was Jayne Wiskowski, and her death had already been written.

I followed her slowly, my boots crunching in the ice and snow even though no one could see me. I didn't see any sign of her impending doom.

The tattoo in my right palm twitched. Something was coming.

One second it wasn't there, and the next second it was, like it had crawled through a fold in time and space to appear directly in front of Jayne.

The creature looked like a long and elegant preying

mantis, albeit one the size of an NBA player. It closed a pincer around her neck and squeezed.

I broke into a run, the sword in my hand before I could think about it. The pincer, sharp as a Santoku, sliced through her neck before I'd taken three steps.

A woman pushing two toddlers in a double stroller a few feet away screeched as Jayne's head fell from her shoulders and rolled onto the sidewalk. Arterial blood spurted as her body collapsed. Her soul poured out in a stream of ecto-plasm, mouth open in the scream she'd never had the oppor-tunity to utter.

The mantis looked at me, and something like a smile ghosted across its alien features. I realized that I was the only one who could see the creature. And it was turning toward the screaming mother and her crying kids.

I didn't have time to think about Jayne's confused soul. I charged the creature and brought the sword down, aiming for the soft, vulnerable joint at its shoulder.

The blade struck true, and the thing gave an ear-shattering cry of pain and anger. Gelatinous goo oozed from the wound.

"What is that? What is that?" the mother screamed, backing away from the sound. She was getting dangerously close to the street, and her kids were freaking out more because their mom was losing it. "What's happening?"

She couldn't see the creature, or me, but she could hear the monster's cries. Behind me I heard the El rumbling into the station. In a minute a bunch of people would get off the train and find Jayne's body. Then there would be a lot of fussing and running to and fro, and the creature would have more opportunities to kill. More opportunities for "collateral damage."

I had to take it out or get it away from the area. I couldn't think about Jayne right now.

The mantis slashed out at me, its pincers snapping at any part of me it could reach. I dodged away, striking back with the sword. The blade slid off the smooth carapace that covered the creature all over except at its joints, so if I didn't strike in those precise spots, I was just wasting energy. I didn't want to start throwing magic around. There were too many people, too many chances for things to go wrong.

I drove the creature toward Newport, hoping to push it off the main thoroughfare and into the alley that was behind the candy store. A couple of concerned citizens had arrived in response to the mother's cries, and had conveniently moved her off to the side, away from both the battle and the street.

There was a hubbub of activity behind me now as more people found the body without a head and a crowd gathered. Sirens blared a few blocks away. There was a police station very close by on Addison, and the authorities would be arriving at any moment.

The mantis clipped at my coat, snagging the material dangerously close to my neck but missing my skin. It cried out in frustration as I slashed at it, forcing it to move away from the crowd of people.

I couldn't do this all day. I could feel my energy flagging, the weariness that came from pregnancy covering me like a veil. I had to take a chance, and there was no one on the street behind the creature.

I dropped the sword to one side, loosely gripping it in my left hand. The mantis lifted its pincer high like it was anticipating the need to block an attack. I stepped forward with my right foot, fluttered up on my wings and reached under the block with my hand, laying it on the visible flesh just under the creature's head.

It was slimy, and soft, a lot like touching an exposed

organ. But I couldn't think about what I was feeling, or give the mantis a chance to attack. I sent electricity careening through my body and out my fingers, into the soft parts of the monster.

It gave a hideous cry, high-pitched and ear-shattering. The hubbub on Southport quieted as several people cried out, "What's that? What now?"

I held tight to the creature as it struggled, its body shaking and trembling, my feet suspended above the sidewalk. The air filled with the smell of cooked insect. I gagged, barely holding on to the pancakes churning in my belly.

After a few moments I let go, and the creature's blackened corpse fell to the sidewalk. I hung in the air for a moment, breathing in and out through my nose until my stomach settled. Then I lowered to the ground and looked at the burned and twisted thing smoking there.

I couldn't leave the corpse in the middle of the sidewalk. No one could see it, but they might step on it. I heaved a sigh and went around behind the mantis to drag it into the alley.

The body was surprisingly heavy. Despite the extra dose of strength that came from being half-angel, it was still a struggle for me to pull the creature about ten feet to the nearest Dumpster.

I stood, huffing and puffing and trying to get my pounding heart under control before I attempted putting the remains in with the other garbage.

"Madeline . . . Black . . ."

I shrieked and jumped back as an eerie, metallic voice came from the monster I'd thought I'd killed.

8

"MADELINE BLACK," IT SAID AGAIN, AND ITS VOICE WAS tinny, fading away.

I raised my sword above my head to finish it off.

"All . . . your . . . fault," it said, coughing. "Here . . . for you."

Was this creature telling me that Jayne had died because of me? That she was a lure to get to me?

"Who sent you?" I demanded.

It laughed, or tried to. It was hideous to watch it try to speak. Burnt flesh and armor fell from its beaklike mouth, crumbling into ash in the bitter wind.

"Find out . . . soon enough," it said.

I heard the rattle of breath, the last exhalation of the dead. But I wasn't taking any chances.

I cut off its head anyway. Then I cut off its arms, and then its legs, and then I began hacking away at its torso, which was much more vulnerable to the slice of my blade now that it was burned up.

After a while the red haze of anger receded. I realized I was dripping sweat over a pile of smoking insect parts. The wind cut through the holes in my battle-damaged coat, and I shivered.

This was stupid on so many levels. I was standing out in the cold, pregnant and exhausted, and while I was mindlessly hacking up the mantis, one of my many enemies could have snuck up behind me.

"At least it's easier to put in the garbage now," I muttered, scooping up the parts and tossing them into the Dumpster.

I adjusted my hat, put away the sword and went to find Jayne Wiskowski.

Her soul, of course, was gone.

There was crime scene tape up around the spot where her body had fallen, and several police officers stood around talking to one another and shooing away the curious. Her body was nowhere to be seen, which meant it had been already transported to the morgue.

Given the trauma of her death, it was unlikely that the soul was still attached to the body. She'd probably broken free of her mortal shell pretty soon after her ectoplasmic self had caught a glimpse of her separated head. Which meant that she was wandering somewhere.

I gritted my teeth, knowing I'd have to hunt for her, and settled in for the long haul. Given all the problems at the Agency, there was no way I could submit paperwork on a lost soul. Of course, the Agency could have helped me out by sending another collector instead of leaving me hanging in the wind.

For half a second I entertained the idea that the Agency

had wanted me to fail, and that was why they'd sent me out on my own even though they knew there was a strong possibility this collection would go pear-shaped.

Then I realized that the constant persecution from enemies known and unknown was making me paranoid. The Agency couldn't be after me, too, could they?

Well, maybe they could, but I couldn't worry about it. I had enough to worry about. I'd limited the monster's kills to one, and if—no, *when*—I found Jayne's soul, I'd have this pickup all tied up with a ribbon, just the way upper management liked it.

Three hours later the wind had frozen me into a Popsicle, and I was dizzy from flying in circles. Jayne had disappeared, and I hadn't the remotest clue where she might have gone.

My face was frozen, my stomach was rumbling and Beezle had probably worked himself up into a tizzy, so I decided to head home.

I cut over to Addison and flew straight west toward my house.

Beezle was on the kitchen counter with his beak in a gigantic sack of Kettle chips. His bottom half stuck out of the bag as he burrowed through like an earthworm. Rapid crunching sounds emitted from inside.

I grabbed him by the ankle and yanked him out. Chips skidded all over the counter. He looked guilty for a second, then covered it with defiance.

"What? Nobody else wanted them," he said.

"I might have wanted some," I said. "I see you were not even remotely worried about me. Where is everyone?"

"Jude had to meet with Wade about some pack thingy. He called and said he would be back soon. Nathaniel is downstairs sulking, as usual. Or maybe he's plotting. It's hard to tell the difference. Samiel is playing Skyrim on the computer."

"Do I want to know what Skyrim is?"

"Probably not," Beezle said, dusting chips off his face.

"I need to eat something," I said as my stomach growled.

"We should get Potbelly sandwiches," Beezle said hopefully.

"No," I said. The closest Potbelly was right across the street from the place where Jayne Wiskowski had lost her head. I didn't need to be reminded of that debacle while I was eating.

"Can we go to Costco and get a hot dog, then?"

"*You* just ate. I'm the one who needs to eat something."

"Those chips are mostly air," Beezle said. "I need something substantial."

A hot dog did sound good. And there was a bookstore on Webster, near Costco. I could stop and get a copy of *What to Expect When You're Expecting a Demon Baby.*

"Okay, we can go to Costco," I said.

"Really?" Beezle said. He seemed disappointed that I hadn't put up a bigger fight.

"Yes, but you only get one item off the menu," I said as he climbed into my coat pocket.

"Just one?" he whined. "How can I possibly choose between the hot dog, the ice cream bar and the churro?"

"Choose wisely," I said. "Because I'm not sharing whatever I get."

Beezle tucked himself under my lapel, grumbling.

The store was packed, as usual. Beezle finally settled on an ice cream bar after much dithering. I took off my coat and laid it over the child seat in the shopping cart so that Beezle could camp under there and eat without attracting notice.

I bought a hot dog and soda and pushed the cart through the store, even though I had no intention of buying anything. I like to walk through the aisles sometimes, looking at things that I'll never be able to buy. I stopped in front of the jewelry case, but the gleam of diamond engagement rings made me twist my wedding band around my finger in an unhappy way, so I moved on.

In the center of the store was a collection of tables displaying new clothing. One of the tables was covered in baby clothes, pinks and purples and blues and greens.

I picked up a tiny infant sleeper and had a moment of panic. Babies were small. Really small.

"How am I supposed to take care of something this small?" I said aloud.

"What was that?" Beezle said. His voice was muffled by my coat and the ice cream in his mouth.

"Nothing," I said, dropping the sleeper back on the table and pushing my cart away.

How could I be responsible for someone so little, someone so breakable? How could I ever keep a baby safe? I'd barely managed to keep myself safe so far.

After Beezle had finished eating an ice cream bar as big as his torso, we ditched the shopping cart and flew over to the bookstore on Webster.

I stood in front of the pregnancy and child-care section, awed by the number of books relating to the birth, care and feeding of children.

Beezle poked his head out of my lapel. "Gods above and below. Who says kids don't come with instruction manuals?"

"Yeah, but how do I know if I'm picking the right one?" I asked.

"No matter what you choose it won't cover your extenuating circumstances," Beezle said. "These books are for human babies."

"What did my mom do?" I asked, my eyes scanning the rows of titles.

Beezle shrugged his little shoulders. "It was the seventies. There were no books on babies in the seventies. You popped the kid out and figured things out as you went along."

I looked down at him. "Was she ever worried about what I would become, being a child of Azazel?"

The gargoyle's face was grave. "She worried, yes. She didn't know if you'd come out of the womb with visible wings or blazing magic. She didn't know if she would survive the birth at all."

"Why would she take that risk?" I asked.

Beezle looked at me pointedly. "Why do you?"

"Because I loved Gabriel," I said, and my heart hurt. "I loved him, and this child is the last piece of him that I have."

"And, as hard as it may be for you to believe, that's how Katherine felt about Azazel. She loved him. She lost him. And you were her last link to him."

It was hard for me to reconcile the idea of Azazel as a longed-for lover with my image of him as a vicious killer, but I supposed that my mother must have never seen that side of him. Or—and this was even more disturbing to contemplate—she had seen that side of him, and made her peace with it.

"If she hadn't loved him, I wouldn't have had you," Beezle said. "And even though you were little and wrinkly and had a terrible temper, I loved you. And still do, even though you never listen to me."

"I love you, too. Even though you eat all of the popcorn."

Beezle rubbed his eyes. "All right, enough of the mushy stuff. Get your instruction manual and let's get out of here."

I smiled. At least I knew I could count on Beezle, who actually had some child-care experience. Presumably he would make sure I didn't screw up too badly.

I chose a book that looked fairly comprehensive, paid for it and left.

As we approached our street, I saw a plume of smoke rising in the air. A cold ball of dread formed in my stomach. There was no good or innocent reason why smoke would be rising from the vicinity of my house.

And I was right.

When I landed on the front lawn, Samiel, Jude and Nathaniel were all standing around the smoldering remains of what must have been a bonfire. All three of them were covered in soot and looked exhausted.

"Is everyone okay?" I asked, rushing to Samiel. "What happened?"

He nodded, his face grim. *We're okay, but I don't know how they managed to build this so fast.*

"Who?" I asked.

"Faeries," Jude spat.

He moved to one side so I could see the scarecrow that lay in the snow. It looked like an oversized rag doll, cloth and stuffing, with long black yarn hair, a black overcoat, and the star of Lucifer upon its face. It was quite obviously a stand-in for me, and I felt my temper rising again, though I struggled to keep it under control.

"Their information must not be up-to-date," I said, trying for a light tone. "Their voodoo doll needs a haircut."

"Don't joke about voodoo dolls," Beezle said, his claws squeezing my shoulder. "If the faeries had put a spell on that scarecrow and these three hadn't managed to put out the fire, you would have been burned to cinders by now."

I stared at the smoke-stained doll that someone had meant to be my death by proxy. My death, and my child's.

"Enough," I said, and heard the anger I couldn't suppress in my voice. "This stops now."

It was just past the middle of the day, but the lawn suddenly seemed brighter as the power of Lucifer flared inside me.

"They are not getting away with this. They are not going to terrorize me or keep me looking over my shoulder for the rest of my life."

"What are you going to do?" Beezle asked as the other three stared at me.

"I'm going to Titania and Oberon's court and I'm going to show them once and for all that I am not to be trifled with," I said.

I could feel the magic surging in my blood, the heat of the sun, the brightness of my anger. If Titania and Oberon wanted me for an enemy, then they could face me instead of hiding behind threats and rag dolls.

"How will you get to the court?" Nathaniel asked. "The pathways are hidden, and fraught with risk. Titania and Oberon do not welcome uninvited guests."

"I think I know someone who can get me in," I said.

"J.B.?" Beezle asked. "You'll put him at risk."

I shook my head. "Not J.B."

I tilted my head back toward the sky, let my power and my anger spill forth. Jude, Nathaniel, Samiel and Beezle covered their eyes as I lit up like the heart of the sun.

"LUCIFER!" I screamed, and my voice was not my own. It was a thing of terrible beauty, full of darkness and sharp as a thousand blades.

A pulse of magic left me like an aftershock, following my voice along the line of blood that connected me to Lucifer. I felt his presence as I had never felt it before. My eyes could see for thousands of miles, and far away, farther than I'd imagined, I saw Lucifer upon his throne. And I knew when he heard me.

His eyes widened, and then he disappeared.

"He's coming," I said, in that same terrible voice. "Go inside."

For once, none of them argued with me. I don't think any of them wanted to get caught in between Lucifer and me. They all hurried toward the house, except for Beezle.

"Where are you, Maddy?" he asked, his face troubled.

"I'm still here," I said, but it felt like a lie. Madeline Black was buried beneath the light of the Morningstar.

"Somewhere," he said. "Don't lose yourself."

Losing myself seemed less important than surviving another day. I couldn't survive if I continued to let Titania and Oberon set the rules.

Lucifer approached, and a storm came with him. Black clouds rolled over the sky, blotting out the sun. The light inside me blazed brighter as the day was cloaked by night.

And then he was before me, magnificent in his darkness, his wings darker than a raven's, his eyes twin pools of starlight.

"Granddaughter," he said, and the ground trembled at his voice. "How dare you summon me thus? How dare you show your power to me in anger?"

"How dare you abandon me thus?" I said, my temper surging again. "Over and over, Titania and Oberon have threatened my life, the life of your grandchild. Would you allow your enemies to destroy me to feed your own purpose?"

"Perhaps I thought you did not need or welcome my

assistance," he said silkily. "You have never been particularly loving toward me."

"Perhaps that's because you've brought nothing but trouble to my door," I replied.

"And what would you ask of me, now that you have me here?"

"I want you to take me to the court of Titania and Oberon, so that I may end their quest for vengeance," I said.

"Do you believe that you can stop them?" he asked, his voice laced with curiosity. "Do you believe that you can match wits with two of the oldest creatures in existence and come away without paying a price?"

"Take me to them and you'll see," I said.

"The ways are hidden to mortals," he said.

"I am not completely mortal," I replied.

"And . . . they are perilous. You may not get as far as the court," Lucifer said.

"Are you refusing to take me?" I asked.

"I can take you to the start of the path, and no farther," he said after a long pause.

"Another test?"

"No," he said impatiently. "I am bound by treaties written long ago, treaties that prevent the old creatures from encroaching on one another. I cannot enter Titania and Oberon's realm without express invitation, as they cannot enter mine without the same."

"Fine," I said. "Show me where to go and I'll take care of them without you. Just as I've taken care of every other problem you've brought me."

"You seem very contemptuous of me, granddaughter," Lucifer said, and he seemed to grow larger. The magic in the air grew stronger, thicker.

But my anger was greater than his, and my power pushed

back. This was the second time I had gone head-to-head with the Prince of Darkness. The last time, he'd backed down because it had suited him to do so.

This time, he didn't.

His power roared up in the darkness, a sudden blaze of fire like an exploding volcano. The blood that connected us turned against me, and I saw before my eyes the horror that Lucifer could bestow upon the world if he so chose.

"No," I said, but instead of shrinking before him, I grew stronger. It seemed that he hesitated for a moment, shocked that I had not withered before his assault.

He had tried to turn the power against me, but he was feeding it. I no longer belonged only to myself. Gabriel's blood was inside me, too. Gabriel's child was closer to Lucifer than me, separated by only two generations, and that child could feel the call of Lucifer's magic, and embraced it.

"You can't scare me," I said.

He diminished suddenly, returned to his normal self, his wings hidden beneath his coat. And then he applauded.

"Oh, yes. Titania and Oberon won't know what to do with you, my dear," he said.

I returned to normal as well, the light and power shrinking in the face of his sudden surrender. I felt as if I'd somehow been tricked again, that Lucifer had gotten something he'd wanted.

"Why is it that I never seem to feel like I've gotten the best of you?" I muttered. Beezle needn't have worried. Madeline Black had returned without any ill effects.

"People often feel that way around me," Lucifer said.

I rubbed my head. "Will you take me to the path, then? Since it seems to suit you?"

"Of course, as it suits you as well," he said, a merry twinkle in his eye. "But I think you should not go alone."

He nodded toward the front porch, and I turned to see Nathaniel standing there as if he'd been summoned. I looked back at Lucifer and shook my head.

"I'd rather have Jude," I said.

"But I would prefer you take Nathaniel," he said, his voice covered in steel.

"Why?" I asked. "What have you got planned now?"

"If you want to go to the path, then you will allow yourself to be escorted by Nathaniel ap Zerachiel and no other," he said.

I glanced back at Nathaniel, standing on the porch with a stony expression, waiting for my decision. Was it worth it to push this, and lose my chance at confronting Titania and Oberon? I already knew I could handle Nathaniel, but why was Lucifer pressing him on me so determinedly?

"Ticktock," Lucifer said.

"All right," I said.

I needed to take one problem at a time. First Titania and Oberon, then Azazel's plot, then Azazel himself. Somewhere in there I'd have to find time to unknot Lucifer's motivations and figure out if the Agency was conspiring against me.

"Beezle is not going to be happy about this," I said.

"I will speak with your gargoyle, and your guard dog," Lucifer said.

"Um, I don't think you want to talk to Jude," I said, thinking of their history.

"Do not worry. Judas and I have dealt with one another before."

"Yeah, that's what I'm afraid of," I muttered. I didn't want Jude to get himself killed going after Lucifer.

Lucifer smiled, and it was not a nice smile.

"Wait here for a moment," he said, and went toward the house. He paused on the threshold, calling Jude's name.

Even Lucifer couldn't get into my house without an invitation. That made me feel a little better.

Jude, Samiel and Beezle must have been lurking just inside the foyer. The door opened immediately.

Nathaniel went down the steps and came to stand near me. I watched Lucifer and the other three confer in quiet tones at the door. I couldn't see Lucifer's expression or hear what was said, but Jude was purple in the face and Samiel's jaw was set.

"He's controlling them by threatening your life," Nathaniel said softly.

"He wouldn't risk me," I said, not mentioning the baby. As far as I knew Nathaniel was still unaware of the pregnancy. "He wants me for some purpose of his own."

"*They* won't risk you," Nathaniel said. "No one can see into Lucifer's heart, and they love you. So they will not take the chance that Lucifer might harm you out of spite."

"Would you let him?" I asked, giving him a sidelong glance.

"No," Nathaniel said firmly.

I was surprised. I'd expected the usual nonsense about having to obey the wishes of his master and whatnot.

"Whatever you may think, whatever my other motivations, you have come to mean something to me. I would not let anyone harm you if I could prevent it."

He seemed sincere, but I didn't know what to think. Just about every angel I'd ever met had seemed one thing and been another. Except Gabriel. He'd always been exactly what he seemed to be.

I didn't know what to say to Nathaniel, so I just nodded

in acknowledgment. This seemed to satisfy him for the moment, and we both looked away.

Lucifer approached us with a satisfied look on his face. Apparently he'd gotten his way. Jude, Samiel and Beezle all appeared angry and frustrated.

"Are we ready to depart, then?" Lucifer said, clapping his hands together.

"Just a moment," Nathaniel said. "I have to discuss something with Samiel."

Nathaniel went up to the porch. I watched him go, bewildered. What on earth could he have to discuss with Samiel?

Lucifer turned to me. "I hope you are prepared, granddaughter, for the trial ahead of you."

"Titania and Oberon can't be worse than you," I said.

He smiled at me. "Not many are."

"Normal people aren't proud of things like that."

Nathaniel returned a moment later, nodding at Lucifer. "My lord."

"Off to see the wizard, then," Lucifer said.

He took hold of my hand and Nathaniel's, and a second later we winked out of sight.

It wasn't like traveling through a portal. Portals are noisy, and windy, and painful. This was like passing through the heart of the universe. It was peaceful, and quiet. Above and beneath and beside us all the worlds unfolded like a beautiful string of pearls. Images passed by at a rapid rate, a flickering film of people, gods and monsters, cities and countries, mountains and oceans. And in one of them, I thought I saw, just for a moment . . .

"Gabriel!" I cried out, and tried to slip Lucifer's hand, to go to him.

"Madeline," he said firmly. "Do not let go, or you will fall into time and space and be lost forever."

"I saw . . . I thought I saw . . ." The wound that I'd thought was scabbed over was bleeding anew. I'd seen him. I was sure of it.

"You saw what you wished to see," Lucifer said.

I didn't say anything further. The moment was gone. I didn't even know which of the dozens of places I'd seen had held Gabriel. But I had seen him, even if Lucifer didn't want me to believe it.

I don't know how much time passed. After a while Lucifer said, "This is the place."

And we were there.

The three of us stood on a high hill. The hill was split down the middle. One side was rocky and barren, and stretched away into an icy tundra covered by a gray sky. The other side was lush and green and dotted with sunshine. We were on the rocky, icy side, and a bitter wind bit through my coat.

"Once you cross this line," Lucifer said, indicating the split, "you will have entered the kingdom of Titania and Oberon, and there is no turning back."

"How will we get home without you?" I asked.

"Either you will negotiate your own safe passage, or . . ." He trailed off.

"Or we won't come home at all," I said.

"I have every confidence in you, granddaughter," Lucifer said, taking me by the shoulders and kissing my forehead.

I felt the usual roil of confusion that I experienced around Lucifer. There was something very fatherlike about him, but then, no good father had ever threatened to sacrifice their child for their own purpose.

He released me and turned to Nathaniel.

"You know what your charge is, Nathaniel ap Zerachiel," Lucifer said, and all the warmth was gone from his tone.

"Yes, my lord," Nathaniel said, bowing.

"See that your duty is done," Lucifer said.

And then he disappeared.

I looked at the happy valley spread out below us. Like all things faerie, I was sure that it was a glamour disguising a lot of terror and ugliness. Knowing that there was danger ahead didn't make it any easier to take that first step.

"Well, I guess it's you and me," I said to Nathaniel.

"Not quite," said a muffled voice, and Beezle crawled out of Nathaniel's coat, looking disgruntled.

"What are you doing here?" I asked as he flew over to my shoulder and made an elaborate show of smoothing his horns.

"Like I would let you go to Titania and Oberon's court without me. How are you supposed to benefit from my intel if I'm not with you?"

I looked at Nathaniel, who watched me with an uncertain expression.

"Thank you," I said.

"I thought you would feel more comfortable if the gargoyle were with you," he said.

"Well, comfort doesn't really factor into it, since I've got to lug him around," I said.

"Information comes with a price," Beezle said loftily. "Now, can we get this train rolling? I need to be back in time for *Dancing with the Stars*."

"Of course," I said dryly. "Nothing could possibly be more important than seeing which D-list celebrity gets eliminated this week."

"It's *awesome*," Beezle said.

I took a deep breath, and stepped over the line. Nathaniel followed.

I was immediately enveloped in warmth. It felt like a

beautiful summer day on this side. The air was lightly scented with flowers. Birds whistled songs that caught in the breeze and carried up to where we stood.

"This is so wrong," Beezle said.

"I know," I replied. "Nothing this lovely or charming could possibly be real. Do you see what's underneath?"

Beezle concentrated, staring at the scene before us. After a while he shook his head. "This glamour is really good, and it's old. It's layered so deep that I can't see with a quick glance. I'd have to look at it for a while."

"It's all right," I said. "We know that we can't trust what we see, so let's just proceed carefully."

"And don't eat or drink anything," Beezle said.

"I know," I said, and we started down the hill.

The hill was longer than it seemed from the top. The descent was gradual but it took much more time than I'd expected to reach the bottom. When we did, both Nathaniel and I were sweating. We were dressed for winter in Chicago.

I pulled off my coat, hat and gloves and gave them a regretful glance as I left them on the ground. Nathaniel followed suit, his wings revealed. He rolled up the sleeves of his shirt.

"There's no point in carrying this stuff around," I said, though I hated to leave things behind.

"The coat is trashed, anyway," Beezle said. "Again. What tore up the shoulder?"

I told Beezle and Nathaniel about the mantis-thing that had attacked the girl on Southport as we walked through a field of knee-high grass. Brightly colored butterflies alighted here and there on tall wildflowers.

"Was the mantis something faerie?" I asked.

"Not that I know of," Beezle said.

"Great. So something else is out to get me?"

"I suppose it could be a sending from Azazel," Nathaniel said. "One of his experiments?"

"Then why not say so?" I asked. "Azazel loves to rub it in my face when he thinks he's about to get the better of me."

"I guess we just have to accept that you've pissed off enough people that we can't tell who's after you without identification," Beezle said.

"Why is it my fault when these immortals come after me?"

"Well, you do keep foiling their evil plans," Beezle said.

"So, I should let them kill innocent people?"

"All I'm saying is that it puts a target on your back," Beezle said.

"Enough," Nathaniel said. "Why did I consider it a good thing to bring you along?"

"That wasn't too bad," Beezle said. "You might want to work on your cutting tone, though. I can't fence with an unarmed man."

"It is a wonder both of you have not yet been killed," Nathaniel said seriously. "How can you hear the enemy approaching over the sound of your bickering?"

"Maddy survives mostly on luck," Beezle said. "I'm not sure being able to hear the monsters approaching would make much of a difference."

"I resent the implication that I'm some kind of half-wit stumbling around in a sea of chaos," I said.

"You said it, not me."

"Gods above and below," Nathaniel muttered.

Beezle winked at me.

We came to the edge of a wood. There was a clear path proceeding through the trees, and the forest looked as bright and happy as the field we'd just passed through. A doe and her fawn stood a short distance away, and seemed unconcerned by our presence as they fed on leaves and twigs.

Beezle gave the deer a good hard stare. Then he leaned close to my ear. "Those aren't deer."

"Do I want to know what they are?" I asked.

"Probably not," Beezle said. "It will just give you indigestion."

I pointed out the deer to Nathaniel. He nodded.

"Should we go forward?" he said quietly.

"There's no other way to go if we want to get back home. Let's just hope they don't bother us," I said, and stepped onto the path.

Both deer looked up as my foot crossed into the forest. They shimmered for a moment, and the deer suddenly weren't there anymore.

But something else was, and they looked far too happy to see us.

9

"YOU WERE RIGHT," I SAID TO BEEZLE. "I'D RATHER not know."

The creatures grew before our eyes until they were the size of the trees that towered in the forest. They looked like a cross between trolls and dogs, with lumpy, misshapen, humanoid faces attached to furred four-legged bodies.

Long canines protruded over their lower jaws, and their disconcertingly human eyes seemed to say one thing when they looked at us.

Lunch.

"Stand and fight or try to escape?" I asked.

"Fly!" Nathaniel shouted.

I didn't need to be told twice.

Beezle launched off my shoulder. I pushed out my wings and shot into the sky above the trees, Nathaniel beside me. We accelerated away from the troll-things, which howled as they saw us taking to the air.

I looked back over my shoulder and gasped. "Oh, that's not fair."

I pulled up for a moment. Nathaniel and Beezle turned to see what I was looking at.

The creatures were growing wings. Huge, reticulated wings sprouted from their bodies. The larger creature narrowed its eyes at us in triumph.

"Fly faster," Beezle said.

"No," I said. "We can't outrun them. Evasive maneuvers."

I dove back into the trees, the other two following me. For a moment we were out of the sight of the monsters, hidden by the thick, leafy canopy. I settled in a sturdy-looking curve of branch, and Beezle landed on my shoulder. Nathaniel hovered in the air beside me.

The monsters both roared in anger as we disappeared. A moment later the ground trembled, and then a gale-force wind hit us as the creatures lifted off the ground. They buzzed over us, shouting at one another in a language I did not understand, clearly searching. They flew in small circles above the trees, and we tensed as they passed above us, then relaxed when the trolls moved on.

"What do you have in mind?" Nathaniel whispered, his face close to my ear so I could hear him over the wind. "We can't hide here forever. They are large enough to grab us from the ground if we stay under the tree cover."

"So if we stay under the trees, they'll grab us from the ground, and if we stay above the trees, they'll catch up to us quickly," Beezle said. "Why didn't I stay home with the TV and the popcorn?"

"We'll have to fly in and out," I said. "And try to blast them with spells while we're at it."

"Oh, great," Beezle said. "We're going to kill something else of Titania and Oberon's, and then they're *really* going to be pissed at us."

"Do you want to get back home to the TV and the popcorn?" I asked.

"Fine, fine," Beezle said. "Have it your way."

"Look—they're staying above the trees for now. So let's try to get as far as we can under the canopy. They make so much noise they should be easy to hear if they approach," I said.

Nathaniel nodded and Beezle squeezed my shoulder with his claws.

"I take it that you're riding?" I asked Beezle.

"I'm not built for evasive maneuvers," Beezle said.

"You left yourself wide-open there, but I'm not going to take advantage on account of the fact that we're in mortal peril," I said.

Nathaniel and I flew quickly and quietly toward the path. The branches of the trees arched over the path and left plenty of room beneath to fly between the two sides. The trolls were still above, roaring at one another.

"We're always in mortal peril, so if you're going to have scruples about things like that, you're not going to be able to keep up with me," Beezle said.

"If that's the case," I started, but I never had the chance to finish.

Something wrapped around my waist and yanked me backward, out of the air.

Beezle cried out as the impact caused him to lose his grip on my shoulder.

A moment later I slammed against the bark of a tree, and

looked down to realize that one of the tree's branches had wound around me. Another branch quickly wrapped around my ankles. Across the path, Nathaniel had also been captured by the trees. The trees began to shake, almost like they were trying to communicate with the trolls.

"Oh, no," I said, annoyed. "I know what to do with you."

My hands were bound tight against my sides by the branch, but I could still wiggle my fingers. Which meant that I could send a blast of fire scorching down the bark of the tree.

The tree loosened its grip on me for a moment. I laid both my hands against the branch and gave it a good solid blast until it ignited.

It let me go and I plummeted toward the ground for a moment until I could get my bearings and start flying again. The air quickly filled with smoke.

"Why don't you just wave at the trolls and say, 'Hey, I'm over here'?" Beezle said conversationally as he reattached himself to my shoulder.

"Should I have let the tree crush me to death?" I asked, flying toward Nathaniel.

He'd blasted his tree with fire as well. That meant that we were both free. For the moment, anyway. The trees were looking very ominous all of a sudden. The two trees that had caught fire were waving their branches around in distress.

"I don't think we should stay under the cover of the trees anymore," Beezle said.

"I concur," Nathaniel said.

"If we go up, we're going to get chased by trolls," I said.

"There are only two trolls and a whole lot of trees," Beezle said. "Let's take our chances."

Up above the monsters paused, their giant wings flapping.

One of the creatures shouted at the other, which headed away toward the direction of the hill.

"Maybe it went to get water to put out the trees," I said.

"Maybe it went to get the rest of its family," Beezle said.

"Okay," I said, and we went up through the canopy.

The trees slashed and grabbed at us, but I kept a steady stream of fire coming so that they couldn't get a good hold. A few moments later we were through the top.

The troll was waiting for us, of course.

I blasted it full in the face with nightfire, and the spell bounced off the troll's skin and careened into the trees, setting some more leaves on fire.

"Oh, yeah, I forgot about that," Beezle said. "Trolls are immune to magic spells."

"Are you kidding me?" I shouted. "You couldn't have remembered this earlier?"

"We will have to try to outrun it," Nathaniel said grimly.

The troll swooped toward us, its mouth open. It looked ready to scoop us out of the air with its tongue and swallow us whole.

I waited until it was so close that I could smell the stink of its breath, and then I dropped rapidly, straight down. Nathaniel chose to go up, and the troll stopped for a moment, seemingly unsure of what had just happened.

I shot straight up again, sword drawn, aiming for the troll's belly. The blade struck true, piercing the creature's abdomen. A gush of fluid poured from the wound, coating Beezle and me. I ignored Beezle's howls and kept a secure grip on the sword, flying toward the creature's back legs. All the while I pulled the sword through, until I'd run a nice neat line through the center of the monster.

More goop poured out, and some large gray things that

might have been organs. I yanked the sword out and got out of the way just in time.

The troll plummeted toward the burning forest, crashing into the trees, tearing branches as it fell to earth.

I hung in the air for a moment, panting from exertion. Nathaniel approached us, a look of concern on his face, and then he stopped when he got close. I couldn't blame him. We smelled like troll guts.

"That was utterly disgusting," Beezle said, wiping at his eyes with his little fists. "You couldn't find a less gooey way to kill the thing?"

"You were the one who said it was impervious to magic," I said. "Let's get out of here before the other one comes back."

The forest below us swayed, and the angry clatter of branches told us that heading back to the ground wasn't an option. Some more trees had ignited, and it seemed like the whole place was on the verge of a full-on conflagration.

"We will have to fly to the edge of the forest," Nathaniel said.

All three of us looked ahead. The trees appeared to stretch on forever.

"It's got to end sometime," I said with a hope I didn't feel.

We started off, flying as quickly as possible, always checking behind us for signs of the other troll.

I don't know how long we flew, but there was no break in the endless expanse of treetops. After a while Beezle started complaining.

"I'm hungry," he said.

"How can you even think about food when you smell like that?" I asked.

"My beak has gone numb, and it's been hours since I've eaten anything," he said.

"That's not true," I said. "You had your face in a bag of chips while I was out trying to find Jayne Wiskowski's soul, and you just ate the world's biggest ice cream bar."

"But it's been a really long time since then," Beezle whined.

"How long has it been?" I asked Nathaniel. I'd left the house without my cell phone, and I didn't own a watch.

"It's difficult to say. I know it only seemed like a few moments that we traveled with Lord Lucifer, but it could have been hours. Time moves differently for him," Nathaniel said.

"Well, we can't eat anything here," I said to Beezle. "So you're just going to have to suck it up."

My own stomach growled uncomfortably, and I desperately wanted a shower. But neither of those things would be forthcoming until we got out of this stupid country, and it seemed like we would never get to Titania and Oberon's court.

Then I looked down and saw the edge of the tree line and, about half a mile beyond, a little cabin beside a lake.

"Thank the Morningstar," I said, and started to descend toward the ground.

I was exhausted. I didn't often do a lot of long-distance flying, and the unfamiliar exercise plus the constant fatigue of pregnancy had worn me down.

"Wait," Nathaniel said, grabbing my shoulder. "We don't know if there are friends or foes in that place."

"I don't care," I said. "I need to set down for a while or I'll never make it."

"Yeah, and I'm going to jump in that lake and wash all over," Beezle said.

"Let me investigate first," Nathaniel urged.

I could see the wisdom of this, so I nodded, hanging in the air while he went to the ground to check things out.

Nathaniel covered himself with a veil, and disappeared from sight.

I couldn't see what he was doing, but no alarm was raised by his actions, and after a few moments he reappeared in front of the cabin, waving us to the ground.

"Bath time!" Beezle shouted, and dove for the lake.

I followed more slowly. By the time I'd reached the ground Beezle had cannonballed into the pool of water and was happily splashing around like a puppy.

"Any sign of who might live here?" I asked Nathaniel.

He shook his head. "The cabin is empty."

I went to the window and peeked inside. There was a fire roaring in the fireplace, a pile of soft-looking furs on the floor before it. Steam rose from a silver bathtub in the corner of the room.

"Did you set all that up?" I asked Nathaniel.

He blinked. "Set what up?"

"The bath and the fire and all that," I said.

"There is no bath or fire," he said. "The cabin is bare of furniture or any sign that anyone might have ever lived here."

I looked back in the window. The tub and the fire and rug were still there.

"Either I'm hallucinating or there's something screwy going on here," I said. "You don't see anything inside there at all?"

Nathaniel shook his head, a line forming between his eyebrows. "If you do, then there must be some magic here to lure you, and we should leave."

The cabin looked comfortable and inviting, as I'm sure

it was meant to do. Especially if one was covered in dried troll slime and totally wiped out from a long-distance flight.

"Let's ask Beezle to take a look," I said. "Beezle!"

Beezle was floating on his back near the shore of the lake, his round belly pointed toward the sun. "What?"

"Come over here and look at something for me," I said.

He heaved a long-suffering sigh and flew out of the water to join us. I nodded toward the window. "Look inside and tell me what you see."

The gargoyle flew closer, peering inside. "Ah. Yeah, you don't want to go in there."

"What is it?" I asked.

"This is the home of a gretewitch," he announced.

"A great witch?"

"Yeah, like 'Hansel and Gretel,' you know. She's trying to lure you inside with something you want. Kids like gingerbread houses, but you would see something else. Once you get in there, she'll pop out from wherever she's hiding and eat you up," Beezle said.

"What do you see when you look in there?" I asked curiously.

Beezle sighed. "An all-you-can-eat buffet."

I laughed. "And you didn't see anything, Nathaniel?"

"No," he said shortly.

I was pretty sure he was lying and, if so, wondered why. Surely he wouldn't want me to get eaten up by a witch? But it didn't seem wise to hang around a witch's house. She might decide not to wait for us to come inside.

"I guess we have to continue on," I said, looking sadly at the sparkling water of the lake. Washing off the muck would have to wait. "I don't think I can fly, though. We'll have to walk for a while."

We set off around the lake, which seemed as large and endless as Lake Michigan. After a very long while we came to the farthest shore. When I looked back I saw that the cabin was far out of sight.

The sun had not moved its position in the sky the entire time we'd been in Titania and Oberon's kingdom. The constant blaze of sunshine was starting to get annoying, and I was thirsty and tired.

Before us was yet another field of tall grass and wildflowers and, at the end of it, a forest. A forest that looked a lot like the one we'd just come through. I could see a mother deer and her fawn foraging at the edge of the field.

"Are you kidding me?" I said, my temper blazing to the surface. I shouted at the sky. "Are you *kidding* me? You want me to walk in circles until I'm crazy? Do you think I'll fall for that?"

"Who are you shouting at?" Beezle asked.

"It's an illusion," I said.

"Well, yes, we knew that. Remember I told you that the glamour was too deep to penetrate?"

"No," I said, shaking my head. "It's not a glamour to make a bad place look good. This whole path-to-the-court thing—it's an illusion. Titania and Oberon are probably watching us walk around like idiots. There's no forest, no hill, no lake, no troll, no witch. It's not here at all."

As I said this, the ground beneath our feet trembled. Nathaniel grabbed my hand as I stumbled. There was the sound of trees falling in the forest ahead.

Then the lake rose up behind us like a tidal wave, and before we could do anything, we were swept away.

10

THE WATER SMASHED INTO US, AND NATHANIEL gripped my hand tight as we went under. I kicked toward the surface and broke through, calling Beezle's name. I couldn't see him or hear him, but Nathaniel clutched my fingers like a vise. He wasn't going to lose me.

The lake had turned into a rushing river that was contained by a gorge. White stone cliffs rose high on either side of the water. We were tumbling through the water, pushed by the roaring current.

"Beezle!" I called. "Beezle!"

The swirls of water slammed us against the sides of the rock wall. I cried out as the jagged points bit through my shirt.

"Beezle!" I shouted again.

"Maddy!" He was behind us, flying above the surface of the water, trying to catch up.

The sound of water seemed to grow louder, and I looked ahead of us in dread as we were tossed about like garbage.

"Of course there's a waterfall," I muttered angrily as we sped toward the precipice and our certain doom. "Of course there's a thrice-bedamned waterfall and I . . . have . . . had . . . ENOUGH!"

My magic burst out of me, hot and angry, and just like that, the river was gone.

Or rather, it wasn't gone. Nathaniel and I stood in a dry riverbed, with the water crashing and pushing on either side without actually touching us. We were both soaked to the skin, and I was furious. I shook my fingers out of his grip.

"Enough games!" I shouted. "I want to see Titania and Oberon, NOW!"

Beezle came and landed on my shoulder just as the ground beneath our feet crumbled away.

We were falling through a long dark hole, and it was freezing. Rocks and debris tumbled through with us. Flying particles of dirt made it hard to breathe. The rapidity of our descent made it impossible to contemplate trying to fly. It seemed like the air was pushing down on us, making us fall faster and faster.

Beezle gripped my shoulder, digging in with his claws. "We're going to die, we're going to die," he repeated over and over.

"We are not going to die!" I shouted, but I was starting to wonder about that. We seemed to be moving faster with every passing second.

"Madeline!" Nathaniel shouted, reaching for my hand again. He grabbed my wrist and pulled me to him, spreading his wings wide.

I automatically struggled against him, but he wrapped his other arm around me.

"Hold still," he said through gritted teeth. "I am not trying to harm you. I am trying to slow us down."

And indeed, I could feel our descent slowing by increments. Nathaniel seemed to be straining hard against the press of the air from above, using his wings both to slow us and to protect me from the crash of rocks. More than once I heard the thud of debris against his wings, and saw the flutter of white feathers torn asunder.

After a while we had slowed to a drift, and it was almost pleasant to float along in the air like a dandelion seed. Beezle's death grip on my shoulder loosened.

The tunnel seemed just as long and endless as everything else in this place, but we finally reached the ground. Nathaniel touched down softly, putting me down with great care. His hands lingered at my shoulders.

"Are you well?" he asked.

"Yes," I said, feeling as awkward as I always did when he was kind to me. "Thank you."

He nodded. "You are welcome."

"Can we stop with the meaningful glances?" Beezle said. "There's another tunnel, for Morningstar's sake."

I pulled away from Nathaniel and looked around. We were, indeed, standing in another tunnel. This one looked like it was part of a rabbit's warren. It was just a path dug through the underground—dirt on all sides, exposed roots, worms and bugs crawling in and out.

It was just barely tall enough for Nathaniel to stand straight, and wide enough for two people. There were torches set at intervals along the path. The flickering flames cast strange shadows on the wall.

"What is it with faeries and their stupid games?" I asked, trudging forward. Shouting at the sky had gotten me nowhere.

"They're old and have lots of time on their hands," Beezle said, fluttering ahead of me.

"I just want you both to know now that I am in a bad mood and I'm probably going to say and do things that are impractical, impolitic or just plain stupid when we finally get to the court," I said.

"We know," Beezle said.

"I would not expect any less of you," Nathaniel said.

"Because I can't stand games. I cannot stand this stupid BS where they try to wear me out because they're too cowardly to face me," I said.

Cowardly?

The voice seemed to come from everywhere and nowhere. It was a part of the earth, but also a part of my own mind.

I stopped and glared down the tunnel. "Yes, cowardly. You're afraid to face me so you've trying to run me like a rat in a cage."

The king of Faerie fears nothing. Especially not Lucifer's half-mortal whelp.

"More like a quarter-mortal, actually," I said. "So if you're not scared, then why are you putting me through my paces? You think you'll break me? I've faced a lot worse than your pathetic illusion."

Oh, really?

In the darkness, away from the light of the flames, something growled.

"You couldn't wait to piss him off until we were out of the dangerous tunnel?" Beezle complained.

"I was trying to get us *out* of the dangerous tunnel by pissing him off," I muttered, drawing my sword.

Beside me Nathaniel readied his magic. I shook my head at him. "You've got to let me handle this."

"Lord Lucifer would have my head if I did not defend you."

"This isn't about your pact with Lucifer," I said impatiently. "Oberon wants me to prove something to him, and I'm going to prove it."

Nathaniel's mouth tightened. "Very well. But do not expect me to do nothing if your plight becomes dire."

The shadows before us seemed to be congealing. I heard a wet sucking sound as the darkness formed into something huge and red-eyed. Silver teeth caught the light from the torches and gleamed.

"Whatever," I said, and ran toward it, sword raised. I pushed my power through the blade and aimed the pointy end toward one of its glowing eyes.

The sword struck true, my power flowing through it and into the monster. The thing of shadows burst, splattering me with muscle and blood.

"Come on, I just got clean from killing the last monster," I said.

"You have gristle in your hair," Beezle said.

"Is that all you've got?" I shouted at Oberon, opening my arms wide.

There was a rustle, a chitter, then the sound of many legs moving. I could see a crowd of eyes moving toward us, close to the ground.

"Rats?" I said. "Rats? Really?"

I blasted them with fire. They squealed, tried to turn, and I blasted them again. A few minutes later there was nothing but rat ash.

"You will not beat me," I said. "I have faced the nephilim in the Valley of Sorrows. I have overcome the Maze. I've fought countless monsters that are worse than anything you've got. I killed the Grigori's Hound of the Hunt, and I defeated your own Hob."

"You might not want to remind him of that since that's the reason they're trying to kill you," Beezle said.

"If you persist in sending these small things instead of facing me yourself, I'm going to get angrier than I already am. And you don't know what can happen when I'm angry. I might just decide to destroy your whole kingdom."

"Getting a little dark, are we?" Beezle asked.

I knew that I was on a slippery slope. I'd done things before that I was not proud of, like condoning Violet's torture in order to get information out of Amarantha. But I'd always justified it by saying there was a greater good at hand.

This time, I was just angry. There was no greater good to fall back on. I was sick of being hunted, of being chased, of being toyed with by immortals. I was sick of dancing to someone else's tune. And I was not going to permit the king and queen of Faerie to plague me and my child for the rest of our lives.

It had to end today, or it would never end at all.

Oberon did not reply.

"Fine," I said. "You asked for it."

I plunged the sword into the ground and called the power of the Morningstar. It flowed easily through me as it had never done before, and I felt the answering beat of my child's wings inside me. I was not just myself anymore. I was a conduit for Gabriel's power, too, in the form of our baby.

All of that magic rushed through me and through the sword and into the earth that surrounded us.

"Grab on to me!" I shouted to Nathaniel and Beezle.

Beezle crawled down the back of my shirt, hiding his face. Nathaniel put his hand around my arm. His eyes widened when his skin touched mine. I was burning hotter and brighter than a star, and I was about to supernova.

Then the walls collapsed, the floor fell away, the ceiling disappeared and we were shooting up, up, up. No, we weren't shooting—we were *growing.* I smashed a mountain out of my way, and knocked over the troll-guarded forest. I ground the gretewitch's cabin beneath my boot.

Then we were standing in the middle of a throne room made of stone, a thousand shocked faces staring at us. I was covered in blood and dirt and brandished Lucifer's sword in one hand. The remains of Oberon's toy lay in shards underneath my feet. Beezle clambered up my back and flew out so that he could glare around.

Two faeries, a male and a female, each more beautiful than any human I'd ever seen, sat upon thrones at one end of the court. Both of them were clothed in velvet and furs and wore jeweled crowns. And they looked just as shocked as everyone else. I shook Nathaniel's hand off my arm and strode toward the thrones.

My movement recalled the king's soldiers to their duty. A platoon of faeries, dressed in armor and carrying swords, assembled in front of me.

I didn't stop to think, or even to really look at them. I just hacked them out of the way.

When I reached the thrones I had more blood on me, and I was barely out of breath.

"Who else will you sacrifice because you're too scared to face me?" I asked.

"How dare you . . ." Titania began.

"For the love of the Morningstar, enough," I said,

cutting her off. "You've tried and failed to kill me several times over. Give it up, or get off your ass and fight me yourself."

"You have done us great insult by entering the kingdom of Faerie without invitation," Oberon said through gritted teeth.

"Do you think it's not an insult to send an assassin after me?"

"You murdered Queen Amarantha in cold blood," Titania said.

"I hear myself saying this over and over, but she was trying to kill me at the time. I defended myself."

"So you say," Titania said.

"Amarantha wasn't up to anything good," I said. "She was stealing people's memories and working in concert with Azazel. She also participated in an uprising against Lucifer, twice."

"What care we for the troubles of Lucifer?" Oberon sneered.

"You don't have to care," I said impatiently. "But if someone takes a swing at me, I'm going to swing back. Amarantha tried me, and she lost. Don't make the same mistake."

"You have killed our champion, entered our kingdom without leave and insulted us before our court. We cannot allow that to pass," Oberon said.

"You should," I said steadily. "You really should."

"You will face a trial by combat for your crimes," Oberon said, standing from his throne.

"I am not a member of your court," I said. "You do not dictate to me."

"Watch yourself, Lucifer's spawn," Oberon hissed. "I

have not yet shown you the full extent of my powers. I could wipe you from the face of the earth without blinking."

"Then do it," I challenged. "I don't think you've got all that much, to be honest."

"I am king. I do not engage with the lower classes," Oberon said, moving to sit again.

"Coward," I said.

His eyes narrowed. They were bright green, the color of a new spring leaf glistening with dew.

"I am no coward," Oberon said.

Titania laid a hand on his arm. "Do not let her incite you."

The king shook the queen's hand away impatiently. "She has insulted me for the last time."

I stepped back, the sword gripped loosely in my right hand, and gave him a challenging look. "Come and get me, then, coward."

All around us the faerie court was murmuring, but I was barely aware of them. I saw only Oberon. I needed to get him to engage, to make a mistake.

And then I would finish this.

"Very well," Oberon said, removing his crown. "We will engage in a trial by combat. No magic. Physical weapons only."

"And when you lose, you will call off your plans for vengeance. No faerie or creature under your command will pursue me or mine any longer. The blood price will be negated. Oh, and you will allow Nathaniel, Beezle and myself safe passage home."

"And when *you* lose, Madeline Black, you will have your guts torn from you before the entire court of Faerie," Oberon said.

"Why does everyone always want my guts?" I asked. "Fine, I agree to your terms if you agree to mine."

Oberon nodded.

"No," I said. "I want to hear you say that you agree to my terms."

I wasn't stupid. Faeries love loopholes.

"I agree to your terms," Oberon said after a long silence.

"And you, too," I said to Titania.

"Disrespectful child," Titania said. "Foolish child. You do not know that which you meddle in."

"Do you agree or not?"

"I agree to your terms," Titania said, her eyes hard as flint. She stood from her throne and clapped her hands. "The trial shall begin in ten minutes. Combatants, you may prepare yourselves."

Oberon and Titania went into an immediate huddle. The courtiers weren't even bothering to hide their shock and amazement. The room was abuzz with talk.

I deliberately turned my back on the king and queen, letting them know that I wasn't afraid. Nathaniel and Beezle waited for me in the middle of the court, both of them looking resigned.

Nathaniel tugged me toward an empty corner of the room. The faeries gave us a wide berth. I didn't know if it was because they were scared of me or because I was covered in blood. Probably a little of both.

"Is this what you intended all along?" Nathaniel said in a low voice. "To provoke Oberon into a fight?"

"No. I was just kind of going with what felt right at the moment," I said. "Oberon is a weak link. His pride is touchy, probably because of the heir question."

"Please do not say such a thing any louder," Nathaniel said. "Do not give them another reason to come after you."

"They're not going to come for me after today," I said. "I'm going to finish this."

"If you beat Oberon, then what?" Beezle whispered. "Remember what we were talking about at breakfast? If you kill him, there will be magical repercussions."

"Oh, yeah," I said, a little of my righteous anger deflating. I wasn't interested in causing the magical equivalent of a nuclear explosion. "Well, I won't kill him."

"So you will defeat him and leave him humiliated before his court?" Nathaniel asked.

"That works for me," I said.

Beezle shook his head. "You have to completely neutralize him or this will never end."

"Look, stop worrying about the endgame," I said. "Just tell me how I can beat him. I'm not allowed to use magic."

"You should be," said another voice, and we all turned to see who was eavesdropping on us.

A youngish male faerie stood there. He was handsome in an impish way, and had black hair and merry blue eyes.

"I should be what?" I asked.

"Permitted to use magic," the faerie said. "Lord Oberon uses magic to maintain his appearance, and he won't show his true face even during combat."

"I'm sure that they'll claim that a faerie's glamour is not the same as using power for destruction, blah-de-blah," I said. "It's probably not worth the argument. Who are you, anyway?"

"Puck," Beezle said thoughtfully.

"I see my reputation precedes me," he said, bowing extravagantly. "As does yours, Madeline Black."

"Is that a good thing?"

"It depends upon who you ask," Puck said. "There are some members of this court who welcome your reputation, and all that comes with it."

"Are you one of them?" I asked.

Puck smiled. "You can't cozen me into admitting treason."

"Is there anyone else around here who can be? A few allies wouldn't go amiss right now," I said.

"You present such a fearful appearance at this moment that I doubt you would get a truthful answer," Puck said.

"Does Oberon's glamour increase his strength or speed?" I asked Puck, getting irritated with this circular conversation.

He shrugged. "Who can say? It has been so long since Lord Oberon appeared without his glamour that he's probably forgotten his true nature."

"That's not real helpful," I said. "Are you here to help or to annoy me?"

"Who can say?" Puck repeated, winking at me.

"Yeah, okay, you're cute," I said, grabbing Puck's shoulders and spinning him around. "Move along."

He glanced back at me. "Remember, Oberon has as much at stake as you do."

Then he disappeared into the crowd.

"That was useful," Beezle said.

"You don't sound sarcastic," I said.

"That's because I'm not. Puck helped you out."

"Maybe I'm delirious from all the monster-fighting, but I fail to see . . ."

"Ladies and gentlemen of the court, the trial by combat will begin in one minute!" Puck announced. "The combatants will now step forth into the ring."

I turned toward the center of the room and was surprised to see an actual boxing ring set on a dais in the middle of the room. Puck stood in the middle of the ring wearing a tuxedo he hadn't been wearing a minute before.

In one corner of the ring stood Oberon. He'd stripped off the signs of his office, the jewels and furs and velvets, and wore only a pair of leather breeches. His chest was thin and milk white, but ropy muscle showed underneath his skin. In one hand he held a broadsword with a basket hilt.

"I'm not stripping down to my Skivvies," I said to Beezle.

"Why not? Oberon might take one look at your little belly pooch and run away in terror," he replied.

"Hark who's talking about a belly pooch," I said.

"Madeline has gotten thinner, in any case," Nathaniel said.

"No, I haven't," I said automatically. How could I? I was overweight to begin with and now I was pregnant. I was only going to get bigger.

"No, she . . ." Beezle said, and then trailed off, frowning as he looked at me. "Actually, you have. I wonder if . . ."

"Madeline Black, please step into the ring!" Puck said in a singsong voice. "Your complete and utter destruction cannot take place without your participation!"

I climbed into the ring, wearing my bloodstained jeans and shirt and holding Lucifer's sword. "You're not as cute as I thought you were," I said to Puck.

"Wait awhile and see if I change your mind," Puck said in an undertone. Then, in a voice loud enough for everyone to hear, he said, "Welcome, ladies and gentlemen of the court and honored guests! Today's entertainment is a trial by combat between our very own high Lord Oberon and the lady Madeline Black ap Azazel, representative of Lucifer's court."

"Uh-uh," I said, not wanting the faeries to use my association with Lucifer as a new excuse to try to kill me. "I'm not representing anyone but me, and I've disavowed Azazel as my father."

"Very well," Puck said. "Madeline Black, then, representative of no one except herself. The rules of combat are these—there shall be no use of magic to harm one another within the ring. Combatants may use physical weapons only, with no assistance from outside the ring. There shall be no mercy offered and none given. This is a fight to the death. If these rules are broken by one combatant, then they no longer apply to the other. Begin!"

Puck spun a quarter turn and disappeared, reappearing beside Nathaniel and Beezle at one outside corner of the ring.

Oberon gave a wild war cry and charged me with his blade out to strike. I parried his blow quickly and slashed under his arms toward his stomach.

As quick as lightning, Oberon danced away from me, the tip of my blade never even coming close to his skin. I spun back to face him just as his sword slashed down at the shoulder of my sword arm.

I was fast, but not fast enough. The sword bit through my thin T-shirt and into the muscle just under the joint. As the sword cut me I felt a little sting of pain in the back of my neck. I clamped my teeth together so as not to cry out as he slid the blade out again. I would not give Oberon the satisfaction of knowing he had hurt me.

I turned on him more aggressively, hacking at whatever I could reach with Lucifer's sword. It seemed he was always just a little faster, just a hairbreadth farther away than I thought.

A dull headache started to pound behind my eyes as my temper rose and I had to suppress my magic. All that power careened around inside me, looking for an outlet, and it took half my concentration just to keep it under control.

Blood dripped down my arm and made my hands slippery on the grip. My shoulder throbbed every time I swung the sword at the faerie king. I was starting to feel woozy. I hadn't considered that it would be so difficult to defeat Oberon without magic. I never realized what a crutch my power had become. If something annoyed me, I just blasted it out of the way. I couldn't do that now.

Oberon had a self-satisfied look on his face. He knew he was winning, and as he feinted and parried and did everything except dance a little jig, I got angrier and angrier.

And, as happened sometimes when I got angry, I suddenly saw what was before me with complete clarity.

Oberon had cheated.

"You cheated," I said loudly, blocking his sword once more.

"Come, now, Agent Black," Oberon said smugly. "We will have none of that. If you lose this battle, it will be because of your own incompetence."

"Or because," I said, and it was getting hard to speak, "you poisoned me."

There was a gasp from the watching crowd as I pulled the tiny needle from the back of my neck. I'd felt something sting me when Oberon had cut me in the shoulder, but I'd assumed it was sympathetic pain from the muscle that connected to the joint.

"Someone, probably your queen, shot me in the neck with this when you cut me," I said, slowly but clearly. "That means, I think, that the rules are forfeit."

I looked at Puck, who nodded, his eyes no longer merry.

Oberon had dropped his blade to his side, the smug look replaced by calculation.

"And if the rules are forfeit," I said, and stepped forward before he could think, laying my open palm over his heart, "then I can use magic."

11

"STOP HER!" TITANIA CRIED.

Oberon's eyes widened as all the pent-up magic inside me released into his body. I had just enough will left to focus that power so that it didn't spill over onto everyone in the court.

A massive stream poured from my hand into Oberon. There was a tremendous flash of light, and for a moment it seemed the universe froze. It took everything I had to keep standing, to give the illusion of strength. The poison worked its way into my blood. I felt it killing me by inches.

There was an explosion of magic, and the shock wave that pulsed out of Oberon's body had enough force to knock down everyone in the immediate vicinity, including me. The magic that was bound to Oberon dissipated into the ether. He was finished.

I struggled to my feet, swaying as the poison made me dizzy. Nathaniel climbed over the ropes at the edge of the ring and came to my side, his arm propping me up. Beezle hovered worriedly.

I felt a subtle warming as Nathaniel pressed his hand over the wound in my shoulder, healing me. The heat ran through my body, burning out the poison, closing all my existing wounds. The child inside me fluttered as Nathaniel's power touched it.

"Thank you," I murmured.

Nathaniel brushed his hand over my cheek. "The claw marks from the Hob still remain. You have quite a dashing scar now."

Beezle landed on my shoulder, squeezing me with his claws. "How are we going to get out of this one?"

All around us the courtiers were murmuring and coming to their feet. Everyone looked around for Oberon, and when they didn't see him there was a collective gasp. Then Titania screamed.

"Get her! Kill her! Avenge your lord!"

There was a clatter of armor as several soldiers climbed into the ring. I spun toward them, ready to defend myself, the sword in one hand, my other hand fisted.

But Puck stood in the way, and none of the soldiers seemed inclined to knock him over. I wondered just what his position was in the court. "My lady, you have already violated the rules of combat by interfering in the fight. Do not worsen your position by ignoring the pact that you made with Madeline Black."

"What care I for that agreement when she has killed my lord?" Titania said, her face a mask of grief and anger. "I am under no obligation to keep to the terms that she made with Oberon."

"I did not kill your lord," I said softly, but my voice carried.

"Then where is he?" Titania asked.

I held up my closed fist, and then opened my palm. In the center of my hand lay a tiny, sleeping faerie, the size of a housefly.

Titania put her hand to her mouth. "What have you done?"

"I didn't kill him," I said. "So there is no blood price, and no vengeance to be had."

All I'd done was remove the eons of glamour and magic that Oberon had used to cloak himself, and reverted him back to his original form.

And his original form had just the smallest fraction of magic compared to the illusion he'd built up over time. It would take him centuries to return to the form he'd used to try to kill me.

"Madeline Black followed the rules of trial by combat as set forth," Puck said. "By your own agreement, you are permitted no vengeance, whatever she has done."

"Where lies your loyalty, Puck?" Titania asked, her eyes narrowed. "With your queen, or with this child of Lucifer?"

"My loyalty lies with my queen, so long as my queen is loyal to her word," Puck replied.

"You would play the jester now, when your own lord has been brought low?" Titania said.

"If the jester is a truth teller, then that is what I shall play for you. My queen, do not jeopardize your court. Do not invite Lucifer's wrath upon us," Puck said.

The doors to the throne room opened, and everyone in court turned toward the sound.

Silhouetted in the sunshine that poured through the door was a tall, broad-shouldered man carrying a bow and arrows.

"Bendith!" Titania cried.

"Mother?" he asked, confusion evident in his voice. "What is happening?"

Bendith stepped into the throne room and his face was fully revealed.

I sucked in my breath, unable to disguise my shock. This was undoubtedly Titania's son. He looked exactly like Titania, except for one feature.

His eyes were the exact same merry blue as Puck's.

No wonder rumors had persisted doubting Oberon's paternity. With eyes like that there could be no doubt who had fathered the heir to the court.

Everyone watched Bendith as he approached his mother. Everyone except for Puck, who was watching me. He nodded at me when I looked back at him, acknowledging the truth that must have been on my face.

"Mother, what has happened?" Bendith asked again. "Why is the combat ring set? Where is Father?"

Titania fell into her son's arms with a dramatic flourish. She wept on his shoulder as he patted her back in bewilderment. It was so patently an act that I could hardly believe Bendith bought it.

"That . . . creature," she said, pointing a manicured fingernail at me. "She has diminished your father."

"Diminished?" he said, a crease forming between his brows. He was handsome, but there didn't seem to be a lot going on upstairs.

Puck held out his hand to me while Titania was distracted by Bendith. I placed Oberon gently in his palm.

As my hand brushed against his, he replaced Oberon with something sharp and hard.

"You may use that for safe passage when the time comes," he said, soft and quick so no one else could hear.

I carefully opened my palm and saw the glint of a small blue jewel there.

"How?" I whispered.

"There's no place like home," Puck said, and winked.

During this exchange Titania and Bendith had continued their conversation in an undertone. Now Bendith stood and faced me, nocking an arrow in his bow.

"Stand aside, Puck," Bendith said. "I will take vengeance for my father."

Puck did not move.

"I did not kill your father," I said to Bendith.

"Yes, and for this you have violated the rules of the trial. This combat was proclaimed to end only with death," he said.

Titania smiled behind him, and I knew who had planted this idea in Bendith's head.

"So you would kill me for showing mercy?" I asked.

"You agreed to show none," Bendith said.

"Your father and mother violated the rules of combat first, so they no longer applied to me," I said.

Bendith hesitated, lowering his arrow a fraction.

"Do not heed the words of a child of the Deceiver," Titania said. She was crafty, much craftier than I had thought. She knew exactly how to twist her son in knots so that she would get her way. "Kill her and take revenge for our family."

"Oh, I've had enough of this," I said, stepping around Puck and blasting Bendith in the face with my power.

It was just a little knockdown magic, not enough to harm him permanently, but Titania started yelling like I'd torn his arms off.

I grabbed Nathaniel by the hand, made sure Beezle was secure, and squeezed the jewel that Puck had given me.

"There's no place like home," I whispered.

And a second later, we were there, appearing in the dining room.

We shocked the hell out of Jude and Samiel, who were playing checkers at the dining room table. Samiel's eyes widened when we appeared. Jude knocked over his chair in his haste to stand up and face us, obviously thinking we might be some kind of threat.

I dropped Nathaniel's hand and rubbed my forehead. "Well, that did not go as I'd intended at all."

Jude looked at me critically. "You're covered in blood. Is any of it yours?"

"Some, but I'm okay," I said. "I want a shower. And food."

"And then you'll tell us what happened," Jude said.

"Beezle can fill you in," I said, dropping my sword on the side table as I walked down the hall to the bathroom.

"Information comes with a price," I heard Beezle say. "How many doughnuts will you give me if I tell you what happened?"

Jude growled in response and I laughed out loud as I shut the door. When I saw myself in the mirror I sobered.

I was covered in blood, and my cute new haircut stuck up all over the place. The gash in the shoulder of my T-shirt was huge, an indication of just how bad that cut had been before Nathaniel had healed it. The four claw marks the Hob had given me had hardened into white scars that ran from my eye to my chin on my left cheek. My eyes were hard. I looked like someone who possessed no mercy. And I was a little afraid that was what I was becoming.

There would be consequences for my actions in the faerie court. I knew it. Titania wouldn't leave me alone now that I had diminished Oberon. No matter what the outcome of that fight, they had no intention of letting me live. I knew that now. Faeries loved loopholes, and you could bet that Titania was finding one in our pact at that very moment.

She would never stop hunting me.

How had this escalated so quickly? I'd started out just wanting to get through a simple diplomatic mission to Amarantha's court, and now I was in a blood feud with the high queen of Faerie. When I looked back on the choices I'd made I didn't see any other way for me to have survived. At every turn Amarantha, then Titania and Oberon, had pushed me, provoked me and tried to squash me beneath their heels.

"What should I have done?" I asked the girl in the mirror. "What could I have done differently?"

I didn't have an answer, so I pulled off my bloody clothes and climbed in the shower. They had tried to kill me, over and over. Over and over I had defended myself, and I had tried to negotiate for a cessation of hostilities.

None of them had been interested in peace.

I'd had to kill Amarantha. I'd diminished Oberon.

Sooner or later I'd have to take care of Titania, too. And then her son would come after me, or someone else.

It would never end, not unless every last faerie was wiped from the earth.

I wondered if that was what Lucifer had in mind all along. To use me as his sword and shield, knowing that I would protect my child.

For when I thought about my baby I knew that I could and would slaughter every last denizen of Faerie if that was what it took to keep him safe.

It was frightening to think of myself that way, as a weapon without mercy. But it was also true. I knew that under the right circumstances that was what I could become.

But I didn't want it to come to that. I didn't want to spend my life always looking over my shoulder. And I especially was not interested in doing anything that might serve Lucifer's purpose.

I sighed. There was nothing I could do at the moment except wait and see what happened. And call J.B., who was not going to be happy with me at all.

I dressed in clean jeans and a sweater and put on a pair of heavy wool socks. The house felt really cold. It was possible that I'd forgotten to pay the heating bill. More than a few important things had slipped my mind lately.

I stopped short as I entered the dining room. "Crap. What day is it?"

"You were gone for about fifteen hours," Jude said.

"So it's tomorrow, then?" I said.

"Whatever that means," Beezle said.

"It was late afternoon when we left, so it's the next day," I said, running back to my room and grabbing my soul collection list.

I scanned the list quickly, then closed my eyes.

I'd missed a pickup.

I couldn't believe it. I'd missed a soul pickup.

That had never, ever happened to me before. I'd managed to lose Jayne Wiskowski yesterday and today I hadn't even made it to the pickup location.

J.B. was really not going to be happy with me at all. Maybe I could call him at some later date and explain. Like three months from now. Unfortunately, I didn't think he would let me dodge him for that long.

My shoulders slumped, I went back to the living room. The front door was open. Jude and Nathaniel were nowhere to be seen.

I looked questioningly at Beezle and Samiel. Beezle had

taken over Jude's half of the checkerboard and was beating Samiel handily.

Beezle negotiated for pizza and wings in exchange for information, Samiel signed as Jude reentered the apartment carrying a delivery bag.

"You didn't have to let him get his way," I said to Jude. "I would have told you what happened today for free."

"You need to eat," Jude said. "You're looking thin."

"You're the third person to say that," I said.

"Yeah, I wanted to talk to you about that," Beezle said, pushing away from the checkerboard and looking at me. "I think it's the baby."

"The baby is making me thin?" I asked. "That would no doubt be a first among pregnancies."

"You've been really tired, right?" Beezle asked.

I nodded. "But I don't think that's so unusual for a woman having a baby while fighting off mortal threats at every turn."

"You have lost some weight, though. I think the baby is eating up more energy than a normal baby."

I blinked. "So I should be worried that my child is going to . . . what? Eat me from the inside out? Like a parasite?"

"The baby is part nephilim," Beezle said. "We don't know what it will do to you."

"He's not a monster," I said angrily. "He's Gabriel's child, and Gabriel was not a monster."

"But he had monster in him," Beezle said.

So do I, Samiel signed, his face stony. *Ramuell was my father, too.*

"You're a known quantity," Beezle said impatiently. "The baby isn't."

"I refuse to believe this child will be like Ramuell," I said. "Gabriel was the gentlest person I ever knew."

"Regardless of what the baby is or is not," Jude said, "we have to acknowledge that it comes from the bloodlines of immortal creatures, and you are mortal. You will not experience a normal human pregnancy."

"Okay," I said. "So I'm losing weight. Although my pants don't feel any looser, so I'll have to take your word for it. What am I supposed to do about it?"

"Eat more," Jude said. "When a wolf goes through many changes in a short period of time, he can lose a lot of weight because of the energy required for the changes. Even a straight human pregnancy would mean extra calorie intake. Given that the child has a magical bloodline, you'll probably have to add in a significant amount of food."

"Food I can't afford," I muttered.

"All of us will help you. And I'm certain some of us can go without if necessary," Jude said with a meaningful glare at Beezle.

"You have no idea how much food I need to get through the day," Beezle said.

"Need and want are not the same thing," I said, going to the kitchen to get paper plates.

Beezle had already gotten into the chicken wings by the time I returned. There was a large pile of bones next to him.

"I hope you placed a double order," I said to Jude, who was watching Beezle in fascination.

"I had no idea something so small could eat so much so quickly," he said.

"Where's Nathaniel?" I asked.

Samiel shrugged as he placed a couple of slices of pizza on his plate. *He went downstairs to clean up, he said.*

"Is he getting a spa treatment?" I asked. "I had more blood on me than he did."

I'll go and see what he's up to, if you want.

"No," I said, shaking my head. "Just leave him alone. He obviously wants to be there."

I didn't need Nathaniel around reminding me that he'd saved my life in the faerie court by ridding me of the poison. Every time he was kind to me, it was harder and harder for me to remember that he had an agenda that did not correspond with mine.

After lunch I went to call J.B.

"Black," he barked when he picked up the phone. "Why did you miss your pickup today? And what the hell happened to Jayne Wiskowski yesterday?"

I explained about the mantis attack, the disappearance of Wiskowski's soul, and my little adventure in Titania and Oberon's court. There was a long silence at J.B.'s end when I finished.

"Are you still breathing?" I asked.

"Yes, although I'm not sure why I bother," J.B. said. "Do you know how much trouble you've gotten yourself into now?"

"I have a good idea," I said.

"I'll talk to you later," J.B. said. "I need to go and see how much fallout there is from this in my own court."

"I'm sorry," I said helplessly.

"You keep saying that," J.B. said, and hung up.

I *was* sorry. I was sorry that I caused J.B. so much pain. But I wasn't sorry for what I had done in the court, and I think J.B. knew that.

I put my phone on the bedside table and crawled under the blankets. It was the middle of the day, but I was wiped out. On the heels of that thought came the memory of Beezle's voice.

You're a known quantity. The baby isn't.

"You are not a monster," I whispered.

The baby fluttered inside me, and I closed my eyes. And, sleeping, I dreamed.

I flew above the world, all the worlds that were, and I could see everything. I could see what had been, and what was, and what would be.

And I could see the path to the person that my heart longed for.

It was a green place, and peaceful, and he sat beside a river that ran as clear and bright as the sun that sparkled upon it.

He turned as I approached, and his face was wreathed with joy.

"Madeline," he said.

The sound of his voice pierced me to the heart.

"Gabriel," I said, and ran to him.

I was complete in his arms, and I wept for everything we had lost.

"Madeline," he said again, and he crooned it over and over until my tears stopped. "I should have known."

"Should have known what?"

He smiled down at me, his hands framing my face. "That you would do something unexpected. How have you come to be here? It is not allowed."

I looked around. There didn't seem to be anything distinguishing this place from any other pleasant green valley. "I thought I was dreaming."

Gabriel shook his head. "Somehow you have defied the order of the universe, of time and space itself. And if anyone would, it would be you."

"I was never very good at following the rules."

"I am not certain you even know what the rules are." His face sobered. "But this is a place of the dead, and you do not belong here."

I took his hand in mine. "I want to stay with you."

Gabriel reluctantly pulled his hand away. "You cannot. You are not meant for this. Not yet."

"Don't send me away," I said. "I need you."

"Madeline," Gabriel said, and his eyes were so tender. "My love will always be with you."

He kissed me, and into his kiss he poured his happiness, his grief, his regret.

"Don't," I begged.

"You cannot stay," he said.

He seemed to grow smaller before my eyes, and I realized he was not growing smaller. He was getting farther away. I was leaving, being pulled by some outside force, by the order of the universe righting itself.

"Gabriel!" I cried out.

He turned away.

"Gabriel!" I repeated, and went into darkness.

And in the darkness I was not alone. His mouth was on the back of my neck, his hands were on my chest, and I smelled cinnamon.

I opened my eyes in my own bedroom, and felt Gabriel moving in the bed beside me.

12

"GABRIEL," I BREATHED, AND ROLLED OVER TO FACE HIM.

His lips covered mine, and that was when I knew something was wrong. I tore away, pushed out of the bed, tumbled to the floor.

"You're not Gabriel," I said, and called nightfire to my hand. "Who are you?"

The ball of flame that hovered above my palm lit the room in an eerie blue light. The person on the bed smiled Gabriel's smile at me, and then it dissolved into the merry, impish smile of Puck.

"What are you doing here?" I demanded.

"Enjoying the company of a beautiful woman," Puck replied, giving his eyebrows a suggestive wiggle.

"Wrong question," I said, and realized I was on the verge of losing my temper. Puck had come into my home and pretended to be Gabriel. He'd manipulated my grief for his own purpose. He'd better have a damned good reason or I'd blast him back to Faerie, despite the fact that he'd helped save my life there. "How did you get here, and why?"

"Which question would you like me to answer first?" Puck asked.

"Don't you dare toy with me, or I'll blow you into a million pieces."

"Temper, temper," Puck said, rising from the bed and approaching me. "That attitude of yours will get you into trouble."

"It already does," I said shortly. "Now tell me why you're here and how you got into the house without waking Jude and Beezle, or so help me I'll—"

"You have my jewel," Puck said, nodding at the blue sapphire he'd given us for safe passage. "I can come and go wherever it is."

I grabbed it off my dresser and held it out to him. "Take it back, then. I don't want to wake up to find you impersonating my husband again. Is that how you got the queen pregnant? By pretending to be Oberon?"

Puck nodded. "It helped them maintain the fiction they needed—that Titania had been loyal to him, and that he had sired a child."

"Does she know that it was you, and not him?"

He shrugged. "It is not what she knows, but what she will admit to herself."

"Why can't you just answer a question in a straightforward manner?"

"Now, what is the fun in that?"

He still hadn't taken the jewel from me. I waved it in front of him. "Take it back."

"I'd rather not," Puck said. "I might want to visit with you again."

"If you don't take it with you, I'll throw it in the garbage can, and next time you come through you'll find yourself caressing rats at the city dump."

"I think you'll find that if you throw it away, it will return to you," he said with a small smile.

I dropped my hand at my side. "What do you want from me?"

Puck wandered around the room, picking up things here and there—the book on my bedside table that I never had time to read, some little silver knickknacks that had belonged to my mother, the plastic hairbrush that Gabriel had used to comb my hair on our wedding night. "I may want to ask a favor of you sometime in the future."

"Really," I said flatly.

He looked up at me, a gleam in his eyes. "Is a favor so much to ask, after I aided you in court?"

"It is a lot to ask if I don't know what the favor is," I said. "And I was under the impression that you helped me out for reasons of your own."

"What would you say if I told you those reasons included wanting you indebted to me?" Puck said.

I closed my eyes. "I'd say that I should have known better than to expect a faerie to help me out of the goodness of his heart."

"Yes, you should have," he said.

"Just who are you, anyway?" I asked. "You seem to have a lot of power in that court."

The air shimmered for a moment, and Puck disappeared and reappeared on the other side of the room.

"I am the voice that dances on the wind," he said.

"Very poetic."

He turned in a circle and threw out a shower of gold sparks. When he stopped he looked like Oberon had before I'd diminished him.

"I am the beating heart of the earth," he said.

He held out his hand and there was a puff of blue smoke that covered him before he reappeared as himself. He seemed more serious as he approached me; the merry light that always danced in his eyes was gone.

"I am older than this earth, older than the stars. I saw Titania and Oberon born. I have walked all the ways of the universe, the hidden paths known only to a few."

He stopped in front of me, and put his hands on my shoulders. "And I have counted Lucifer as my enemy since time untold."

"You are not a faerie," I said, my heart trembling.

He shook his head. "No. I am not. And I find you, Madeline Black, very interesting."

For just a moment, I thought I saw the shadow of wings behind him. Then he winked, and disappeared.

I sank onto the bed and stared at the jewel in my hand, the jewel that had purchased my safe passage and that now bound me to some ancient creature that despised Lucifer.

It glittered in the light of the ball of nightfire that floated aimlessly in the room. The glittering reminded me too much of Puck's eyes, and I stuffed the jewel in the drawer of my bedside table.

I glanced at the clock. It was a few minutes past five in the evening. The darkness outside made it seem much later. I went out into the hall and down to the living room.

Samiel, Jude and Beezle looked like a guy cliché, all three of them ensconced on the couch. Samiel and Jude had their shoes off and their feet propped on my coffee table. Beezle sat in between them. On either side of my gargoyle was a plastic bowl filled with junk food. One bowl had popcorn, and the other had potato chips.

Beezle looked like he'd found heaven. I heard the sounds of gunfire coming from the TV.

"*Aliens*?" I asked.

"I love this movie," Beezle said.

"Shh," Jude said. "I've never seen it before."

Samiel had looked up when I entered the room, and with his usual perception he realized something was going on.

What's wrong?

"I hate to interrupt your party, but Puck's just been to see me and I thought you'd want to know that there's a hole in our security."

"What?" Jude asked.

Beezle paused the movie with the remote. "Puck was here?"

I told them that Puck had appeared in my room because of the jewel. I didn't mention that he'd appeared in the form of my dead husband and that he'd groped me.

I realized I was trembling all over. Puck had violated me. He had burrowed into my memory of Gabriel, had stolen the intimacy that we'd shared, an intimacy I'd never shared with anyone else.

Samiel was at my side in an instant, his arm around me. *What did he do to you?*

I shook my head. I couldn't tell them. "Nothing," I said through chattering teeth. "I'm just c-c-cold. Can you get me a blanket?"

Samiel looked like he wanted to push it, but decided not to. He led me toward a chair and covered me with a crocheted afghan.

I'll get some tea, he said.

"We need to get rid of that jewel," Jude said.

"I already tried that," I said, still shaking. "I was told that it wouldn't have much effect."

"So we just have to accept that he can come and go as he pleases in this house?" Jude said angrily.

There was a knock at the back door, and I heard Samiel letting Nathaniel in the kitchen. Nathaniel entered the room, followed by Samiel carrying my tea.

"All you all right?" Nathaniel asked. He looked harried. "I felt the presence of something unnatural here, but I couldn't get upstairs to you."

"You felt Puck?" I asked, interested.

"You know, it's funny," Beezle said, shoving potato chips in his mouth. "We decided to watch the movie maybe fifteen minutes before you came out. We all had the same impulse simultaneously."

And we didn't even argue about what movie to watch, Samiel added.

"So Puck managed to neutralize all of you so that you couldn't help me if I needed it," I said. "You three didn't seem to be aware of him at all. Nathaniel knew he was here but wasn't able to help. How did he keep you downstairs?"

"Every time I tried to walk to the stairs, go out the front door or fly out a window, I felt some force turning me away," Nathaniel said. "It was maddening."

"I wonder why you could feel him and the others couldn't," I said thoughtfully. "You don't have faerie in your blood, do you? I can usually feel Lucifer when he's approaching."

Nathaniel drew himself up haughtily. "I am the only child of two first-generation angels."

"Okay, okay," I said. "I wasn't casting aspersions on your character. Just curious."

Beezle looked curious, too, but he didn't pursue it. No use getting Nathaniel annoyed over nothing.

"Puck as good as told me that if I tried to throw away the stone, it would come back to me," I said. "But there has to be some way to prohibit him from entering without permission."

Beezle tapped his chin. "He got around the threshold rule by giving you the jewel in the first place. That implied permission when you accepted it, even if you didn't realize it."

"Faeries love loopholes," I muttered.

"And so do fallen angels," Nathaniel said. "We cannot get rid of the jewel, and we cannot prevent Puck from entering the house, but we can bind the stone in such a way that it will imprison Puck when he enters."

"I don't want to imprison him," I said, thinking of Puck's speech about his origins. I wasn't up to making any creature that old angry with me.

"Not imprison forever," Nathaniel said. "He would be able to return easily to his own realm. But he would not be able to enter your home and walk about freely. He would be confined to one space unless you gave him express permission otherwise."

I nodded. "Like a holding cell. I like it. How can we do it?"

"First decide where you would like to place the jewel," Nathaniel said.

"As far from Madeline as possible," Jude growled. "The basement. Or the shed outside."

"That's not going to work," I said. "I want to know when he's here. It should be someplace visible to anyone who comes through, like in this room."

"You want Puck popping up when we're in the middle of dinner?" Beezle asked.

"It's better than him showing up in my bedroom when I'm asleep," I said.

"Very well," Nathaniel said. "Bring me the jewel and I will perform the binding."

I started to stand, realized my legs were still shaky, and sat down again.

"It's in the drawer of my bedside table," I told Samiel.

Samiel disappeared for a few minutes, then reappeared, shaking his head.

It wasn't there. Did you put it somewhere else?

"I just put it there a half hour ago," I said. "Where did it go?"

I pushed to my feet, and Jude came to support me so I wouldn't fall. "Let me look."

Jude and I led the parade down the hall to my bedroom, where I was forced to suffer the indignity of everyone pawing through my belongings looking for the stone.

"It's not here," I said finally, sitting on the bed in defeat.

"Puck must have enspelled it to make sure that we couldn't change the terms of the magic," Nathaniel said.

"That sneaky little so-and-so," I said.

"I guess he knows more about loopholes than you do," Beezle said to Nathaniel.

Nathaniel glared at Beezle, but said nothing.

"Okay, so we can't solve the Puck problem right now," I said.

"What problem *can* we solve now?" Beezle asked. "We still don't know where Azazel is or what he's up to. You've really ticked off Titania, and the solution for that issue doesn't seem to be in sight. You forgot your pickup this morning and lost the soul from yesterday. I think the only thing you can do right now is go into work and fill out forms that express your incompetence as an Agent."

"Why is it that when you speak a feeling of hopelessness descends upon me?" I asked. "Has Chloe been around here lately?"

Samiel shook his head. *I haven't seen her since she left yesterday with the binder.*

"Hopefully she's working on deciphering it," I said. "I'll call J.B. and see if he knows anything."

I dialed J.B. and waited while the phone rang. Everyone watched me.

"Don't the rest of you have something to do?" I asked.

"No," Beezle said. "Your life is our life."

"Maddy," J.B. said as he picked up the phone. He sounded worried. "I was just going to call you."

"Why?" I said, a feeling of dread coming over me. "What's after me now?"

"It's not that," J.B. said. "Something's happened. I need you to meet me downtown."

"Where?" I asked.

"One fifty South Wacker," he said. "There's a plaza between two big office buildings there. You'll have to leave Jude at home. You need to come under a cloak so no one sees you."

"I'll be there as soon as I can," I said.

Jude was already shaking his head. He'd heard every word of the conversation. Wolf hearing is incredible.

"You're not going alone," he said.

"I don't have to," I replied. "Samiel can go with me."

"Or I can," Nathaniel said.

"Samiel can go with me," I repeated. I didn't want to be alone with Nathaniel right now. I wanted to be with someone I was sure I could trust. I was still feeling a little unsteady after my encounter with Puck, and I hadn't even had time to contemplate the implications of my dream of

Gabriel. "He can fly and he knows how to cloak himself. The rest of you stay here."

"And do what?" Jude said. "Twiddle our thumbs?"

"Don't worry. I'm sure something will show up to attack me sooner or later, and you can destroy it if I'm away."

"I don't want to destroy things," Jude growled. "I'm here to keep you safe."

"And you do," I said. "I feel much safer knowing that you are here."

I didn't say that the reason I felt safer was because Nathaniel was hanging around the house and I knew Jude would take care of him if necessary, but I didn't have to. Everyone seemed to know this without my saying it aloud.

Nathaniel's face hardened. "Since I do not seem to be needed or wanted, I will return to my room and await your further instructions."

"You do that," Beezle said.

Nathaniel went out of my room and into the kitchen. He slammed the back door so hard that I heard it bounce off the frame.

"And that's another problem you can't solve," Beezle said.

"Don't remind me," I said. "You stay here, too."

"Aww," Beezle whined. "But I want to see what J.B.'s being all secretive about."

"You'll find out when I get home," I said. "My life is your life, remember?"

"But it's so much more fun when I can actually be there instead of experiencing things vicariously," Beezle said.

"Look at it this way. If you stay, you can finish off the potato chips before Samiel comes home and gets a crack at them."

"Good point," Beezle said.

Fifteen minutes later Samiel and I were on our way downtown under a veil. The few stars that were visible through the ambient light of the city shone in the dark sky. Cars moved below us as people headed home after work along Lake Shore Drive.

We cut across the Loop, following the curve from East Wacker to South Wacker Drive, which was presently a big pit instead of a working road. It seemed like it had been under construction forever and there was no sign of completion in sight. There were detour signs everywhere and snarled traffic as drivers, cabs and cyclists tried to negotiate the limited options left available to them.

The address that J.B. had given us was on the east side of the Chicago River. As we approached I saw that Adams had been closed off to traffic by several police cars, their lights flashing. There were a lot of ambulances, and a large crowd of curiosity seekers strained to see over the yellow crime scene tape that had been run across the entrance to the plaza.

Samiel and I lowered carefully to the ground inside the tape and looked around for J.B. We didn't have to look far. He was standing in the center of the plaza, surrounded by bodies.

They were everywhere—men and women, mostly wearing the business suits that marked them as white-collar workers. Their limbs were broken; their heads were twisted the wrong way. And every single one of them had their neck torn open. There was an unbelievable amount of blood.

Briefcases and laptop bags had broken open and papers were strewn across the plaza, blowing in the wind. Uniformed officers and EMTs stood in little clumps, waiting for the crime scene techs to finish their work. It seemed like they would be waiting a long time.

I felt sick as I approached J.B. Whatever had done this had slaughtered these people without mercy.

J.B. had his hands in the pockets of his overcoat, and he wore earmuffs in concession to the bitter cold. He looked sadder than I'd ever seen him. His shoulders were slumped, like he was carrying a heavy weight, and his face was tight with stress. His wings curled around him, like he was trying to comfort himself.

"What happened?" I asked, putting my arm around him.

"Vampires," he said briefly.

I gazed around in shock. "Vampires? Out in the open like this?"

He nodded. "They were waiting at five o'clock when most of the people who work in these buildings were leaving. The early sundown worked to their advantage. We knew that something big was going to happen, but not exactly what. There were Agents here to collect the souls, and they saw the whole thing."

"The prophets knew that the vampires were going to massacre all these people and they didn't do anything? They didn't warn the Agents?" I asked.

"Don't act like you don't know the rules," J.B. said. "The deaths were foreseen. We were bound not to interfere."

I looked around at the piles of twisted, broken forms. "That's BS, and you know it."

"How are these deaths any different from any others?" J.B. said impatiently. "What gives you the right to decide what deaths are right and which are wrong?"

"Because these aren't normal human deaths," I said.

"They were killed by something they couldn't understand, and had no defense against."

"People have been killed by vampires before," J.B. said.

"Not like this," I said.

"So the number of people killed is what matters?"

"No," I said. "Why are you picking a fight with me? You know that the Agency is wrong. You know that the prophets shouldn't have sent the Agents here without warning them."

J.B. turned his head away, but not before I saw the glitter of tears behind his glasses. "You're right. They should have warned them. Maybe they wouldn't have been so unprepared when . . ."

"What else happened?" I asked.

"Only some of the Agents returned," J.B. said.

"Agents were killed, too?" I asked, a cold ball of dread forming in my stomach.

J.B. shook his head. "They were captured."

"By the vampires? Why?"

"One of the Agents that escaped said that there was a man with the vampires. A man with black hair, and black eyes, and . . ."

"Black wings," I finished. "Azazel."

I rubbed my hand over my face, trying to think. The carnage before us was hard to process, and now my father was involved. Again.

"What was Azazel doing while the vampires were killing everyone?" I asked.

"Neutralizing the Agents," J.B. said. "The ones that got away said it was pure luck. He was casting a spell, and the spell missed them."

"How many escaped?"

"Of the twenty-two Agents that were sent here, only six made it back. And all of the souls of the dead are gone. Azazel took them, too," J.B. said.

"Why?" I cried. "What is he doing? Is all of this part of his insane experiment?"

"I don't know," J.B. said. "And I'm not sure we'll be able to figure it out now, in any case. He took Chloe, too."

13

SAMIEL WENT RIGID BESIDE ME. THEN HE GRABBED J.B. by the lapel. *What was she doing here in the first place?*

"She's an Agent; you know that," J.B. said.

She told me she hardly ever collects souls anymore, that she spends most of her time working on tech projects in the basement.

"Hardly ever doesn't mean never," J.B. said. "The upper management requires all Agents, even me, to do several pickups a year. This was one of hers."

"Stand down," I said to Samiel, trying to pry his fingers off J.B.'s coat. Samiel looked like he was going to strangle J.B. on principle. "You know it's not J.B.'s fault."

The light of fury in Samiel's eyes faded. He let go of J.B. and stepped back, covering his face with his hands.

"We have to find them," I said. "We can't leave them to Azazel."

"Management has ordered me not to pursue Azazel," J.B. said, his eyes bleak.

I stared at him. "Are you kidding? They're just going to let sixteen Agents go without a fight?"

"They do not want to get involved in 'fallen business,'" J.B. said. "I told you that before."

"This isn't fallen business. Azazel led a rebellion against Lucifer. He's gone completely rogue."

"They don't care about the particulars," J.B. said. "They saw what happened when Ramuell and Antares got into the Agency. They're not going to risk more lives."

"So they're just going to let all those Agents go? Azazel is probably torturing them right now. I can't believe that they would allow that just because they don't want to get 'involved,'" I shouted.

"Do you think I like this?" J.B. said. "Those are my people that were taken. I know them. I know their families."

"Then why are you going to stand for this?" I said.

"I'm not," he said. "I said that they ordered me not to pursue Azazel. And I'm not going to. But they didn't order me not to look for the Agents under my care."

"Okay, then," I said. "We'll find them."

"You should know that you've been expressly ordered to, and I quote, 'stay out of this matter entirely,'" J.B. said.

"Like I give a shit," I said.

"That's what I figured you'd say."

So where do we start? Samiel asked.

I took my phone out of my pocket. "Let me see if Granddaddy has any useful intelligence. He's got to be tracking Azazel himself, right?"

I dialed Lucifer's number and waited, listening to the phone ring. After a while it clicked over to voice mail.

"Hello, you have reached the voice mail of the Morningstar. Please leave a message and I will get back to you when my schedule permits."

I hung up the phone and stuffed it back in my pocket. "Why is he never around when I want him to be, but he always shows up when I don't want him at all?"

"I'm sure it has something to do with being the Prince of Darkness," J.B. said.

"Right," I said. "Look, can we finish this conversation at my house? Beezle and Jude will have some ideas, and it's hard for me to think here."

The sight of all the mangled bodies was making it difficult for me to collect my thoughts. And I couldn't help thinking that if I'd found Azazel already and killed him as I should have, none of these people would be dead.

I'd gotten distracted by the faeries, and forgotten my promise and my purpose. Finding Azazel—and the missing Agents—was now priority number one.

"I have to go back to the office and finish some paperwork first," J.B. said. "You'd better come, too, and fill out the forms for the souls you lost."

"Why bother?" I asked. "The Agency is going to be royally pissed at me when they find out I'm tracking Azazel. What's the difference if a couple of papers don't get properly filed?"

"How about you try following the rules for a while so as not to arouse their suspicion?"

"You're talking logic here," I said. "I don't do logic."

"Indulge me," J.B. said.

I tapped Samiel on the shoulder. He was facing the crime scene techs as they did their gruesome work, but I knew he wasn't really seeing them. He was seeing Chloe. It took a few seconds for him to focus on my face.

"I'm going with J.B. to pretend to be a good Agent," I

said. "Can you get home and fill in the others? We need to put together some kind of plan to find Azazel."

Samiel nodded.

"I'll be back soon."

He took off, flying north toward home. I hadn't realized he was in love with Chloe. Maybe he hadn't realized it himself, until she was taken.

"Let's walk," J.B. said. "The office isn't that far from here. We can unveil once we get across the street."

"Okay," I said, sensing that he needed some time to brood. I did, too. Even though I'd disavowed any relationship with Azazel, it's hard to acknowledge that the person who fathered you is responsible for organizing the killing of dozens of people. Beezle would no doubt tell me that I was being absurd, but I felt a little tainted. Like I had bad blood in me.

"You are being absurd," I muttered to myself. Because if I had bad blood, then so did my baby. And I refused to have either one of our lives dictated by the actions of our forebears.

"Did you say something?" J.B. asked as we walked in the shadow of the Sears Tower.

Far above us the red safety lights of the tower glowed. Most of the restaurants that served the nine-to-five crowd were closed up for the night. I could see workers through the windows at Starbucks mopping the floor and cleaning the espresso machines.

"Nothing," I said. "Just thinking out loud."

"You should probably know that I received an official missive from Titania shortly after I talked to you," J.B. said.

"And?"

"She's holding me responsible for your behavior in her court."

"Well, that's just dumb. I flat-out told them that I represented nobody but myself."

"It's apparently my fault that the situation escalated because I didn't punish you immediately as I was supposed to," he said.

"And it's your fault that I don't file paperwork on time and let souls get lost, too, I suppose," I said.

"That's how the Agency sees it," J.B. said.

"I know I keep saying this, but I'm sorry," I said.

"You're sorry, but you won't change, either," he said.

"I'm not changing for anyone, especially not the faerie queen. Or the Agency. Upper management can take this job and stick it up their butt, as far as I'm concerned."

"Titania has ordered me to appear in her court next month to receive my punishment for your actions. On Valentine's Day," he said.

I stopped in the middle of the sidewalk, tugging J.B.'s sleeve so that he would stop. A man walking behind us huffed as he was forced to take one step sideways to go around us.

"You're not going, right?" I said.

J.B. shook his head at me. "I have to."

"No," I said, grabbing his shoulders. "You don't *have* to. You have to stop thinking that way. You don't have to do anything you don't want to do."

"The alternative is to watch her hound you until you're dead," J.B. said. "Do you think that's acceptable to me?"

"Do you think it's acceptable to me that you are going there to be tortured and quite probably killed in my place?" I shouted. "And what makes you think she'll leave me alone even if you do nobly sacrifice yourself? She's already proven that no agreement is sacred to her. She'll kill you and then come after me anyway."

"I love you," he said, and I froze.

"I love you," he repeated. "So I will do whatever I think is necessary to keep you safe."

"J.B.," I said, closing my eyes.

He took both of my hands in his. "Don't say anything. Don't tell me that I'm just a friend to you. Don't tell me that you still love Gabriel. Just don't. I know all those things, but it doesn't change the way I feel. And it can't change the fact that I'll always look at you and think that if I had just tried sooner, if I just stopped being afraid that you would say no, that you might be mine now instead of grieving him."

"What can I say when you tell me things like that?" I asked, my heart breaking for both of us.

"Tell me that you'll keep yourself safe, that you'll stop taking crazy risks," he said.

"I can't promise that. My enemies will make sure of that."

He put his hand on my face, on the white scars that covered my cheek. I nestled my head in his hand for a moment; then I pulled away.

"If you insist on going to Titania's court, you're not going alone," I said.

"You don't need to piss her off any more than you already have," J.B. said.

"You're not going alone," I repeated. "Besides, I think I have an ally in court. Maybe. Possibly. Of course, his help comes with a price."

We started walking again and I told J.B. about Puck. When I finished he seemed stunned.

"Why would Puck take an interest in you?"

"That seems to be the question of the hour," I said as we approached the front doors of the Agency.

"Puck never takes an interest in anything except himself, and maybe Titania," J.B. said as we entered the lobby.

We had to go through the usual screening process—biometric scan, metal detector, abandonment of anything that resembled a weapon. I was glad I'd left Lucifer's sword at home. It really bothered me to leave it with security. And now that the Agency management had decided I was persona non grata, it was possible that they might decide to confiscate it, and then I'd really be up a creek. That sword had saved my life more times than I could count.

"I don't know why he's interested in me," I said as we entered the elevator just past the reception desk. "But I should tell you that I'm not certain he's a faerie. Or at least, not only a faerie."

"What do you think he is?" J.B. asked.

"He told me that he was older than Titania and Oberon, and said he'd been Lucifer's enemy forever," I said. "What could possibly be as old as Lucifer?"

J.B. looked troubled. "Not a lot."

"That's what I was thinking, too. Either he's an angel or a demon in disguise, or he's some creature we've never seen before."

"Why would a creature of such power hide himself in Titania and Oberon's court for centuries? Why would he pretend to be inferior to them?" J.B. asked as the elevator rose to our floor.

I shrugged. "You got me. Apparently I don't think the right way. Every time I turn around I find machinations within machinations, and in case you haven't noticed, being sneaky is not my strong suit."

The elevator opened and we stepped out. There were still a fair number of people working at their cubicles, even though the hour was late. Death never slept.

"I'll call you when I'm finished," J.B. said, heading toward his office. "Be a good girl for an hour or so, will you?"

"Define 'good,' " I said, but he was already out of earshot.

It was hard not to notice that other Agents gave me a wide berth as I walked to my cubicle. Chloe had told me I'd developed some kind of reputation in the Agency. I was hardly ever there anymore, and when I was it seemed that something crazy had happened around me, so I could see why nobody was interested in saying hello to me.

My desk was covered in a thin layer of dust. Apparently even housekeeping was afraid to enter my space.

There were a bunch of forms in my in-box, most of them related to pickups that I'd done over the last two months. I hung my coat on the hook in the corner of my cubicle and sat down with a sigh, pulling the papers toward me and taking a pen out of my drawer.

The Agency is pretty well locked in the mid-twentieth century, technology-wise. The forms have to be filled out by hand or typed on a typewriter, and there are four copies of each attached in different colors.

Many Agents had suggested that paperwork would be less onerous and more efficient if we could fill out the data on a computer, but upper management was not in the least interested in efficiency. They did not like change. Change implied that something had been done incorrectly before, and management did not like to be told that they had done something incorrectly. Which was probably one of the many reasons why they didn't like me.

After about forty minutes of laborious printing, I dropped the pen on my desk and pushed my chair back. I was rubbing the cramp out of my right hand when I realized someone was standing in my cubicle behind me.

I whirled around and came to my feet, ready to defend myself if necessary, my hand automatically groping for the sword that was not there. My chair rolled on its casters and crashed into my desk.

A man stood there, a rather heavy man with an amused expression on his face. He was only a little taller than me, and his stomach was round and protruded in front of him. He had hangdog jowls, very little hair and small blue eyes.

"I assure you, Agent Black, that no violence is necessary."

I dropped my hands to my sides. "Who are you?"

"My name is Sokolov, and I am the assistant to the chairman of the board of the Agency."

"Really? The chairman?" I said, leaning back against my desk and crossing my arms. I was surprised that one actually existed. I'd always figured he was a figment of J.B.'s imagination. I'd never seen him. "What does the chairman want with a lowly Agent?"

"You are hardly lowly, Agent Black," Sokolov said. "The chairman has asked me to tell you that your first responsibility is to the souls of the dead, irrespective of the complications of your paternity. As such, you are hereby ordered not to engage in any pursuit of Azazel the fallen angel, particularly as it relates to the incident of today."

"The 'incident'? You mean the one where a bunch of your Agents were kidnapped and a whole lot of innocent folks were killed because the upper brass wants to stick their fingers in their ears and say 'la-la-la'?" I asked.

"It is not for you to question the actions of your superiors," Sokolov said.

"Too bad I don't think anyone is superior to me," I said.

"You should be careful, Agent Black. You have people that you care about, do you not? You wouldn't want to see them hurt because of your inability to take orders," he said silkily.

I pushed away from the desk and marched up to Sokolov, getting in his personal space. He smelled like peppermint and onions.

"Don't you dare threaten me," I said, my temper snapping. "You don't know what I'm capable of."

"On the contrary, the Agency knows precisely of what you are capable. As a further notice, you are hereby warned that any further adventures beyond the Door will result in your immediate death at the hands of the Retrievers," he said.

I blinked. "I haven't gone beyond the Door. No Agent can."

"You set off the alarms at headquarters at approximately four eighteen p.m. this afternoon. Your excursion was of ten minutes in length," Sokolov recited.

"Four eighteen p.m.? But I was asleep . . ." I started to say; then my voice faded. That was when I'd dreamed of Gabriel, and Puck had appeared. I thought it had just been a fantasy implanted in my head by Puck. Had I really gone beyond the Door?

Sokolov nodded, as if he'd confirmed some suspicion. "Despite the fact that you were unconscious of your actions, you are not permitted to go seeking the soul of your loved one in the land of the dead. Should this occur again, you will be punished accordingly."

"Going to send your bogeymen after me?" I asked.

"I would not sneer so if I were you, Agent Black," Sokolov said. "The Retrievers would not be kind to you."

"You've delivered your message. Now move along," I said.

Sokolov's face hardened. "You should take the Agency

more seriously, Agent Black. We have the power to destroy you utterly."

The Agency's messenger boy turned on his heel and retreated from my cubicle. I pulled on my coat like I didn't have a care in the world. I was sure they were watching me on the security cameras, and I didn't want anyone to think I'd been even remotely affected by Sokolov. I picked up the sheaf of papers I'd filled out and walked toward the drop box where all the soul forms were collected. I pushed the forms through the slot and continued on to J.B.'s office.

His secretary was missing from the outer office, gone home for the day like a normal person who had a life. I knocked on the closed door and opened it before he could respond.

J.B. looked up, his brow furrowed. "I thought I said an hour."

"I'm hungry now," I said, trying to send him a meaningful glance. "Where's that dinner you promised me?"

He buried his head in paperwork again. "I still have some stuff to do here."

"Are you really going to let me get home by myself?" I asked.

"You fly by yourself all the time," he mumbled.

Gods above and below, he could be so dense sometimes. Especially if he was focused on paperwork. It was like it had some kind of magical sway over him.

"J.B.," I said loudly, hoping my tone would cut through the fog caused by the delight of completing forms in triplicate.

He looked up again, and this time it seemed like his eyes finally focused on me. He seemed to realize I wanted him for something.

"I'm coming, I'm coming," he said, putting down his pen and grabbing his coat. "I lost track of time."

"I'm used to it," I said.

"So where do you want to eat? You want a pizza?" J.B. said, playing along as we walked past the cubicle maze on the way to the elevators.

"We eat enough pizza at my house. Beezle thinks take-out is one of the four food groups," I said as the elevator doors opened and we stepped in.

"The four food groups are over," J.B. said. "Now there's a plate or something."

"I thought it was a pyramid?"

"Nope, that's come and gone already."

We continued talking about nothing in particular until we were outside the Agency and a block away.

"Let's fly," I said, and we both pushed our wings out.

We disappeared from the sight of ordinary people, but any Agent would still be able to see us. I glanced behind to see if anyone was following us. There was nobody I could see, but the back of my neck tingled. Maybe it was just the lingering effects of Sokolov's visit.

"What's up?" J.B. asked after a few minutes.

"Wait until we get home," I said, and he didn't press me.

We landed on the lawn. Everything looked normal. There were no monsters waiting to attack, no effigies burning on the front walk. The lights were on in Samiel's apartment. I could see the flickering blue light of the television set through the front picture window of the upper floor. It looked like every lamp had been turned on as well.

"Beezle should know better," I said. "He's going to kill my electricity bill."

Curiously, I could also see lights on in the basement,

and the shadow of someone moving around behind the curtain.

I pushed open the foyer door and unlocked the door to my apartment. J.B. followed me upstairs.

"Hello?" I called as I entered, expecting a chorus of greetings in reply. But no one answered.

"Hello?" I repeated, dropping my coat on the table as I went toward the back of the house.

No one was in the kitchen, and the back door was open. I went to the top of the stairs and heard Nathaniel's, Jude's and Beezle's voices.

"Where did it go?" Nathaniel shouted.

"That way, that way, you idiot!" Jude roared.

"What's going on?" J.B. asked, standing behind me.

"Search me," I said, starting down the steps.

"Watch out!" Beezle said. "It almost got into the pipes again."

"Why don't you help instead of telling us things we already know?" Jude said.

"I am helping. I'm watching—there it goes! Toward the washing machine!" Beezle said.

"Sounds like there's a mouse in the house," J.B. said.

"Yeah, but why would they be freaking out over a mouse?" I said as we entered the basement.

My basement is not the cleanest part of my house. It's just one big room, and I've got a lot of junk stacked in boxes all over the place. There was an old pullout sofa at the far end. An ancient washer and dryer stood a few feet from the bottom steps.

Nathaniel had pushed the washer away from the wall and was on his hands and knees, reaching with a tennis racket. Jude crouched on the other side of the washing machine, his hands cupped and close to the ground. They both looked sweaty and harassed. Beezle fluttered over to J.B. and me.

"What are you doing?" I asked.

"Trying to catch the rat-demon that got in the house," Beezle said.

"Gah," I said with a shudder. I'd seen the internal organs of many a monster without blinking, but the thought of rats in the house gave me the heebie-jeebies. "Where's Samiel?"

"Waiting upstairs at an entry point in case the thing escapes through the wall," Beezle said. "There's a big hole in his apartment near the heater."

"Yeah, I keep meaning to fix that," I said. "Why don't you just blast the thing and be done with it?"

"Because," Nathaniel said, as he swatted at the squeaking thing with the tennis racket. "It is immune to magic. That is how it managed to get in the house in the first place. It found an opening in the outside wall and was able to construe that as an invitation."

"What are you going to do with it once you catch it?" I asked.

"Question it," Jude said grimly. "It's a spy."

"I didn't know either of you spoke rat," I said, and Jude spared me a dirty look.

There was an increase in the pitch and frequency of the demon's squeaks. I shuddered again. There's just something about rats that makes even the most easygoing person cringe.

"Ha!" Nathaniel said as he swung the racket one last time. Jude gave a satisfied grunt and stood up. The creature squealed, and Nathaniel pulled the handle of the racket along the floor as the little demon made horrible noises.

When the head of the racket emerged from behind the

washing machine, I saw why the monster was howling so. Nathaniel had basically squashed it to the ground under the netting, so the rat-demon was imprisoned between the wire of the racket and the floor. It was pressed so flat I was surprised it wasn't dead already.

"We need a jar or something to keep it in," J.B. said as the demon tried to wriggle out of the cage Nathaniel had made.

"There's that empty plastic container from Costco that had all those cheese puffs in it," Beezle said. "I don't think it went out to the recycle bin yet."

"You ate all those cheese puffs already?" I shouted after him as he went upstairs to get it.

"Where do rat-demons come from?" I asked Nathaniel.

"They don't ally themselves with any particular creature or particular court. They're mercenaries, willing to work for whomever will feed the nest," he said.

I crouched down and looked in the thing's beady black eyes. Up close it appeared less ratlike and more like a demon. What I had thought was fur was actually tiny scales. It stared at me with such malice that I felt goose bumps break out. "So how do we talk to it? Don't we need a translator or something?"

"No," Nathaniel said. "It can understand every word we say. And the squeaking is for effect. It can speak English, and just about any other language you can think of."

I suppressed my revulsion and leaned a little closer. "Who sent you?"

14

THE VOICE THAT CAME FROM THE CREATURE'S MOUTH was high-pitched and eerie. "A horror that you cannot imagine, Madeline Black."

"Yeah, like I've never heard that before," I said, sitting back on my heels.

Nathaniel pressed down harder on the netting and the demon squealed even louder. "Answer the question."

"You're going to squash it," Jude said mildly, but he didn't sound like that would be particularly upsetting.

Beezle returned with Samiel in tow. My brother-in-law carried the cheese puff container. A few tiny holes had been punched in the red lid so the monster wouldn't suffocate.

Samiel opened the top of the jar and kneeled on the floor next to Nathaniel.

Quick as lightning, Nathaniel lifted the racket, grabbed the rat-demon's tail and dropped it inside the jar. Samiel screwed the top closed while the thing was still scrabbling around inside.

"Who sent you?" I repeated.

The rat-demon ignored me. It bared its teeth and started scraping at the plastic.

"Can it chew its way out?" I asked the room in general.

"Probably," Beezle said. "A regular Chicago alley rat can chew through concrete."

"That is disgusting," J.B. said.

"Yeah, and you'd better wash your hands," I said to Nathaniel. "The gods know where that thing has been."

Nathaniel scowled. "I'll be right back."

"We really can't use magic on this thing?" I said.

"It would be pointless," Beezle said. "It's too small to be affected."

"Well, that's annoying," I said. "You're the one who told me that most things don't like . . ."

I trailed off, and Beezle's eyes gleamed.

"Yeah," he said. "That ought to do it."

"What?" Jude asked.

"Bring that thing upstairs," I said to Samiel, and led the parade up to my apartment. Nathaniel joined the crowd in my kitchen a few moments later.

I rummaged through my pantry until I found an old sauté pan that I wouldn't mind throwing away afterward. Then I put it on my gas stove and turned the flame underneath very high.

"Put the jar in the pan," I said to Samiel.

He looked slightly revolted, but he did it.

The demon squealed some more, frantically scratching at the sides of the jar with its claws.

"This is going to smell," J.B. said.

"And it will probably set off the smoke detectors,"

Nathaniel added, taking the detector in the hallway down and opening the case to release the batteries.

Jude opened all the windows in the kitchen, letting in the frigid air from outside as the acrid odor of burning plastic filled the air.

"I can't help but feel like we've reached some kind of low," Beezle said. "We've got an angel, a half-breed nephilim, a werewolf, a gargoyle and a couple of Agents of unusual bloodline, and we're all standing around the kitchen watching a rat-demon get burnt."

"You're not wrong," J.B. said.

"You wouldn't think it's a low if that creature had escaped back to its master with information you'd thought was confidential," Nathaniel said. "Or if it had completed its mission and then returned with the remainder of its nest."

"I would burn the house down before I would live here with a rat infestation," I said.

"Given your penchant for burning buildings, this does not surprise me in the least," Beezle said.

The bottom of the jar started to melt as the heat in the pan increased. The demon screamed as its clawed feet were scorched. The air blowing in from outside barely disguised the stench of burning chemicals mixed with rat. Smoke billowed around the kitchen, and we all covered our faces with our sleeves.

"Let me out, let me out, LET ME OUT!" the demon screamed.

"Who sent you?" I repeated for the third time.

"Antares! Antares!" it said.

"So he is still alive, then," I said. "Is he working with Azazel? Are they together now?"

The rat screeched in pain as the jar began to melt more

rapidly. Hot plastic dripped from the top and sides onto the demon's scales.

"Let me out, let me out!"

"Where is Antares?" I demanded.

"In the Forbidden Lands!" the rat-demon screamed.

"Is Azazel with him?" I asked.

"No! No! Let me out! Let me out!"

"Where is Azazel?" I asked.

The rat-demon howled. Its legs were almost entirely encased in melted plastic, and I think its feet were attached to the bottom of the pan.

"Where is Azazel?" I repeated.

"I don't know, I don't know! I told you what you wanted to know—now let me out!"

"I never said I would let you out," I said.

The rat-demon's eyes widened in terror. The six of us stood and watched as Antares' minion was killed by inches.

It took a long time. Jude went to open more windows.

When it was nothing but a blackened husk, Nathaniel scooped up the pan and took it outside to the Dumpster in the alley.

"I feel dirty," Beezle said as Nathaniel came back inside.

"Yeah, it doesn't exactly feel like a victory, does it?" I said tiredly.

The back of my neck tingled, and again I had the sensation of being watched.

"Let's get the windows closed," I said. "And, Nathaniel—is there some way to put a veil over us so no one can eavesdrop from outside?"

"Paranoid much?" Beezle asked.

"I don't think it's that outrageous. We just had a rat-demon in our house trying to spy on us for Antares," I said. "I'd rather our plans were not generally known."

"It can be done, yes," Nathaniel said. "But we would all have to stay in the same area, under a bubble, so to speak."

"Let's all sit around the dining room table," I said.

"If we're sitting at the table, then we should bring snacks," Beezle said. "It only makes sense."

"How much popcorn did you eat while I was out?" I asked.

Samiel held up three fingers. *He snuck the last bowl when I wasn't looking.*

"You don't need any snacks," I said.

We all collected around the table, and Nathaniel cast the spell. I had the uncomfortable sensation of my ears popping as the veil surrounded us, and I cracked my jaw so I could hear properly.

They already knew about Azazel and the vampire attack, so I filled everyone in on Sokolov's threats at the Agency. J.B. seemed shocked.

"I can't believe they sent him personally to threaten you," he said. "They must really think you're high-risk."

"I don't intend the Agency any harm," I said. "I don't know why they won't leave me alone."

"You're a danger to their order," J.B. said. "If they let you run wild, then other Agents might start getting ideas about defying their authority."

"Yeah, well, I don't really care about the Agency and their control issues except to the extent that they get in my way. I think somebody followed us home," I said.

It makes sense that they would have you under surveillance, Samiel said.

"It's a waste of resources. Why follow me and wait for me to screw up? Why not use every available Agent to find their missing coworkers?" I said.

"Because . . ." J.B. began.

"I know—they don't want to get involved. We don't need to go over it again. It pisses me off. There are two things we need to focus on now. The first is finding the Agents. The second is finding Azazel."

"With any luck they'll be in the same place," Jude said.

"Have you tried asking Lucifer for help?" Beezle asked. "Because you're his Hound of the Hunt."

"Yeah? So?"

"If he ordered you to find Azazel, you would be compelled to hunt him until you found him, and you would have the knowledge to help you do so," Beezle said.

I stared at him. "You couldn't have mentioned this earlier? I would have asked Lucifer to help me when he was here last instead of taking me to Titania and Oberon. And I wouldn't have bothered with that debacle at Azazel's mansion."

Beezle shrugged. "You went to the mansion without telling me you were going, and anyway, I thought you knew that would happen if you were the Hound of the Hunt. Everyone was so depressed when Lucifer bestowed that office upon you. Besides, I figured you wouldn't want to use that skill except as a last resort. I didn't think you'd like being under Lucifer's compulsion."

"Well, no, I wouldn't. But I would put up with it if that meant I could find Azazel. And now my useless grandfather isn't picking up his phone. Again," I said. "You'd think he would have told me that he could do that."

"Which means that he has some reason of his own for not wanting you to find Azazel easily," Jude said.

"I don't even want to think about what that reason might be," I said grimly. "Either this rebellion is a farce, or he's looking to profit from Azazel's actions in some way that I haven't yet figured out."

"Lord Lucifer's ways are mysterious," Nathaniel said. "But the rebellion was not a farce; that, I can tell you. Azazel despises Lucifer."

"So he's hoping to profit from Azazel's insanity," I said. "And in the meantime it suits him to have me running in circles trying to find Azazel."

"Does that mean we shouldn't try to find the Agents?" J.B. said.

"No. I won't leave them to Azazel's tender care," I said, thinking of the humans that had been caged in his labs.

"So the best lead we have is Antares in the Forbidden Lands," J.B. said. "If we can find him, maybe he'll lead us to Azazel."

"Have you ever been in the Forbidden Lands?" I asked. "Because I have. It's a giant wasteland, and in between deserts there are mountain ranges with a thousand nooks and crannies to hide in."

Samiel rapped the table so that we would look at him. *I grew up there, remember? I know some places that he might hide.*

"We've got to try," J.B. said.

I rubbed my eyes tiredly. I was getting a headache again. "Did Chloe tell you if she'd found anything in the notebook?"

"She said she thought she'd cracked it, but she wasn't able to tell me what she'd found. We were in the office and there were a ton of other people around," J.B. said.

"I wonder if she left any notes in her apartment," I said.

"I don't think breaking and entering would look very good to upper management if you are being followed," J.B. said.

"I don't have to break and enter," I said. "I'm the Hound of the Hunt. I can pass through walls and all that good stuff, even if Lucifer doesn't tell me to do so. If Chloe left some notes, we may be able to figure out what Azazel is doing. And if we can figure out what he's doing, then maybe we can work out where he's hiding."

"And if that doesn't work?" Jude said.

"Then we'll go to the Forbidden Lands and see if we can find my cockroach of a half brother," I said. "But first we have to get rid of this tail. I don't want some Agency stooge hanging around when I expressly disobey Sokolov's orders."

"It's strange," Jude said thoughtfully. "I believe you when you say that you're being followed, but I didn't smell anything unusual outside when I opened the windows."

"And what does that mean?" I asked. "Why does everything that happens to me have to be mysterious? Why can't I just have a straightforward situation—Agency wants me followed, Agent follows me, we neutralize whatever sad sack got stuck with the job? Why does there have to be something weird?"

"Obviously because the Agency is terrified of you, and thus has sent their best and most unique Agent to follow you," Nathaniel said.

"I wonder . . ." J.B. said, his eyes widening.

"What?" I asked.

"I wonder if it's Bryson," he said.

"Bryson the invincible?" I asked. I put my head in my hands. "No. No, no, no. I don't need any super-soldiers hunting me. Doesn't my life already suck? Do I need this, too?"

"Who's Bryson?" Jude asked.

"He's like the ultimate Agent," I said. "He's got a perfect record—never a ghost or a lost soul in the thirty years he's been collecting. And for the last ten years he's been leader of some elite unit that takes only the most difficult cases. He's awesome."

"But so are you," Nathaniel said. "Do not underestimate yourself. You have surely overcome creatures far more powerful than a mere Agent."

"I've overcome those creatures through a combination of luck, willpower and magic. Most of the time I take advantage of their emotions, like I did with Oberon. But you can't do that with Bryson. He's like a robot."

"In other words, he's the exact opposite of you. You're emotional and impulsive," Jude said.

"Don't forget prone to pyromania," Beezle added.

"He's logical and orderly," Jude said, continuing as if Beezle had not spoken. "So we play to your strengths in order to disarm his."

"You're suggesting that if she acts like her usual spastic self, it will throw this guy off the scent?" Beezle said skeptically. "That doesn't seem like much of a plan."

"This may come as a surprise to you, but most of the things I do don't have much of a plan," I said.

"That is not any surprise to me at all," Beezle said. "I always suspected you just did whatever came into your head at the moment."

"I do not think we should assume this super-soldier, as you call him, is the one following you," Nathaniel said. "It may be someone else entirely."

"No," I said. "J.B.'s probably right. Bryson is likely the only one who could effectively hide himself from Jude."

"But now that I know he's out there somewhere, I can find him," Jude said. "Lack of scent is just as powerful a signature as a strong smell."

"You mean you would be able to sense where he is from the empty space, so to speak?"

Jude nodded.

"Okay," I said. "Let's get rid of Bryson, and then I'll go to Chloe's."

"You're not going alone," everyone said, and Samiel signed it for good measure.

"Yes, yes, I know you all have to pretend I'm small and helpless so you can feel more confident in your masculinity," I said.

"Nobody here believes you helpless," Nathaniel said.

"But you are small," Jude said.

"Definitely the smallest one here besides Beezle," J.B. said.

And Beezle's not that much smaller than you are, Samiel added.

"All right, all right. You've all had your fun at the expense of the short person. Listen, I don't want Bryson hurt," I said.

"How are we supposed to neutralize him without hurting him?" Nathaniel said. "He will surely fight."

"Don't hurt him any more than necessary," I said. "He's not malicious. He's just following orders. He doesn't know any other way to be."

So what's the plan? Samiel signed.

"The first thing is that we've got to get Jude outside so he can sniff around, but Bryson can't suspect."

"I could put Jude under a veil while also cloaking myself," Nathaniel said. "Then we could explore to our heart's content without his knowledge."

I shook my head. "Too complicated. Besides, I bet he'll have some way of detecting the presence of a veil. He's a super-soldier, remember? We don't want to spook him."

"How about you go outside and stare longingly at the stars like you're missing Gabriel, and the rest of your entourage follows you out because they're worried about you?" Beezle suggested.

"Then everyone is standing still, and how will Jude sniff around? We need to all be outside and moving around, but not in a way that will make Bryson suspicious."

We all fell silent, trying to come up with some logical reason for us to be outside in the snow on a frigid January night.

"Let's make a snowman," I said.

"A snowman?" Jude said, looking skeptical.

"Yeah, a snowman. We'll all be outside running around the yard collecting snow, so you'll have plenty of opportunity to sniff around. Bryson will have no reason to suspect that we're trying to find him."

"I thought we'd reached a low when we tortured the rat-demon. Now you want to try to trick Mr. Awesome Agent by playing in the snow?" Beezle said.

"You were the one who said I should be my usual spastic self," I said. "Building a snowman gets all of us outside. And Nathaniel and Jude don't even have to actually do the building. You can stand around and look bored, or sneer, or whatever. It will look like you want to keep an eye on me but don't want to participate."

"I don't want to participate, either," Beezle said. "Rolling around in the snow is not my idea of fun."

"Then stay inside. But you're not getting anything else to eat."

None of the others looked too thrilled with my idea, either.

"If anyone else has a suggestion, I'm happy to hear it," I said.

"I guess it could work," J.B. said reluctantly.

"It will totally work," I said with a confidence I did not

feel. The truth was, I thought it was kind of a dumb idea, too. But a lot of my dumb ideas seemed to work out. I laid out the basic plan and everyone agreed.

I pushed away from the table and said to Nathaniel, "Drop the veil now."

My ears popped as the veil disappeared. I made a big show of being annoyed.

"Fine, the rest of you do what you want," I said loudly. "I'm going outside."

"Yeah, go outside and get yourself killed by another thing from Faerie," J.B. said. "That's real smart."

"I'm not going to stay locked up in this house forever just because you think I should live under glass," I said, grabbing my coat and stomping toward the back door.

Samiel followed me. *Maybe you should listen to J.B.*

"Not you, too," I said, and clattered down the steps toward the outside door.

I threw the door open with a huff and went out to the back porch. I looked around for a moment, like I was trying to gather my thoughts. I couldn't see any sign of Bryson, but my spider-sense was tingling. He was here somewhere.

Samiel tapped me on the shoulder, holding up my hat and mittens.

Forget something? he asked. He was already bundled up.

I took the hat and gloves from him. "Thanks. I'm sorry I lost my temper."

I went down the three stairs to the yard and kicked the snow around, doing my best imitation of a person torn between depression and anger. It wasn't that big of a stretch. I missed Gabriel every second of the day, and I was angry at constantly being hounded by threats and assassins.

Samiel tapped me on the shoulder, holding out a small, perfectly formed snowball. *Want to make a snowman?*

I smiled at him, like I was letting him cheer me up. "Sure."

We started rolling the snowman's bottom half. A few moments later Jude and Nathaniel came outside.

"Where's J.B.?" I asked.

"He left," Jude said.

Actually, J.B. had gone around front and intended to circle back by way of the alley. I felt that Bryson had to be flying or resting somewhere at second-story height, because he would want to see and hear what was going on inside my apartment. My hope was that he would be focused on me and not paying attention to J.B.'s approach from the alley.

Jude prowled around the perimeter of the yard like he was bored. Nathaniel walked to the fence that separated my property from the alley and leaned against it, watching us.

After a while Beezle came outside. He couldn't stand not being in the middle of things. He had a scarf wrapped around his horns and another one wrapped several times around his middle.

"Why is it we're outside freezing our butts off?"

"Can you not see that we're building a snowman?" I said.

"I can see. I just want to know *why*," Beezle said.

"I needed some air."

"You needed air that's only seventeen degrees?"

"Go back inside if you're going to be annoying," I said.

At that moment, Jude leapt over my head. As he did, he transformed into a shaggy red-and-gray wolf.

Nathaniel launched after Jude. I heard the sound of a wolf slamming into a human body with tremendous force. I spun around and saw the veil that was hiding Bryson fall away as Jude attacked.

The Agent slashed out with the knife he gripped in his right hand, but Nathaniel was there before the blade could strike Jude. The knife fell into the snow. The angel held Bryson's wrists to the ground and Jude stood on his chest, growling.

J.B. flew over the fence and landed beside me. "Did I miss all the fun already?"

"Yup," I said, approaching the three men in the snow.

Bryson stared up at me with cold blue eyes. His gray hair was buzzed close to his head and he had the wiry, tough look of a lifelong soldier.

"What are you doing here, Bryson?" I asked conversationally.

"You know the answer to that, or else you wouldn't have even suspected I was here," he said. His voice was low and gravelly, like that guy who does the voiceovers for truck commercials.

"Were you supposed to just watch and report, or did Sokolov have something else in mind?" I asked.

Bryson said nothing.

"Right," I said. "You can't say."

"If you're going to kill me, do it now," Bryson said. "You'll get nothing from me by torture."

"I'm not going to torture you," I said, offended.

Bryson narrowed his eyes skeptically. "I saw what happened to the rat."

"The rat was a demon, and it was spying on me," I said. "I wouldn't do that to another Agent."

"I'm spying on you."

"You act like you want me to set you on fire," I said, annoyed. "Look, all I want is for you to back off. Go home and tell Sokolov that I stayed home all night like a good little girl."

"That would be a violation of protocol," Bryson said.

"Listen, what did Sokolov tell you I was up to?" I asked. "Because I'm not doing anything bad here. I'm trying to find and rescue the Agents that were kidnapped today."

"You've been ordered to keep out of it," Bryson said.

"Yeah, and the Agency won't do anything to rescue those people. Does that really sit well with you?" I asked.

His mouth tightened, but he didn't respond.

"So you don't like it, either, but you won't do anything about it. Is that it?"

Bryson continued with the silent treatment.

"Fine. If that's how you're going to be about it," I said. "Tie him up and put him in the basement. Samiel and Nathaniel, take turns standing guard. And make sure you search him—I'm sure he's got weapons in every pocket."

"You will regret this," Bryson said as Nathaniel hauled him to his feet.

"I don't think so," I said. "I know that you're under orders, and you think you can't defy the Agency. So I'm not going to hurt you. But I can't let you report back to Sokolov, either."

His eyes burned as Nathaniel and Jude dragged him in the house, and I knew that I had made yet another enemy.

15

"HOW LONG ARE YOU GOING TO KEEP HIM HERE?" J.B. asked. "Sooner or later someone from the Agency will come looking for him."

"Just until the morning," I said. "That will give us time to search Chloe's apartment."

"And what then?" Jude asked.

"We'll kick Bryson loose, and he'll have to go back to Sokolov and say that he failed. But they'll have no proof that I did anything wrong," I said.

"What if we have to go into the Forbidden Lands?" J.B. said.

"If Bryson really wants to follow us into the Forbidden Lands, then he's welcome to it. But I don't think he'd be able to. We'd probably have to go through a portal, and we could easily prevent him from entering. So again, no proof that we're doing anything wrong."

"I don't know," J.B. said. "Somehow I don't think Bryson or Sokolov are going to take this well."

"I can't worry about Bryson's feelings," I said. "Or Sokolov's, for that matter. They're the ones who came after me. I can either roll over and let them have their way, or I can defy them and save the missing Agents."

J.B. scrubbed his hands through his hair, always a sign that he was under stress. "I know. But the fallout . . ."

"Will be what it will be. You knew that when you asked me to come downtown and see that massacre. You knew that I would go after Azazel."

"But that was before the Agency sent one of their goons to threaten you," J.B. said. "The stakes are higher now."

"I'm not leaving Chloe, or any of the others, to Azazel," I said steadily. "Bryson's out of the picture for now. Let's work the problem a step at a time."

"Is this how you get through the day?" J.B. asked. "By only looking at what's directly in front of you?"

"Since my typical day involves conspiracies of the fallen, Agency and faerie nature, regular attempts on my life and a cascade of shocking revelations, yes. If I tried to take in the big picture, I'd probably lose my mind."

"So what are we doing now, then?" Beezle asked. He still sat on the railing of the porch. I'd forgotten he was even outside.

"You go inside and help Samiel and Nathaniel," I said. "Me, Jude and J.B. will go to Chloe's."

"I'm not a guard dog," Beezle sniffed.

"You know, your job description includes the words 'home guardian.' "

"That's not guarding the home. That's guarding some guy who knows two thousand ways to kill me with a toothpick."

"Look, I want you to do what you do best," I said.

"Make nachos?" Beezle said hopefully.

"No. I want you to badger and annoy Bryson until he gives up information on Sokolov's plans for me."

"That's diabolical," Jude said. "I thought you said you weren't going to torture him."

Beezle gave Jude a dirty look. "What makes you think he'll crack?"

"I know you," I said.

Beezle flexed his claws. "Fine. But I want compensation."

"In the form of some trans-fat-laden pastry, no doubt," I said as Beezle flew back inside.

"Where does Chloe live?" I asked J.B.

"Not far from here, actually," he said. "Near Belmont and Paulina."

"By the frozen custard place?" I asked.

"No, closer to the library," he said, giving me a funny look.

"What? Beezle likes custard," I said. "I can't help it if my mental map of the city has all the sweets shops as landmarks."

We decided to walk since Jude couldn't fly and it wasn't worth the effort to carry him there. He changed into wolf form so that we would look like a couple walking their dog late at night.

"We should have a leash or something, though," I said.

Jude growled at me.

"Okay, okay. I was just trying to complete the illusion. Stay close to us so nobody gives us a hard time."

"I don't think that's going to be a problem," J.B. said. "Most normal people aren't out and walking about on a night like this."

Chloe's apartment was about a ten- or fifteen-minute walk from mine. There was very little traffic on the street, and we saw no pedestrians from my house to hers. Most homes were darkened, their residents already tucked in bed for the night. I thought longingly of my own bed, but hard on the heels of that thought came the memory of Puck disguised as Gabriel.

Maybe I would sleep on the couch for a while and give Jude my room.

Chloe's apartment was on Melrose in a white-siding two-flat not much different from my own. We walked up the porch and peered at the names on the mailboxes. Chloe was on the first floor, which was handy.

"I'll go in through the wall and come out to let you two in," I told Jude and J.B.

They nodded, and I laid my hand on the exterior door.

"I am the Hound of the Hunt, and no walls can bind me," I said softly.

My hand slipped through the door like water, and the rest of me followed with it. I turned around and let the other two into the foyer, and then repeated the process on Chloe's door.

A few moments later we were inside. I flipped on the light switch that was near the front door.

The place was trashed.

The apartment was an open studio with a small galley kitchen at the far end and a little corner reserved for a bathroom.

There were clothes everywhere, papers scattered willy-nilly and an open futon covered in tools and bits of metal. Her storage system seemed to consist of cardboard boxes and old milk crates, and they were used for everything from underwear to books. The sink was piled high with dirty dishes, and I think there was mold growing on the coffeemaker.

"Has someone been here before us, or does she live like this?" I said, horrified.

"You've never seen her cubicle, have you?" J.B. said. "This is actually somewhat organized for Chloe."

Dismayed, I looked at all the paper all over the floor. "You don't think she took the sheets out of Azazel's binder, do you?"

Jude, who had been sniffing around the room, gave a short bark. He stood near a small, two-person card table that Chloe had shoved under a window.

Azazel's binder rested on one of the chairs. I opened it up and found it empty.

"You've got to be kidding me," I said, scanning the mess on the floor. "We have to go through all this junk."

J.B. sighed. "It's you, right? Nothing can ever be easy."

We spent the next hour or so on our hands and knees, crawling around collecting pieces of paper and sorting them into two piles—"Azazel" and "not Azazel."

After a final walk-through we were pretty sure we'd gotten all of the documents. I'd noticed as we were collecting them that Chloe had made oblique notes on several of the pages in purple marker.

I shoved the papers back through the rings of the binder and shut it. "Let's bring this home and look it over. I can't take the smell of this place anymore. Hasn't she ever heard of disinfectant?"

I shut off the lights and sent Jude and J.B. outside first so that I could lock the interior door. Not that Chloe would notice if someone broke in, but it seemed like the right thing to do.

•

I drifted through the outside door and saw J.B. and Jude waiting for me on the sidewalk.

We started walking north back to my place. J.B. carried the binder under his arm, and Jude trotted a little bit ahead, sniffing as he went.

We were on Lincoln, across from the Burrito House and near the public play lot, when Jude stopped.

"What is it?" I asked.

He whined, pawing at the metal fence that surrounded the play lot. I reached around him and opened the gate.

He darted inside, nose pressed to the ground, and crossed between the swings and the slide. The playground was bordered by a high wall that supported the Metra tracks that ran through the neighborhood.

Jude went right up to the wall, sniffing and whining so that we would follow him. J.B. and I followed, bewildered.

After a few minutes Jude stopped and barked. He pointed with his nose toward the wall.

There, inscribed in the metal support, was a tiny symbol—a circle topped by an upside-down *V*.

"The sigil of the charcarion demons," I said.

Jude barked.

"This is probably a portal," I muttered. "But why put it so close to my house? Why risk my finding it?"

"If it's a portal, can you open it?" J.B. asked.

I stared at the symbol. The last time I'd opened a portal like this, I'd found the wolf cubs that had been taken from Wade's pack. If I went through the portal now, would I find the missing Agents? Would I find Azazel?

Or was it a trick, a trap planted by Azazel? If I went through the portal, would I find nothing but my own doom?

I looked down at the tattoo of the coiling snake on my

right palm. There was no tingle of magic, no prompting to open the portal.

Then again, my little parasite had been rather quiet lately. Not that I'd noticed, what with everything else that was going on.

"Better not try to open it now," I said finally. "We don't know where it goes."

"It could lead to Chloe," J.B. said.

Jude barked.

"Or it could lead to a nest of charcarion demons," I said. "We don't know how long that sigil has been there."

"But—" J.B. said.

"No," I repeated. "I've reached my limit of foolish, impulsive decisions for the last twenty-four hours. Let's go home and try and see if Chloe left anything useful for us. We know that the sigil is here, so if we don't come up with any other options, we can always come back to it."

"If you don't want to go through it now, maybe you should seal it," J.B. said with obvious reluctance. "It's right next to a playground. What if Azazel decides to send a bunch of demons through during the day when kids are playing here?"

That was a terrifying thought.

"I'm not sure I want to risk leaving it open, in that case," I said.

"Either we should go through now, or we should seal it," J.B. said.

Would I be sealing Chloe and the other Agents behind my spell, never to be found? Could I take that kind of chance?

Alternatively, could I risk the lives of innocent children who might fall prey to some wild plan of Azazel's?

There wasn't really a choice when I put it in those terms.

"Stand back," I said, and lifted my hand to the sigil.

My tattoo lay quiet on my skin, but I didn't need its help for this spell anymore. The metal glowed hot and yellow beneath my touch, and when I pulled my hand away the sigil was blackened, closed forever.

None of us spoke as we continued home. We all knew there was no other real option than to close the portal, but it was hard to feel good about that choice.

I only hoped that whatever Chloe had discovered in Azazel's notebooks led us to her and the other Agents, and I wouldn't have to regret closing the sigil.

Beezle buzzed into the living room as soon as we walked through the front door.

"I have been as annoying as I possibly could be. I think Nathaniel wants to kill me, but Bryson hasn't given up anything interesting yet," he said.

"Keep working on him," I said. "I don't want to let him go until sunrise."

Beezle shrugged. "Okay."

He went back downstairs while I settled in at the table with the binder. Jude went into the bathroom and came back out as a human being. He'd taken to keeping a pair of jeans in there.

I opened the binder and divided the papers into three stacks, one for each of us. I grabbed some yellow legal pads and pencils from the side table and gave one each to Jude and J.B. "Now the fun part begins. Write down any notes that Chloe made and the context, if you can understand it."

It was slow and tedious work. Chloe had written a lot of formulas in the margins, and her formulas made as little sense to me as Azazel's. She'd also written cryptic things like "beam?" and "how to hold it internally?"

I heard Jude sighing a lot. J.B. just got that fixed, long-suffering look that he usually had after dealing with one of my escapades.

As I was nearing the end of my pile, I came across a sheet that had a large purple box around the word "SUNSHINE." Chloe had surrounded this word with many, many more exclamation points than were strictly necessary.

"Sunshine," I said, and looked back over my notes. "How to hold it . . ."

I thought about Azazel's own cryptic notes. Blood donors. Vampires. Sunshine.

"Gods above and below," I said. "He's trying to make vampires immune to the sun."

"He can't do that," Jude scoffed. "Vampires are destroyed by the sun."

"He's doing it," I said grimly. "Or at least he's trying."

"How would he do something like that?" J.B. asked.

"I'm not sure, because math is definitely not my strong suit, but I think that he's trying to inject the power of sunlight into human donors. Then he's letting the vampires drain the humans."

"And over time the vampires will build up an immunity to the sun?" Jude said skeptically.

"Well, I don't think it's worked so far," I said. "Because we saw the vampires at his mansion. The vampires were getting crisped in the sun, just as they should."

"So maybe it's not possible," J.B. said. "He's just wasting his time."

"Or maybe," I said slowly, "he had the wrong kind of donors."

"The kidnapped Agents? What would they have that ordinary humans wouldn't?"

"Agents' magic is tied to the dead, right? And vampires

are essentially dead," I said, warming to my theory. "So an Agent's blood might be better tolerated by a vampire, especially when something that would normally kill the vamp is running in the blood."

"And once vampires had built up an immunity to sunlight, then what?" J.B. said.

"I think the massacre that we saw today was just a little taste," I said.

"Vampires roaming free during the day, terrorizing the city?" Jude asked.

I nodded. "And since it's Azazel, you know that's only the smallest part of the plan. The vampires would probably be a distraction for some bigger splash he'd intended."

"If you're right, then the kidnapped Agents are probably being drained by vampires as we speak," J.B. said.

"More importantly, if it works, then Azazel will want more Agents," I said.

J.B. stared at me, his green eyes filled with horror. "The whole Agency is at risk."

"I told you that the upper management was being shortsighted," I said. "They need to put some resources into this."

J.B. shook his head. "I'll never convince them."

"You have to," I said. "They don't want a repeat of what happened with Ramuell and Antares, right? So why would they tolerate their Agents being picked off one by one?"

"From their point of view, it's not a problem. If an Agent dies, then the next person in their bloodline will be activated. Dead Agents are less troublesome than missing ones," he said.

"They're going to start having morale issues if they think like that," I said. "And they won't be able to threaten every Agent with Bryson or the Retrievers."

"The problem is that we have no proof of this," J.B. said.

"Sixteen missing Agents at the site of a vampire attack isn't proof?"

J.B. shook his head. "You don't know how stubborn upper management can be."

"I've got some idea," I said. "Well, the good news is we know what Azazel's intentions are."

"You think," Jude said.

"Let's just assume I'm right. The bad news is that we still don't know where he is."

"Try Lucifer again?" J.B. asked.

"I've got a feeling he's not answering his phone for a reason," I said, but I tried anyway. And got nothing.

"So it's the Forbidden Lands, then," Jude said.

"Yeah, but not for you," I said, and pointed to J.B.

"Why the hell not?" he asked.

"You've got to stay here and try to convince the Agency that other Agents are at risk," I said. "No matter how unlikely the outcome may be. If we can get the Agency to come around to our side, then we'll be better prepared for whatever Azazel's planning."

"We can hardly take on an army of vampires with just the five of us," Jude said.

"Six, if you count Beezle. And he usually doesn't show up for the combat situations," I said pointedly.

"So the four of you can manage Antares and whatever he's got hidden in the Forbidden Lands?" J.B. asked.

"Our options are limited," I said. "I think it would be better if you were here trying to work on the Agency. Start with Bryson."

"Bryson's been listening to Beezle for the last couple of hours and he hasn't broke," J.B. said.

"Don't try to break him. Try to reason with him. You're management. He's got to respect you."

"As a midlevel supervisor, my status is roughly on par with his."

"What do you want to do, then? Give up? Watch our colleagues get taken by Azazel and used for vampire food?"

"No. It's just . . ."

"All the alternatives suck, no matter how we try to play this. If you hang around me long enough, you get used to stuff like that."

J.B. smiled briefly. "Let's go get Bryson, then."

We agreed that J.B. would hold Bryson here until the rest of us had safely departed for the Forbidden Lands. After that he could release Bryson or take him elsewhere to try to convince him to help.

As we went down the stairs I heard Beezle holding forth on the merits of cheese popcorn versus caramel popcorn.

"Of course, you can always blend the two, à la the famous Chicago mix, but I prefer not to mix my salty and sweet together. You wouldn't put a doughnut in a bowl of potato chips, would you?"

Bryson was gagged and tied to an old metal chair that must have been found in the piles of junk. His eyes were glazed over and his jaw set. He looked like a man who'd had a tiny drop of water falling on his forehead continuously for the last couple of hours. Beezle hovered in front of his face, talking endlessly.

Samiel had dealt with Beezle simply—by not facing him. I'd often thought that the reason he tolerated Beezle so well was because he couldn't hear. He stood behind the gargoyle, arms crossed, staring at Bryson.

Nathaniel leaned against the wall to Bryson's left, and he appeared to be at the end of his rope. He seemed to be contemplating Beezle's slow demise.

"That's enough, Beezle," I said, and Nathaniel shot me a grateful look.

Bryson sighed in relief.

"We're remanding you into J.B.'s custody," I said, taking the gag off the Agent. "He's got some important things to tell you."

I jerked my head so that Nathaniel, Samiel and Beezle would follow me.

"Agent Black," Bryson called after me.

"Yes?" I said, turning back. Maybe he'd had a change of heart while listening to Beezle drone.

"I won't forget this," he said, the light of fury burning once again in his eyes.

I nodded, though my heart sank. I couldn't care less about Bryson's threats, but with an attitude like that he'd be impossible to convince. And I was sure that the Agency would be more receptive to Bryson than to J.B. or me.

Once the rest of the troops were assembled upstairs, I explained what had happened at Chloe's and at the playground.

"So the four of us are going after Antares," I said.

"What about me?" Beezle asked.

"I just assumed there was some important TV show you needed to watch, or perhaps you wanted to get into the pantry unhindered," I said.

"Like I would miss this," Beezle said.

"All aboard for the Forbidden Lands," I said.

16

WE STOOD ON A LONG ROAD WITH A CRACK RUNNING down the center. In the distance were jagged peaks of mountains under flashes of silver lightning. And in the foreground, a giant leafless tree scraping white claws against the sky.

I'd been here once before, when my crazy many-greats grandmother had brought me here to kill Ariell, Samiel's mother, who hadn't been the sanest creature herself.

I'd died here, too, for a little while. Ramuell had torn my heart out. For a moment I thought I could feel it again, feel his clawed hand pushing through flesh and bone and closing over my beating center. Then I took a deep breath, and let it go. I had to.

"There's no other way inside?" I asked Samiel.

His eyes were bleak. I could tell that he wasn't reliving happy family memories.

The Grigori closed all the paths to the nephilim save the way through the tree after they re-bound their children.

"But Azazel had two nephilim in his mansion," I said. "So he may have opened another passage."

"But do we have time to search for it?" Nathaniel asked.

I sighed. It was my own reluctance that was keeping us from moving forward. I didn't have any happy memories of this place, either.

"Let's go," I said.

The air wasn't as frigid as Chicago's winter, but it felt significantly less friendly. There had always been a sense of malice in the air here, and as we walked down the barren road, dread settled upon me like a cloak.

Beezle was tucked inside my coat, only his horns and eyes peeking over the lapel. Even he didn't have any smart remarks to offer.

After much loud discussion, we'd decided to go first to the Valley of Sorrows where the nephilim were held. Azazel had already freed at least two nephilim, and there was a fair chance that he was using that cave as the base of his operations. I'd argued that it was far too obvious a place, but Jude had pointed out that at least it was somewhere to start, and better than roaming aimlessly over the mountains.

So to the cave of the nephilim we would go.

The tree loomed larger against the sky as we got closer and closer. As we approached it, sweat trickled down the back of my neck. I did not want to go in there again.

No one spoke. I think we all could feel the menace of this place, and wanted to avoid attracting its attention.

After a long time, we reached the tree. Samiel opened the secret door, and we went into the underground tunnel. I was heartily sick of tunnels and passages and secret ways, especially after my assorted experiences with the fae. There had never been anything good waiting for me at the end of a tunnel. The last time I'd walked through this tunnel, I'd been following the ghost of Evangeline, and she'd left me alone when I reached the door to the cave of the nephilim.

The door was before us sooner than I wanted it to be. It was some heavy metal, warm and burnished like ancient gold. There was no knob but there were seven bolts to be drawn.

I reached for the top bolt. Jude stayed my hand.

"Wait," he whispered, his head cocked to one side. "I hear something."

I couldn't hear anything except the sound of my own breath, and the rustling of Beezle shifting inside my coat.

The tunnel had an odd hushed quality about it, like it was soundproofed. But a wolf could hear for miles.

"The nephilim?" I asked in a low voice.

He shook his head. "Whatever it is, there are a lot of them. Hundreds of them."

We all stared at the door.

"It can't be more nephilim," I said, horrified at the thought. "The nephilim are the children of Grigori and human women."

"How do you know Azazel hasn't been breeding more?" Beezle asked quietly.

I really hoped that wasn't true. I was sure that if Azazel had been breeding nephilim, then the human women who birthed them were not willing participants. The thought made me feel sick.

"We've got to see what's in there," I said.

"If you open that door, then whatever horde is standing behind it will surely descend upon us," Nathaniel pointed out.

"Then I'll veil myself and go through the wall as the Hound of the Hunt," I said.

"No," Jude and Nathaniel said. Samiel shook his head.

"Look, I'm not going through there to pick a fight. I'll be under a veil. I'll do some surveillance, and then I'll be right back."

"I'm not surveilling anything," Beezle said, climbing out of my coat and flying to Samiel's shoulder. "If you want to go into the room with the hundreds of whatevers, be my guest."

"Why must it always be you to take the risk?" Nathaniel said. "Why not one of us?"

"You can't pass through walls," I pointed out. "And we didn't come all this way to stand and stare at a door. I'm going. I'll be back soon."

"Then let me veil you," Nathaniel said. "Your own veil may not be enough."

I stood still while Nathaniel muttered the spell. His magic draped over me, warm and comforting, and I felt a surprising burst of tenderness toward him.

"Can you see me?" I asked.

They all shook their heads.

"I won't do anything stupid," I promised.

"Then you wouldn't be you," Beezle said. "Just come back in one piece. And with no more pieces missing."

I smiled at that, glancing down at my left hand. I'd once promised Beezle I'd come back in one piece, and returned with two fingers missing. Lucifer had sworn that the digits would return, but they never had. The skin there had grown smooth over the place where the sword had cauterized the wound.

I put my right palm against the door and spoke the invocation of the Hound of the Hunt. A moment later I was through the door.

And bumped into the charcarion demon that stood there.

I went still, holding my breath, as it turned around. Seeing no one behind him he smacked the head of the demon that stood next to him, saying something in a harsh, guttural language.

I could see why he thought that another demon had bumped into him. There were hundreds of them crammed into the cave of the nephilim. The cages that had imprisoned the Grigori's monstrous children hung empty at the ceiling. Charcarion demons covered every inch of the floor, crawled up the walls, dangled from the top of the cavern.

It was like being inside a massive, seething hive of insects.

Very carefully, I spread my wings and took flight. I felt like I threaded a very fine needle, trying to pass over the heads of the demons on the floor and below the demons that were suspended above.

The nephilim's cavern emptied into another, smaller chamber. This was the place where Ramuell and Ariell had lived, and where I had died. I lowered to the ground, pulling the veil tighter around me.

The charcarion demons confined themselves to the larger cavern. This one was empty. There were signs that someone had been living here—a mattress, some scraps of food on the floor.

And a large wooden cupboard. A cupboard a lot like the one that . . .

Antares entered from the opposite side of the cavern, a bow in one hand and a quiver of arrows slung across his shoulder. My half brother looks like a medieval priest's idea of a demon—large, curving black horns, red skin, claws, cloven hoofs, the works. I noticed with some satisfaction that there were several scars on his chest, the result of his battle with Gabriel a couple of weeks before.

I felt so secure under the veil that it didn't occur to me that Antares might be able to see me. So it took me by surprise when he shot an arrow straight for my heart.

I dodged out of the way at the last moment, and the tip of the arrow buried itself in my left shoulder instead.

"Hello, little sister," Antares crooned. "Come for a family visit?"

I pushed Nathaniel's veil off me and shot a bolt of nightfire at Antares. It bounced in the air about a foot away from him, and rebounded back at me. I dove out of the way again and the nightfire smashed into the cavern wall. The arrow dug painfully into my shoulder as I rolled on the floor. I reached up and broke off the shaft, but the tip was still buried inside. I'd have to remove it later. If I had a later.

Antares giggled. "No magic for you, sister. My mother's spell protects me."

"Too bad you didn't think to have Mommy protect you when Gabriel was taking pieces of you," I said, coming to my feet and drawing Lucifer's sword.

"Yes, well, never let it be said that I don't learn from my mistakes," Antares said. "But the thrall is dead, and I still live."

"I can take care of that problem," I said, running toward him with the sword upraised.

He shot another arrow at me, and I knocked it away with

the blade. Antares dropped the bow and pulled a charm from a small bag that hung around his neck.

I quickly muttered an incantation and tossed up a shield as Antares threw the charm at me. The spell smashed into the shield and melted it, but the magic didn't hit me. Which was good. Because I had no desire to be melted.

I swung the sword at Antares and he danced away, the blade just skimming across his right arm. That meant that his shield blocked magic, but I could still hurt him with the sword.

Some of the charcarion demons in the other cavern had taken notice of the battle, and a cry went up inside the hive. Several of them poured out and surrounded us so that Antares and I were locked inside a ring. Their chitters and howls echoed loudly inside the cave and made it hard to think.

I needed to get rid of Antares' advantage. I couldn't use magic against him, but he could throw his mother's spells at me all day. I ducked out of the way of another flying charm that hit the crowd of demons behind me. Three of the demons burst into flame. I stepped forward, jabbed upward with the sword, aiming for his jaw.

Antares jerked his head away, but I managed to slice through the cord that held the spells and pull it away with my sword.

"Now what, baby brother?" I said, smiling grimly.

Antares backed away as I stalked toward him. He shouted to the crowd, and one of the demons tossed him a sword. His blade clashed against mine as I swung forward for the kill.

I hacked and slashed and took chunks out of him, and he always managed to move at the last moment. His sword flashed, slicing my leg, my side, opening wounds that bled and weakened me, while the wound from the arrow festered. I was getting tired.

Even if I defeated Antares, I'd still have a room of charcarion demons to deal with, and I didn't think they were going to just let me go.

"Jude," I said, and hoped that he could hear me. "Jude."

"Who are you calling for now, sister?" Antares taunted. "There is no one here to save you, and you are growing weak."

He was so confident, so sure of his ability to defeat me. And why shouldn't he be? He'd always managed to escape me before.

My vision blurred, and for a second it looked like there were two Antares standing there. He slashed with the sword, and I just barely managed to block him.

"You have always been weak," he said. "Small, human, beneath me. My father knew this. That is why I have been chosen to rule."

Small. Human. Weak. His words echoed in my ears as I desperately tried to fight him off. I wasn't attacking anymore. I was fading fast. I just needed to keep him away from me. I needed to live.

The child inside me fluttered its wings frantically.

A wolf howled, and from inside the other cavern came the sound of charcarion demons screaming as they met their death.

Antares paused for a moment, turning toward the sound in surprise.

And I had him.

I stabbed upward, and the sword pierced his heart.

His eyes widened in shock, and when he opened his mouth to speak blood poured from his lips.

The sword pulled free as he fell to the ground.

"Impossible," I heard him say.

He turned over, tried to crawl away from me, a pathetic and broken thing. Crimson liquid spread in a widening pool beneath his body. The charcarion demons that surrounded us had fallen silent in shock even as their brothers fought for their lives against Nathaniel, Samiel and Jude.

There was no mercy in my heart for Antares. He was my half brother, and he had tried to kill me countless times since I had first met him. I knew with a certainty that if I did not finish this now, he would rise up again like the cockroach that he was, always hunting me.

My blade flashed once more, and a moment later Antares' head rolled away from his body.

"Who's laughing now?" I said.

Then the charcarion demons descended upon me.

I didn't have to worry about shields on demons, so I started blasting away with every spell that I had. If a demon came close enough, I hacked at it with the sword.

"Maddy!" Beezle cried, flying over the heads of the demons. "The others are coming!"

I nodded so that he would know that I heard and kept throwing every last bit of magic I had in me. But I was still bleeding, still weakened from my battle with Antares.

Lucifer's tattoo still lay silent on my palm, and I knew that I would not be able to draw upon the power of the Morningstar to help me.

The cavern filled with the cry of a terrible voice, a voice filled with anguish. Everyone stopped, and the charcarion demons looked around, fear in their eyes, but I knew who it was.

"Missing something, Daddy?" I said.

I curse you, Madeline Black, least beloved of my line.

You shall never know peace, for you have taken that which is most precious to me.

"Do you know how many times in the last couple of days someone has sworn that they will hound me until I'm dead? Get in line."

You shall know pain like no other.

"How about you say that to my face?" I said. "Where are you hiding, coward?"

Silence. Wherever Azazel was, he wasn't here. I suspected that he was watching from afar somewhere. Wherever he held the Agents, and his pet vampires.

There was the sound of rock shifting, and then a loud crack. Huge boulders tumbled down the sides of the cavern. The charcarion demons desperately tried to escape the crush of falling rock, knocking one another over and trampling other demons in their haste. I fought to stay on my feet, saw Nathaniel and Samiel flying toward me over the heads of the demons.

One demon, either smarter or more dedicated to the cause than the others, took advantage of my momentary distraction. It closed its claws around my neck, shutting off the passage of air.

I barely had any energy left to fight. I reached up with my hands, tried to pry the demon away, but it held on with fierce glee. Black spots danced in front of my eyes.

"Madeline!" Nathaniel cried, and for a moment he sounded like Gabriel. His voice was full of anguish.

Why so sad? I thought as my vision narrowed to just the demon's vicious, triumphant smile. *It's not as if you really care . . .*

I gasped as the demon's grip was abruptly loosened. Nathaniel stood before me, panting, holding the demon's head in his hands. He tossed the demon's remains away like garbage and scooped me up, flying to the narrow exit that every demon was fleeing toward. The exit was barely as tall as a man and narrow enough that only one person could pass through it. Hundreds of demons were bottlenecked in the door. We wouldn't be able to get out that way.

I looked over Nathaniel's shoulder and saw Samiel carrying Jude in his wolf form. Beezle clung to Samiel's shoulder. There was a sound like thunder, and a lot of screaming as the nephilim's cave collapsed. We wouldn't be getting out the way we came in, either. The cavern around us rumbled ominously.

Nathaniel sped toward the exit.

He calmly blasted the demons out of the way and swooped through the tiny exit, the others on our heels.

The exit was only a few feet from a high precipice that stood above a valley. The demons that did manage to escape the cavern were pushed by the crowd over the edge, falling to their deaths far below.

Nathaniel flew straight across the valley to an outcropping that jutted from the mountain on the other side. There was just enough room for all of us to huddle there as we listened to the sounds of the cavern folding in on itself. The stream of charcarion demons pouring from the exit trickled to a halt.

Nathaniel put me on the ground. I am embarrassed to say that I fainted. In my defense, I was pregnant and heavily injured.

I woke to a feeling of warmth spreading throughout my body, and Nathaniel's lips pressed against mine. For a moment I forgot who he was, and what he was doing, and I kissed him back with a passion.

Then I remembered, and opened my eyes, and pulled away. His eyes were steady on mine. I didn't know what to say. My feelings for Nathaniel got more confused every day.

"Thank you," I finally said, just to break the silence.

He nodded. "You're welcome."

As he stood I saw that he held the broken shaft of the arrow that had pierced me in his hand, but instead of throwing it away, he tucked it in his pocket.

I started to ask him why, but Beezle landed on my chest. He scowled at me.

"I thought you were just going to do some surveillance?" he asked. "What was up with the gladiator routine?"

"Antares saw through my veil," I said. "It wasn't my fault."

"Now, how did he do that?" Jude asked, giving Nathaniel a suspicious look. "I thought you veiled her because your spell was more powerful than hers."

"It was," Nathaniel said, looking surprised. "I do not know how Antares was able to penetrate it."

"Maybe," Jude growled, "you didn't do such a great job. Maybe you wanted Maddy to get hurt so you could swoop in and save her, present yourself in a better light to Lucifer."

A second before, I'd been thinking that maybe Nathaniel wasn't so bad after all. Now Jude's words forced me to consider him in a different light.

Nathaniel shot an angry look at Jude. "I assure you, I would not risk Madeline's life in such a manner. You saw the veil's effectiveness for yourself."

"How do we know that you didn't set that spell to fade after a few minutes?" Jude asked.

"How was I to know that Antares would be there just in time to see Madeline? Think about what you are saying, wolf," Nathaniel replied.

"All I know is that it's mighty convenient that your spell failed just as Maddy needed it most."

"Enough," I said, covering my eyes for a moment. "Just enough."

I looked between Nathaniel and Jude. Jude made a good point, but he was inclined to mistrust Nathaniel. I wasn't completely certain of Nathaniel's agenda, but I had to believe that he didn't intend me any harm. If he did, he could have easily left me in the cavern, or dropped me as we passed over the valley.

I had plenty of troubles without suspecting Nathaniel, too. I was going to have to trust him, at least for now.

"So," I said, trying to cover up the tension. "Antares and his army of demons are gone, but Azazel is still out there somewhere."

"And if Antares is dead, then our best chance of finding Azazel is gone," Beezle said.

Samiel shook his head. He reached in his pocket for something and held it out to the rest of us.

It was Antares' spell bag.

Look inside, Samiel said.

I opened the bag. Inside was a collection of charms and spells hidden inside small stones. Each stone had a rune on it.

"The runes probably told Antares what spell was which," Beezle said.

"Can you read them?" I asked.

Beezle shook his head. "Nope."

I can, Samiel signed. *My mother taught me the old language.*

"What good will this pile of stones do us?" Jude asked.

Samiel took the bag from my hands and rummaged through it until he found what he was looking for.

He held the stone out in front of him. It was small and shiny and black, like a pressed piece of coal.

Inscribed upon it was a symbol—a five-pointed star. Crossed over the star was a sword with a rose wrapped around its hilt.

Azazel's mark.

17

"IT'S A PORTAL TO AZAZEL?" I ASKED EXCITEDLY.

Samiel nodded.

"How can we be sure?" Nathaniel asked.

"It makes sense," I said. "Antares had no magic of his own. This is like the portal charms that the lesser demons use. How else could he quickly and easily come and go from Azazel's side?"

"How did you get this?" Beezle asked.

I saw it on the floor of the cavern as we flew overhead, and I used my will to draw it to me.

"You did a Jedi mind trick?" Beezle said, awe in his voice.

"That's handy," I said to Samiel. "You'll have to teach me how to do that."

He nodded, grinning.

"So now it's off through this portal to the unknown again?" Nathaniel said. "Do you really think that's wise?"

I glared up at him. "What other option do we have? I won't leave the missing Agents to Azazel."

"But—"

"No," I said. "I'm tired of being crossed every time I make a decision. We have a lead. We're going. If you don't like it, then go back to Lucifer and explain why you're not with me."

Nathaniel narrowed his eyes at me. "Your gratitude didn't last very long."

"Are you coming, or are you going?" I asked.

I appreciated that Nathaniel had saved my life, and that he had healed me. But I was sick of arguing with all and sundry. They'd made me the leader, so they'd damned well better follow or go the hell home.

"Of course I am coming with you," Nathaniel said.

"Fine," I said, and looked at the charm in my hand. "Take us to Azazel."

I threw the charm in front of me, and a portal appeared in the air where the charm had been. All of the men immediately shouldered their way in front of me. I didn't even try to argue. Let them work out who would go first.

Samiel won, followed by Jude, and then Nathaniel.

Beezle climbed inside my coat.

"Wake me when we get there," he said.

"Oh, I'm sorry. Is this cutting into your naptime?" I said.

"I already missed my snack time," he grumbled. "I'm not missing my nap, too."

I stepped into the portal, felt the familiar squeeze of air pressure, fought the nausea that rose with it.

And emerged a few minutes later in a tumble. No one was there to catch me. They were all facing away from the portal.

I stood up, grumbling, and dusted myself off. "So much for chivalry. What are you all staring . . ."

My voice trailed off. We were on the back lawn of Azazel's mansion, just inside the shelter of the forest there, and hidden from the sight of anyone in the house.

It was the middle of the day, and the house buzzed with activity. I could see the shadows of many creatures passing to and fro behind the windows.

The lawn was covered in tents. Demons and fallen angels bustled back and forth carrying supplies. I smelled woodsmoke, and heard the ringing of metal on metal.

This was an army. Azazel's army.

"I can't believe he came back here," I whispered.

"Doubtless he assumed it was safe. We have been here once before, and found him gone."

"A smart rabbit knows how to circle back behind the wolf," Jude said.

"He's no rabbit," I said, watching the tremendous amount of activity going on before us. "Is he planning on storming Lucifer's residence?"

"Whatever he's planning, we can't let him do it," Jude said. "Anyone who gets in Azazel's way will be crushed."

"But how will we stop an army with just the four of us?" Nathaniel said.

I stared hard at the orderly movements of the soldiers, thinking. Then I smiled.

"By causing chaos, of course."

"This isn't another stupid snowman plan, is it?" Beezle said from inside my coat.

"That plan *worked*," I said, and explained what I was

thinking. "Remember, the important thing is not to destroy the army. It's to find the Agents, and neutralize Azazel."

"I love it when you use euphemisms," Beezle said.

"Just stay inside the coat," I said. "On the count of three. One, two, three!"

Nathaniel, Samiel and I simultaneously blasted different sections of the lawn. Tents immediately caught fire, and there was a moment of confusion as everyone ran around trying to figure out what had happened and where the threat was coming from.

Jude ran up the center of the lawn, taking out demons whenever he encountered them. The rest of us followed, swords clashing and spells flying.

By the time we reached the side door of the mansion, almost all the tents were ablaze, and several soldiers lay dead behind us.

The door was open since so many soldiers and demons were coming and going from the house to the tent city. Several more soldiers were emerging in response to the cries for help from outside.

Samiel led the charge through the door, blasting whatever was in front of him. Nathaniel followed, and I came behind them, slashing with the sword. Jude galloped in behind me, blood on his muzzle.

Nathaniel and Samiel had engaged fighting the soldiers in the room, but I didn't care about them. If we got caught here, we would be overwhelmed by the sheer numbers of Azazel's men.

"Forget about them!" I shouted. "Keep going! Jude, can you sniff out Chloe?"

Jude barked and dashed through the room, pausing only to tear the throat out of a charcarion demon that made the mistake of getting in his way.

I expected Jude to lead us toward the top of the house and Azazel's labs. After all, he already had cages ready for new prisoners there.

But instead Jude led us through a large kitchen I had never seen before. We shocked the hell out of one of Azazel's soldiers making a sandwich. I slit his throat so he wouldn't raise an alarm.

"Wow, that was cold," Beezle said.

I felt a pang of regret. He hadn't threatened me or mine, and maybe he didn't deserve to die in a pool of his own blood while doing something as mundane as making a sandwich. For a moment I wondered where my humanity had gone.

Then I remembered that the soldier was willingly serving Azazel, and that innocents would die if we didn't stop my father.

After that I decided I wouldn't feel guilty about anything I had to do while I was in Azazel's mansion. Or at least I would save my guilt for later, when it wouldn't risk my life or my friends' lives. Because I was sure that any of these soldiers would kill me without hesitating if Azazel said so.

Jude pushed through a swinging door at the far end of the kitchen and led us down a set of stone steps. The sound of running feet clattered on the floor above but nobody pursued us. They didn't seem to have realized where we'd gone yet.

It got quieter and quieter as we descended, like we were falling into the heart of the earth.

"He's leading us toward the cells," Nathaniel whispered. "The ones that Azazel reserved for his worst offenders."

"And they're guarded by mute soldiers," I remembered.

"Yes, so that they could never reveal what they may have overheard from the prisoners."

"So Azazel could protect his own butt," I said. "I'm sure

that at least some of those prisoners were not offenders but people who'd discovered facts that Azazel would prefer to keep hidden."

"You have so much disgust for him," Nathaniel said, and something about the tone in his voice made me think this was the first time he'd really noticed.

"Of course I do," I said. "He's killed innocents for his own purpose. He tried to use me, bend me to his will. He's the kind of creature that would cut out the tongues of his loyal soldiers just to make sure they'd never cross him. Of course I have disgust for him."

"And so these feelings encompass your feelings toward me, as well," he said. "Because I have long been associated with Azazel. Because I participated in acts which you find repugnant."

"Well, yes," I said, feeling flustered. "But you've done some good things, too."

"But not enough to overcome my past," Nathaniel said.

"This really isn't the time to discuss this," I said. I wanted to stay focused on the mission, not get distracted by the confusing feelings I had about Nathaniel.

"Very well," he said, and fell silent.

The stairs seemed to go on forever. Finally, we reached the bottom. A stone passage stretched away from us, set at intervals with candles encased in glass. The air was dry and smelled like rotten meat.

"Another tunnel," Beezle observed.

"Another tunnel." I sighed. "Stolen from a Vincent Price movie, no less."

It was wide enough that Samiel, Nathaniel and I could walk comfortably abreast. Jude trotted ahead, his nose to the ground. He seemed to be working harder now to follow Chloe's scent. The rotten-meat smell was getting stronger.

The passage came to a T-junction, and we all looked expectantly at Jude. He went down each side of the junction a little ways, circling and coming back over the same ground a few times. He looked up at me and whined.

"You can't tell which way she's gone?" I asked.

He barked in reply.

I looked down each passage. Nothing seemed to distinguish these stone tunnels from the one we'd just come through.

"Maybe we should . . ." I began.

Don't you dare say that we should split up, Samiel said.

"It would be more efficient," I pointed out.

"We are not dividing the group," Nathaniel said.

I heaved a sigh. They were both right. Dividing our forces was not a good idea. I'd seen enough horror movies to know that.

"What do you think?" I asked Beezle, who was peering down each passage with interest.

He clapped his claws over his eyes and pointed with his other hand. "Eenie-meenie-minie-moe. That way."

He pointed right.

Nathaniel raised an eyebrow at me.

"We don't have anything better to go on," I said. "Maybe Jude will pick up something as we go farther along."

After several moments the rotting smell intensified to the point where my eyes were watering. I pulled the neck of my sweater over my mouth and nose. Beezle hid inside my coat with his claws over his mouth, breathing shallowly. Nathaniel coughed every few minutes in a way that told me he was trying to keep from heaving.

Jude, especially, looked miserable. I think the stench was starting to dull his sense of smell.

We all suspected what was causing the smell, but nobody wanted to say it out loud.

The passage came to an abrupt end at a wooden door. There was no lock, key or doorknob, and no window to see what was behind it.

I touched my hand to the door, and it swung open. A blast of stinking air hit me in the face, and I turned away, gagging.

I wished I'd never seen what was behind the door.

The room was long and narrow, and there was another doorway at the far end. Bodies were everywhere in between, tossed like dirty laundry. Most of the bodies were not intact. There were arms and legs, fingers and ears, random bits that used to be people. No matter where I looked I saw exposed bone and ragged flesh.

"Azazel's been feeding the nephilim," Beezle said quietly.

"There's no point in going in," I said, reaching to close the door.

Jude sniffed the ground outside the door and barked, pointing his nose inside the room.

"She's in there?" I asked in dread. I did not want to search through the piles of corpses looking for Chloe.

Jude ran into the room and stopped at the far door. He barked again and disappeared through the doorway.

"I thought we didn't want to divide our forces," I mumbled as we jogged after him.

The next room was about the same size and shape as the previous one, but it was empty. There were copper-red stains on the stone floor.

Jude had already gone ahead to the next room. I heard him bark, and the sound of a sword clashing against stone.

I ran ahead and through the doorway, my own sword drawn. I needn't have worried. Jude had already killed the soldier there and left him on the ground. The wolf turned around, his face covered in blood, his tongue hanging out in a macabre doggy grin.

This room was much like the others, except that each side was stacked floor-to-ceiling with cages. And inside the cages were the missing Agents. They all appeared to be sleeping.

Samiel was already running to Chloe, whose vivid purple hair practically glowed in the gloom. He tore the cage door off its hinges and lifted her out. A second later I was at his side, feeling for her pulse.

Her heart was still beating. On her neck were two puncture wounds. I opened her mouth with my fingers to make sure that she hadn't been turned, and was relieved to see ordinary human canines.

Jude had transformed back into a human and was opening the other cages. Nathaniel lifted the sleeping Agents out and placed them on the floor while I checked to see if they all still lived. I also checked to see if they were all still human.

Two of them had the sharp, pointy canines of a vampire.

"Better take care of them now," Beezle said.

"How can I do that?" I said. "They're no threat to me."

"They were turned by vampires working with Azazel," Beezle said. "If you leave them, it will be two more soldiers you'll have to kill later."

I knew that what Beezle was saying was right, but it didn't make it any easier. These were my colleagues, people I'd worked with at the Agency. They had been kidnapped, likely tortured, and turned against their will.

Killing them didn't seem like the preventive medicine that Beezle made it out to be. It seemed like murder.

"I'll do it," Nathaniel said, holding his hand out for my sword. His eyes were very grave.

I shook my head. "No. I should do it."

As I brought the sword down to their necks one by one, I wondered whether their deaths had been foreseen, and if so, where were their Agents?

I saw their souls emerge, but no Agent appeared to take them to the Door. They both looked at me expectantly, one man and one woman, both about my age. I thought the man's name was James and that his cubicle was on my floor, but I wasn't certain.

"I can take you to the Door," I said, "but I have some things to do first."

"Whoa, Madeline Black is here for us?" James asked. He seemed impressed for a moment; then he looked down at my right hand. "Wait—you killed us?"

I'd forgotten I was holding the bloody sword. "You were turning into vampires."

"And you killed us even though we'd done you no harm?" the woman said. "No wonder you have such a bad reputation."

"Look," I said. "I'm sorry I killed you, but it was pretty likely you would have died in this war Azazel is about to wage. If you'll come with us, I'll take you to the Door once we get the other Agents out of here safely."

"I don't want to go with you," the woman said. "I'm an Agent. I can take my own self to the door."

"Yeah, I think I can handle it," James said.

They both broke free of their ectoplasmic cords without my assistance, and floated upward through the ceiling.

"Well, that's just great," I said, kicking James' body. "I'm sure the Agency is going to harass me for allowing their souls to escape."

"I thought we'd agreed that the Agency was going to harass you no matter what you do," Beezle said. "The bigger problem is this—how are we going to get fourteen sleeping Agents out of here?"

"Wake them up?"

Jude shook his head. "I already tried. It's like they're sedated."

"And I'm sure we can't do something easy, like make a portal out of here," I said to Nathaniel.

"Not as long as we are on Azazel's property," he said.

"We can't call J.B. for help, because the Agency people are being jerkwads," I said, ticking off points on my fingers. "Lucifer is conveniently out of touch again. We can't make a portal. What can we do?"

We all stared helplessly at one another.

"I can't believe it's come to this," I said angrily. "We've found the Agents but we can't get them home?"

"It's only a matter of time before Azazel sends someone down here to see where we've gone," Nathaniel said. "And I don't think it's a good idea for us to go back upstairs through the army."

"I agree," I said, and then stopped.

Something was coming. I could hear it moving slowly through the outer rooms. The ground trembled slightly as it approached.

"Meeeeat," it crooned.

"Oh, no," I said.

We could probably hold off the nephilim. We might even be able to kill it. But that would cause a lot of ruckus and attract the attention of Azazel and his army.

"Come on, think of something!" Beezle said, flying out of my coat and smacking the back of my head. "Where are your Morningstar superpowers?"

"I don't know," I said, looking at the tattoo on my hand. "It's like those abilities have gone quiet since Lucifer disappeared."

"You do not think the Morningstar is dead, do you?" Nathaniel asked.

"No," I said. "But it's like he's a blank, like he's gone under . . . ground . . ."

I looked down at the floor, and back up at Beezle.

"This is another snowman plan, isn't it?"

"Meeeat," the nephilim said, its voice louder as it approached.

"More like an earthworm plan," I said. "Nathaniel, come help me. Samiel, you stand by the door and keep the nephilim from getting in here."

I kneeled on the floor a little distance away from the sleeping Agents, my palms flat on the stone. Nathaniel joined me, looking dubious.

"You want to blast a hole in the floor?" Beezle said. "That's your plan? Haven't we spent enough time in tunnels?"

"If we can dig a tunnel off Azazel's property, then we can take a portal out of here," I said. "And it's a better option than trying to fight our way through the soldiers upstairs while protecting all the Agents."

"We still have to transport them out of here," Jude said.

"Yes, but we'll have a good chance of keeping them safe underground. If we get them all down there, then we can move them in small groups, leapfrogging down the passage. And we easily pick off anyone who comes into the tunnel behind us." I looked at Nathaniel. "Okay, let's do it."

I summoned all the strength and will that I had, and sent a blast of power through the floor and into the earth beneath. Nathaniel followed suit, and the floor buckled underneath us before the stones collapsed. I fell about ten feet into the hole, the breath leaving my body, brick dust raining down on my face. Nathaniel peered over the edge, bemused.

"I do not know how you do it," he said. "How can one person be so clumsy?"

"Yeah, yeah," I said, getting to my feet. I was damned lucky that I was part angel or else I was sure I'd have a broken bone. I gave my belly a little pat and felt the reassuring answer of beating wings.

"MEEEAT!" the nephilim cried, and I smelled nightfire burning. A moment later I heard the sound of something heavy knocking up against a solid wall.

"You'd better start digging, rabbit," Beezle said, flying down to my side. "Samiel's put up a shield, but the nephilim is making so much noise that it's sure to bring the rest of the house down on us."

"We have to get to the woods that are across the road from the front of the mansion," I said. "That's definitely off his property. If we go behind the house, we'll never get out. Gabriel told me that Azazel's woods stretch on for miles in that direction."

Beezle frowned at the packed earth, spinning around in all directions. He stopped moving after a moment and pointed.

"That way."

"Are you sure?" I asked. "Because we really can't afford to mess this up."

"Trust me," Beezle said. "Do you think I would put future doughnut deliveries at risk?"

"True," I said, and started blasting in front of me. "Go

up and tell Jude and Nathaniel to start bringing the Agents down."

Nathaniel floated down a few moments later with Chloe and two other agents held in a fireman's carry. I had blasted about thirty feet of tunnel, and he brought them up and rested them just behind me.

Jude followed with two Agents, and I continued blasting as they went back and forth. I could feel tremors above me, and I suspected that some of Azazel's soldiers had finally noticed the howling nephilim.

Beezle flew down with the update. "A company of soldiers came down to see what the nephilim was freaking out about. Fortunately for us, the nephilim was so crazed from being denied fresh meat that it turned on the soldiers. They're duking it out as we speak."

"Good," I said, sweat pouring over my face as I blasted another ten feet of tunnel.

Samiel came up behind me. *I'll help you clear the tunnel. The other two will move the Agents.*

I nodded. It was faster going with Samiel's help. Nathaniel and Jude had the tedious job of running back and forth, collecting Agents, dropping them off near us, then running back for the others.

On one of these trips Nathaniel said, "I created an illusion in the room to look like the stone floor was still there. It won't fool Azazel, and if anyone steps on it, they will still fall into the tunnel, but perhaps it will hold them off."

"Maybe they won't go all the way into the room. If they see the Agents are missing and we aren't there, then hopefully they'll just go back upstairs to raise the alarm. Good thinking," I said.

Nathaniel smiled briefly and went back for more Agents.

I don't know how long we were underground, dirt and

insects falling in our faces, laboriously moving a few feet at a time, but finally Nathaniel said, "That's enough."

I looked back at him. He was crouched low in the tunnel like Samiel and Jude were. I had only blasted a path maybe six feet high and a few feet wide, and it was a tight squeeze for anyone not pocket-sized.

"We've passed beyond Azazel's property line," Nathaniel said.

"So we can make a portal?" I asked.

He stepped close to me, put his hand on the dirt in front of me and said the words of the spell in an undertone. I was caged between his body and the dirt wall in front of me, and could feel the heat that emanated from him. I stood as still as possible and tried not to think about how close he was.

A portal opened before us, and I turned around, giving Nathaniel a little nudge in the shoulder with my hand so that he would give me some space.

"The Agents go through first," I shouted.

The noise from the portal was deafening in the small space, like being closed up in an elevator with a running vacuum cleaner.

Samiel signed to me before scooping up Chloe. *I'll go through with her. You push the others through one by one and I'll catch them.*

"At twenty-second intervals?" I said, trying to mentally calculate the time it would take for him to catch someone, lay them on the ground and turn around for the next Agent.

He nodded and squeezed past Nathaniel. I pressed up against the side of the tunnel, and he went through the portal.

"Jude, start passing them up to Nathaniel," I said. "I'll keep watch."

Beezle flew up and landed on my shoulder as I pressed past Jude, looking anxiously back the way we had come. Jude and Nathaniel started passing the sedated Agents through the portal.

"What are you worried about?" Beezle asked. "Your earthworm plan worked. As unlikely as it seemed."

"Yeah," I said, but I couldn't shake the feeling that it had been too easy. Someone had to have figured out by now that we'd gone underground.

"This is the last one," Jude called. "Let's get out of here. I'm starting to feel like a badger."

He went through the portal with the last Agent in his arms, and Nathaniel turned back to me, his hand outstretched.

That was when the roof of the tunnel blasted open.

18

IT WAS LIKE BEING INSIDE A TORNADO. NATHANIEL, Beezle and I were scooped up by a howling wind, spun in circles and slammed to the ground in the blazing sunshine.

We were in a little clearing in the woods surrounded by leafless maples. Snow had melted in patches and revealed green moss underneath.

I pushed to my feet, dizzy from being twirled like a top, and stared across the open chasm at my father.

He'd always appeared young and handsome, but while he hadn't aged at all, his face was changed. He was pale as death, and long lines of grief were etched in his face. I'd have expected him to be surrounded by flunkies, but he stood alone. His dark eyes, the mirror of my own, were lit with flame.

"You killed my son," he said.

"You killed my husband," I replied, my fingers curled at

my sides. I had desired this from the moment Gabriel had fallen into the snow, his lifeblood running from his body.

"I curse the day that I met your mother, that I allowed myself to be seduced by her," Azazel spat.

"Oh, fuck you," I said. "You were no damned innocent."

Nathaniel had warily come to his feet beside me and was slowly backing away. At least he had the sense not to get between us. Beezle had flown up to a branch high above and watched us with bright eyes.

"You will suffer like none other," Azazel said, and he flew toward me.

I didn't bother to banter with him. I blasted him with nightfire.

He knocked my spell away easily, like he was batting away a softball, and landed on the ground in front of me. I slashed out at him with the sword and he shot me with a bolt of lightning that knocked the sword from my hand.

"Now you can no longer use Lucifer's shield," Azazel said, and he grabbed me by the shoulders, lifting me from the ground.

His hands were covered in flame, and I screamed as the heat burned through my skin like I was being branded. I kicked Azazel in the ribs with all my strength and he squeezed harder. I could smell my own flesh cooking, and my baby beat its wings in distress.

Azazel's eyes went wide and he dropped me to the ground. I knew he'd felt the presence of the baby. I didn't wait for him to get over the shock. I shot him in the face with electricity, aiming for his eyes.

He screamed, covering his face with his hands, and stumbled backward toward the pit. I struggled to my feet, my shoulders still burning. I could feel Azazel's spell working through the layers of muscle down to my bones.

I blasted him again, and he fell backward into the tunnel.

"Madeline!" Nathaniel cried, and he tossed me the sword.

I barely caught it with my crippled left hand as Azazel flew up out of the hole again. I pushed out my own wings and rose to meet him.

He conjured a blue sword from nightfire and met my strike with his own. He slashed at me furiously, his anger seeming greater than ever now that he knew I was carrying Gabriel's baby.

It was strange. The angrier Azazel became, the calmer I felt. I knew from long experience that when I was angry, I made mistakes. And I didn't want to make a mistake. I wanted to see Azazel staked by my sword.

Maybe then my heart would be at peace.

I shot nightfire at him with my left hand while hacking with the sword in my right. He parried me easily, but his movements were becoming more frantic. I managed to slash open his forearm, and blood dripped on the hilt of the sword.

Another thing that I knew was that if your hands were slippery, it was harder to hold on to your sword. Azazel's fingers slipped, and the nightfire sword tumbled away, disintegrating once it was disconnected from the source of its magic.

I thrust forward, thinking I had him.

But I'd never been that good at seeing all the angles. That was why Lucifer was always outsmarting me.

Azazel closed his hand over the blade—heedless of the fact that it laid open the skin there—and sent a pulse of magic through it.

It slipped under my palm, raced through my body in

time with the frantic thrumming of my blood and covered my heartstone with a suffocating clutch.

I gasped for breath as Azazel grinned maliciously and let go of the sword.

"And so goes the least wanted child of my line."

The blade fell away as I covered my chest with my hand. I couldn't breathe. I could feel my heartstone being squeezed by an invisible grasp, and soon, very soon, it would burst.

And when it burst, I would die. And so would my child. The magic was an invader under my skin, and I rejected it with everything I had. I'd done this once before, when I'd thrown Evangeline from my body and undid her possession of me. I drew on that now.

"No," I said, and grabbed Azazel's bleeding palm, pulling him to me in one swift motion. "This you can have back."

I summoned all my will, all the strength that I had remaining. No light of the Morningstar lit in my blood, but I didn't need it.

I pushed the spell back at Azazel and poured it into his open wound.

His eyes went wide, and purple veins stood out in relief all over his face.

And still, he smiled at me. "It's too late. It's already begun. There's nothing you can do to stop it."

"Bye-bye, Daddy dearest," I said, and sent a blast of electricity to follow Azazel's own suffocating spell.

It zoomed through his veins and pierced his heartstone, already squeezed to the limit.

Azazel exploded from within, and as he did all the magic that had been stored inside his body for centuries exploded outward as well.

"Madeline!" Nathaniel shouted, and he snatched me out

of the air, flying us back into the open pit and covering me with his wings as the world above us went supernova.

"Beezle!" I shouted. "Beezle!"

"I have him," Nathaniel said, his voice taut with strain as he protected us from the storm above, and Beezle crawled from inside Nathaniel's coat to me, clinging to my neck.

The explosion seemed to go on forever. Nathaniel hunched over us, sweat dripping into his eyes, holding me close.

After a very long time, it seemed the storm had passed.

Nathaniel still held me, his teeth clenched.

"Nathaniel," I said. "You can let me go now."

His arms seemed like they were locked in position.

"Nathaniel," I said again, getting impatient and trying to struggle out of his grip. "Come on, let me go."

"Yes," he said, and his arms went suddenly limp.

I rolled out of his embrace and into the dirt, and came up spitting. Beezle flew upward so he wouldn't get crushed by my flailing limbs.

"What the hell . . ." I started.

That was when I saw the tree branch embedded in Nathaniel's back. It was as long as Lucifer's sword, and a dark scarlet stain spread from the point of impact.

"Gods above and below," I said, reaching for the branch, pulling it from him.

He gave a wet, gasping breath and went still.

I fell to my knees, covered the wound with my hands. "Nathaniel, wake up. What do I do? What do I do?"

"You have to heal him," Beezle said.

"Heal him? But—I don't know how. Gabriel never taught me how," I said.

I swiped at my face, wondering why I was crying. It couldn't be because I cared about Nathaniel. It couldn't be, because that would mean that I was letting Gabriel go, and I could never do that.

But I couldn't let him bleed out under my hands. I couldn't let that happen again, not to someone who'd saved me over and over.

I put my hands over the wound and searched for the flickering candle that was the source of my magic. It was low now, tired from all the energy I'd expended fighting Azazel. But I thought I had enough left to help Nathaniel.

I remembered the warmth that I always felt when I was healed by an angel, the light of the sun that ran through them and into me. The sun was inside me, too, pulsing inside my heartstone.

I pushed my power through my heartstone, letting the light of the sun fill me up and flow through me, and as I did I felt my own wounds healing, too.

The blood ceased flowing, and the gap in Nathaniel's skin closed before my eyes.

"Nathaniel?" I said, turning him over so I could see his face. "Nathaniel?"

He opened his eyes blearily. "Madeline?"

"Are you okay?" I asked.

He sat up, putting his hand over his heart. "Did you . . ."

I nodded.

"I can feel you," he said softly. "I can still feel you inside me. And something else. Your baby."

I sucked in a breath. I hadn't wanted Nathaniel to know about that yet.

"Why did you keep the knowledge from me?" he asked.

"I didn't know how you would react," I said. "I wasn't sure if I could trust you."

"But you must trust me now," Nathaniel said. "You

saved my life. You could have let me die, and you would have been free of me."

"I couldn't do that," I said.

"Why not?"

I shook my head. I wasn't ready to face this. I'd thought of Nathaniel as an enemy for so long that it was difficult for me to think of him as an ally, much less a friend.

"I can see why Lucifer is so invested in you," he said finally, when I didn't answer his question. "A child born of two of his lines. You must be very precious to him."

"I'm only precious to him as a breeding instrument," I said. "Once the baby's born, he couldn't care less about me."

"I don't think that is true," Nathaniel said.

"Then why won't he answer my damned phone calls?" I said. "Why is it that he entangles me in an avalanche of problems and then disappears? His little parasite isn't even talking to me now."

"Hey, guys," Beezle said, and his voice sounded far away.

I looked up and saw him perched on the rim of the hole. "You might want to come up here and see this," he said.

I flew up to the forest level, Nathaniel behind me. Then I stopped. And stared.

The forest was gone. The grass, the trees, the moss, the rocks. Gone. So was Azazel's mansion, every last stick of it. So were all of the demons and soldiers that had populated his army. Everything, for miles around, was gone. There wasn't even ash to show that something had once stood there. It was like everything had disintegrated into molecular particles.

"Gods above and below," I said. "It's like a nuclear bomb went off here."

"It did," Beezle said grimly. "Azazel was old. Very, very old."

"The other Grigori will not be pleased with you," Nathaniel said.

"Please. He led a rebellion against Lucifer. Why should they care?"

"For the same reason the faeries cared that you killed Amarantha, even though most of them did not agree with her actions," Nathaniel said. "Because Azazel was one of them, and you are not."

"I don't care," I said, and heard the fierce joy in my voice. "I don't care. Azazel deserved to die. I swore that he would, and I did it. If the Grigori want to come after me, then they can have a taste of what Azazel got."

"The Grigori will fear you now," Nathaniel said. "I'm sure that none of them suspected that you had such power inside you."

"They'd better be afraid," I said. "I've had enough of taking shit from them and everyone else. Titania, the Grigori, the Agency. All I've ever wanted is to live a quiet life, and they won't let me."

"What will you do?" Beezle said, looking worried.

"Whatever it takes," I said.

We all stared at the bleak ruin that had once been Azazel's shining court.

Beezle sighed. "Well, our work here is done. Maddy's destroyed yet another building, so let's portal it home."

"Yeah," I said, and my stomach growled. I couldn't remember the last time I'd eaten something. "I think I want some doughnuts."

"Oh, no," Beezle said, looking alarmed. "Don't tell me you're going to get pregnancy cravings now and start eating all my doughnuts."

"There's no reason for you to eat a dozen doughnuts all by yourself," I said.

"There's every reason," Beezle said. "I need to check all the flavors to make sure they're still good."

"Children," Nathaniel said, and he opened a portal. "After you, my lady."

I went through the portal, Beezle still shouting in my ear about the necessity of buying two boxes of doughnuts. I crashed into my back lawn with my usual grace, and stood up, dusting snow from my legs. It was getting dark now, the sun very low behind the city skyline.

And heard the slide of a semiautomatic handgun very close to my ear.

"Agent Black," Bryson said. "You are under arrest for crimes against the Agency."

"What crimes?" I asked, holding my hands up. I didn't want to make any sudden movements with Bryson holding a weapon to my head.

Nathaniel came through the portal behind me. I heard the soft landing of his boots in the snow.

"Don't come any closer!" Bryson shouted. "Or I will kill her where she stands."

"Listen to him, Nathaniel," I said.

Guns scared me. There was something so final about a bullet. Magic could be undone, as I'd shown with Azazel's spell. But a bullet through the head couldn't be taken back.

The house looked cold and silent. I assumed Jude and Samiel had taken the Agents somewhere to be tended. I wondered why they weren't back yet, and what they had thought when Nathaniel and I hadn't followed them through the portal.

"You can come with me quietly and cooperatively," Bryson said, "or you can make a fuss and give me a great deal of pleasure."

"I understand," I said. And I did. It didn't take a genius

to realize it would give him a great deal of pleasure to end my days on this earth. "Nathaniel and Beezle, you stay here."

"Your conspirators are also under arrest," Bryson said. "We have already captured the wolf and the mute. Bennett was arrested hours ago."

"You leave them out of this," I said fiercely. "If the Agency has a gripe with me, that's one thing. But you leave them out of this."

"That is not for me to decide," Bryson said. "The angel and the gargoyle come, too."

"Little Agent," Nathaniel said, and there was malice in his tone. "What makes you think I have to do anything you say?"

Bryson slid his eyes away from me toward Nathaniel, but he was too late.

Nathaniel moved faster than any human could. All I saw was a blur out of the corner of my eye, and then Bryson was on the ground and Nathaniel stood above him, holding the gun.

I dropped my hands. Beezle glared down at Bryson from my shoulder like an angry parrot.

"Where's J.B. and Jude and Samiel?" I asked.

"I will tell you nothing," Bryson said, his eyes snapping with anger.

I looked at Nathaniel. Nathaniel kicked Bryson so hard that I heard one of his ribs break.

Bryson coughed, but did not cry out. "I will tell you nothing," he repeated.

"I didn't want you for an enemy," I said. "You could have helped us. We saved fourteen missing Agents."

"And killed two," Bryson said. "You are an Agent of death, not a bringer of it."

"How do you know about that?" I asked. If Bryson knew, then the deaths of those Agents had to have been written somewhere, and that meant that the Agency had known before they'd sent Sokolov to threaten me that I would go to Azazel's mansion. And that also meant that they knew I would find the Agents, and they did nothing to help me.

"I know more than you think. I'm not just a tool for Sokolov, as you seem to believe."

"Then stop acting like one," I said. "Did it really sit well with you that the Agency was willing to let their own people die just because they have some grudge against me?"

"The Agency has their reasons," Bryson said.

"And I have mine," I said. "Tell me where the others are. Don't make me hurt you."

"Are you a monster, then, like the things you claim to despise? Will you torture me for your own ends?"

"I am not a monster," I said, and I don't know who I was trying to convince—him or me. "But I won't let you or the Agency or anyone else run over me anymore. I want to know where Jude and J.B. and Samiel are, and believe me, I will break you to get to them."

"That line just keeps getting grayer and grayer, doesn't it?" Beezle murmured, for my ears only.

"You will not break me," Bryson said.

"She may not be able to, but I can," Nathaniel said, and then he gave me a very serious glance. "Look away."

I did. I was sure I wouldn't want to see.

Bryson didn't scream, but he made the most piteous noise I'd ever heard.

I was grateful for the rising darkness, grateful that it was unlikely that anyone could see what we were doing in my backyard. Of course, maybe the neighbors didn't even bother to call the police anymore. They'd seen me carrying bodies into the basement and I hadn't been arrested, so it was possible they'd given up and learned to keep their curtains shut.

"Where have you taken Madeline's companions?" Nathaniel asked.

He sounded cruel. He sounded like a man without mercy or conscience. I'd never heard him like that before, not even when he was trying to kill me. This was the right-hand man of Azazel, the hammer that Azazel had used on his enemies.

I tried hard to remember that I had saved his life for a reason, and that he was doing what he was doing for me.

Bryson whimpered, but he didn't answer Nathaniel.

"This is really okay with you?" Beezle asked quietly.

"I can't leave J.B. and Samiel and Jude to the Agency," I said. "I can't."

"You're losing yourself," Beezle said.

"No," I replied. "I'm finding myself."

"I hope you like the person you find," Beezle said.

Nathaniel did something else, and this time Bryson did scream.

"Where are Madeline's companions?" Nathaniel asked again.

"The Agency, the Agency!" Bryson yelled.

"Where in the Agency?" I asked, turning around.

Bryson's eyes were bleeding. I did not want to know how Nathaniel had done that. The super-soldier looked pale and broken, all his defiance gone. I was sorry for that. I was so sorry that it had come to this.

"In the rooms where they kept the crazy people," Bryson said, and he started to cry.

"In the basement, near the Hall of Records," I said to Nathaniel. "Let's go."

I pushed out my wings, took off toward downtown. Beezle climbed back inside my coat for warmth. Nathaniel flew at my side, blessedly silent. I didn't know what I might say to him right now. How do you thank someone for torturing a strong man until he's broken?

"Better cloak yourself," I said to Nathaniel. "I want to go in the front door, and you'll scare the locals if you land on the sidewalk with those wings out."

He nodded, and a short time later we stood on the sidewalk in front of the Agency doors. Even though I was under the veil, other Agents could see me, and they gave me a wide berth as they exited the building.

Beezle poked his head out of my coat. "How are you going to play this?"

"I'm just going to go in there like I belong. Which I do," I said, and then to Nathaniel, "Try to stun anyone who gets in our way. I've had enough of bodies today."

We pushed open the doors of the Agency and walked inside.

19

AS SOON AS WE ENTERED, NATHANIEL DROPPED HIS veil and I pushed my wings back in. The security guards, who looked like they were half-asleep as Agents went through the checkpoints on their way out of the building, stood up abruptly.

I strolled up to the checkpoint and smiled at the guard there.

"Agent Black," he said carefully. He had one hand in the air, and the other hand was creeping toward the gun at his hip. Where did all the guns come from? Why had I never really noticed them before?

"You don't want to do that, Agent Hill," I said. "Because I am in a really bad mood, and I don't want anyone else to get hurt today."

"Our orders are to take you into custody," he said, his fingers brushing the holster.

"Do you have kids, Agent Hill?" I asked conversationally.

He looked confused. "Yeah."

I leaned close to him, and my smile became a baring of teeth. "Do you want to see them again?"

His hand dropped to his side and he took a step back. "Let her through."

"Smart man," I said, and walked through the metal detector. The alarm was set off by the sword on my back.

"What are you doing?" one of the other guards shouted, running toward us.

Nathaniel, who was following closely behind me, turned around and stunned the guard who had shouted. The man fell to the ground, the gun in his hand spinning away on the shiny marble floor.

"Any other takers?" I asked to the room at large.

The secretary, the other two guards and the few Agents who were in the lobby all stood very still.

"That's what I thought," I said, and went to the elevators.

"They're going to have every Agent in the building come down on your head in a minute," Beezle said.

"I don't care," I said. "In a minute I'm going to have J.B. and Samiel and Jude with me."

"And then what?" Beezle said. "Fight your way out of another impossible situation?"

"No," I said. "They're going to give me the other three, and then we're going to walk out of here."

"What insanity do you have planned this time?" Beezle asked as we stepped into the empty elevator.

I pressed the button for the basement level one. "Don't worry. It doesn't involve anyone bleeding. Probably."

The doors opened. The hallway seemed suspiciously quiet.

"The rooms where the lost souls were kept are this way," I said, going left.

We walked past the Hall of Records. The door was closed. No one moved up and down the corridor.

At the end of the hallway was a set of double doors. Behind the doors was a conference room that had been modified into a padded cell for the people I'd found in the warehouse with their memories stolen.

No one stood outside the doors. I kicked them open.

Sokolov sat at the head of a table like a preening little king. On one side of the table, lying on the floor, were Jude and Samiel, bound and gagged.

J.B. was on top of the table, shirtless, and two Agents held him down while a third sliced a knife across his chest.

Everything stopped when we entered the room.

"Maddy," J.B. said, and his voice was full of despair.

"Let them go," I said to Sokolov.

"Agent Black," he said, coming to his feet. "I am surprised you would dare show your face here after what you have done today."

"Let them go," I repeated.

"I don't think so," Sokolov said, indicating to the Agents that they should come after me. "I think you'll be joining your friends."

"Where do you get your dialogue?" I said. "Cheesy Villains R Us?"

The three Agents approached Nathaniel and me.

"I don't have time for this," I said, and I blasted all three of them in the face with nightfire.

They fell to the ground, clawing at their faces and screaming. I would have felt bad about the fact that I'd set their eyeballs on fire, but I'd seen them cutting up J.B.

"Cut the other two loose," I said to Nathaniel. I went to J.B., who was trying to sit up, and put my arm around him.

Sokolov narrowed his eyes at me. "What is it you think you will accomplish by this act, Agent Black? You have repeatedly defied the express wishes of the Agency. You have harmed other Agents. You have demonstrated that you have no respect or care for your office or your sacred duty. You have become a rogue, Agent Black, and as such you will be given into the custody of the Retrievers."

Nathaniel finished loosing Samiel and Jude, and the three of them came around to help J.B. to his feet. I walked toward Sokolov, who stood impassively as I approached him, secure in his belief that he would defeat me.

"You know what?" I said. "I've had a long day, and I'm really sick and tired of listening to threats from little creatures who think they're more powerful than me. I killed Antares today. I wiped out Azazel's army, the army he'd intended to use to gain dominion over the world. And I killed Azazel."

Sokolov's eyes widened slightly. So he hadn't known about that yet. Good.

"I killed one of the oldest Grigori, the angel that had sat at the right hand of Lucifer since time unknown. And right now, what I really want is to go home with my friends, take a nap, and eat Chinese food until I feel sick."

"Pork dumplings!" Beezle said from the inside of my coat.

"So here's what I am telling you, and believe me, this is no empty threat. If you don't let us walk out of here unharmed, I will burn this building and everyone in it to the ground. And I will start with you."

"She has this thing about burning buildings," Beezle

said. "She seemed normal as a kid, so I don't know where this obsession comes from."

"You are an Agent of death, Madeline Black," Sokolov shouted, and for the first time he looked a little afraid. "You must submit to our authority."

"No," I said, and I knew what I had to do. "I don't. Because I am no longer an Agent."

Sokolov's eyes bulged in his piggy face. "You cannot do that. No one leaves the Agency."

"I break all ties with the Agency. I renounce the mantle of Death," I said, and my back tingled as I spoke. "As of today, you can command me no more."

My words echoed in the room. Sokolov looked stunned. Suddenly, I doubled over in pain. The building trembled in its foundation, like an earthquake had rolled beneath it.

"What's happening?" J.B. said. "What's the matter?"

I couldn't speak. It felt like a thousand swords were plunging into my body. My throat was filled with magic, choking me.

I opened my mouth, and all the magic that I had possessed as an Agent poured from me in a stream. At the same time, there was a rending sound as the back of my coat and shirt tore open. I screamed as pain ripped down both sides of my spine, falling to my hands and knees. Beezle flew out of my coat.

And then it was over.

"Gods above and below," Nathaniel said.

I stood up, feeling sick, and turned around. Jude, Samiel, J.B. and Nathaniel all stared at the ground.

My wings lay on the floor, the roots that had dug into my back torn free. I could feel the blood running down my back, pooling at the base of my spine.

I'd lost my wings, and for a moment I felt despair.

Sokolov chuckled behind me. "What will you do now, Madeline Black, without your magic?"

I turned slowly back to face him. "I may not have my Agent's magic any longer, but I am still the goddamned granddaughter of Lucifer."

I blasted him with nightfire, and he flew across the room, smashing into the wall.

"Well, that was unexpected," Beezle said, fluttering beside my shoulder. "What now?"

"They're going to let us walk out of the building," I said. "Everyone here felt that tremor, and they're going to know who caused it."

Nathaniel took off his overcoat and wrapped it around me. I looked like a child, the hem dragging on the ground. Jude and Samiel helped J.B. back into his shirt and jacket.

"We'll have to do first aid later," I said apologetically.

J.B. nodded. "It's fine. I don't want to spend any more time here than I have to."

"Going to renounce your wings, too?" I said. "Come on, be a rebel."

He gave me a half smile. "How about I just not show up for work tomorrow?"

"It's a step," I said. "Pretty soon you'll be a wild and crazy rule-breaker like me."

He shook his head. "There's no one like you."

"Thank the Morningstar," Beezle said. "Because I don't think this city could handle two of her."

The six of us hobbled into the hallway in various states of disrepair. The passage was still empty. I was surprised there weren't five dozen Agents waiting to take custody of us.

"So what happened?" I asked Jude as we waited for the elevator.

"They were waiting for us when we came through the portal," Jude said. "Bryson and a bunch of his buddies. Sokolov's cronies had come for Bryson and taken J.B. before we got there."

They took the Agents and then arrested us, Samiel signed as we piled into the elevator. *We were just glad that you hadn't come through the portal yet.*

"Did you really kill Azazel?" Jude asked.

"Oh, yes, she did," Beezle said.

"And blasted his whole army into smithereens," I said. "So that problem's gone."

"I don't know," Nathaniel said. "Focalor is still out there. He was working closely with Azazel, remember?"

"With any luck Focalor was in the mansion when it disintegrated," I said.

"I don't think you're that lucky," Beezle said as the elevator doors opened.

A bunch of special-ops Agents stood there with machine guns raised.

I calmly stepped out of the elevator. All the Agents backed up.

"Guys," I said softly. "Since I'm here and Sokolov isn't, what do you think will happen to you if you don't let us by?"

Nobody spoke. I walked toward the exit. Dozens of Agents blocked my way.

They all moved aside as I passed them. The others followed me, the lobby tense and hushed.

I pushed open the doors of the Agency and went out into the cold night air. The lights of the city shone like stars.

The others gathered around me on the sidewalk.

"How will we get home?" J.B. asked. "You don't have any wings to fly."

"I can carry you," Nathaniel offered.

"Jude can't fly, either," I pointed out. I took a deep breath. "Let's walk home."

"Walk?" Beezle said. "It's, like, six miles from here."

"What do you care? You'll probably get carried most of the way. Anyway, this is my city," I said. "And I want to see it from the ground."

"Oh, it's your city, now, is it?" Beezle said, settling on my shoulder. "Now you're getting delusions of grandeur."

"I'm the one who keeps it safe," I said as we turned north. "So that makes it mine."

"If it's your city, does that mean all the Dunkin' Donuts belong to you, too?" Beezle said hopefully.

My laughter rang out in the darkness, and for a moment everything seemed a little brighter.

Hours later, when everyone had been fed and watered and had bandages applied, I sat on the front porch by myself, wrapped in a blanket, looking up at the sky. My coat had been destroyed again. I was going to have to ask Lucifer for a new one—if he ever answered my phone calls.

I'd showered off the layers of blood and dirt and felt shiny pink and clean, like a newborn seeing the sun for the first time. My own child fluttered contentedly inside me.

Everything I had done in the last few days I'd done for my baby, to keep this child safe. I knew that things were not over with the faerie court, and that Focalor was probably still lurking about somewhere, waiting to pounce.

But I'd killed Azazel.

I'd thought that when Azazel was dead, I would feel complete again, that the empty place inside me would be filled up by the satisfaction of vengeance.

It wasn't.

Gabriel was gone, and killing Azazel hadn't brought

him back. The hatred that had driven me had faded with Azazel's death, and now there was nothing in its place.

Just the ache where Gabriel had once been, and would never be again.

"Okay," I said, my throat tight with unshed tears. "Okay. I love you. I will always love you, and I'm letting you go."

I put my face in my hands and cried.

For the first time in days, the snake tattoo on my right palm wriggled.

I looked up, and there was Lucifer.

"Where the hell have you been?" I asked. "I thought you were dead."

"No need to sound so hopeful," Lucifer said, coming to sit beside me. "You killed Azazel."

"He was . . ."

"Trying to kill you at the time. I know. I've heard this before," Lucifer said.

"It's still true," I said. "You could have made things a little easier on me."

"By sending you after him as Hound of the Hunt?" Lucifer said, his eyes bright. "But then you would not have found the missing Agents; nor would you have destroyed Azazel's army."

"You could have sent me after him before he took the Agents, before he raised the army," I said through my teeth. "Don't you care about the innocents that could have been harmed because you want to play games? What if I'd failed?"

Lucifer shook his head. "You would not have failed. You have caused quite a stir, my dear. Quite a stir. The Grigori are most displeased with you."

"Rein them in, then," I said. "That's your deal, not mine."

"The Grigori don't see it that way," Lucifer said.

"They can come and have a go at me if they think they're hard enough," I said.

"So fierce," Lucifer murmured. "Do you really believe you can defeat whatever comes your way?"

"I have to believe that," I said. "Because every time I turn around there's something else."

"And how is my grandchild?" Lucifer asked lightly.

"None of your damned business," I said. "I told you, he's not yours."

"So sure it's a boy, then?"

I thought about it for a moment, realizing I wasn't just calling the child "he" by default. "I know it is."

"Lucifer is a wonderful name for a boy," he said.

I snorted. "Keep dreaming. Where have you been hiding, anyway?"

A voice came out of the darkness. "He's been going someplace he shouldn't. He's been a naughty, naughty boy."

Lucifer came to his feet, his face alight with anger in a way that I'd never seen it before. "You."

Puck strolled into the pool of lamplight on the sidewalk in front of my house. He grinned, his eyes merry. "Me."

"Leave now," Lucifer said. "Else I will be forced to break the covenant you hold so dear."

I looked back and forth between Puck and Lucifer, wide-eyed. What had I gotten into the middle of now?

"I came to visit with your granddaughter," Puck said. "She owes me a favor."

Lucifer turned on me, eyes blazing. "What bargain have you made with this creature?"

"I helped her when you would not," Puck said mildly. "She would not have escaped Titania and Oberon's court without me."

"Is this true?" Lucifer demanded.

"More or less." I shrugged. "Although I did my share of the heavy lifting."

Puck acknowledged this with a little bow. "Indeed. The diminishment of Oberon was all your own."

"You diminished Oberon?" Lucifer said.

"What, you didn't get the news flash wherever you were hiding?" I asked. "You seem to know about everything else."

"I told you, he's been somewhere he should not be," Puck said.

"You shall speak no more of that matter," Lucifer said. "You have no dominion over me."

"As you have none over me," Puck said. "So we are at an impasse, as always."

Lucifer stared at Puck for a moment longer. I could feel waves of hatred pouring from the Morningstar.

"We shall speak another time, granddaughter," Lucifer said. "But I warn you—do not trust whatever he tells you. He has his own agenda."

"Like you don't?" I said.

There was a faint pop, and Lucifer disappeared.

I gave Puck a speculative look. "Did you really come to ask for a favor, or did you just want to give Lucifer a hard time?"

Puck winked at me.

I stood up, pulling the blanket tight around my shoulders. "Next time you want to tweak the Prince of Darkness, leave me out of it. I've got enough troubles."

"Yes, you do," Puck said, sobering. "Indeed you do."

"What now?" I asked, dreading the answer.

"There's something coming," Puck said.

"There always is."

"And even you will not be able to stop it," Puck said. "I

came to tell you that if you need assistance, you need only call for me."

"And owe you some other favor in return?" I asked. "No, thanks."

"You may change your mind," Puck said. "Remember my offer."

"How can I forget?" I muttered.

He laughed, and disappeared as Lucifer had.

I stretched, wincing as the scabs on my back twinged. Nathaniel had tried to heal them, but they'd refused to be closed magically, and Jude had ended up pouring disinfectant in them and covering them with gauze.

"You'll always have scars there," Nathaniel had said, and touched my cheek as he said it.

"What's another couple of scars?" I'd replied.

The scars on the outside don't come close to the ones on the inside, anyway, I thought, and went back into the house.

As I climbed the stairs I could hear the sound of Nathaniel and Jude arguing, and entered the living room to see them playing Monopoly with Samiel, J.B. and Beezle.

I stood in the doorway and watched for a while, happy that we were all safe, and sad because the person I most wanted there was missing.

Beezle flew away from the game for a moment and landed on my shoulder.

"I know you think you made some necessary choices," he said in an undertone. "But you should think about the lines that you're crossing. Remember that Lucifer's kingdom lies where there are shades of gray."

"I'm not going dark side," I said, stung.

"And I'm not so sure about that," Beezle replied, and flew back to the game.

I headed for my bed, and sleep, and tried not to be troubled by what Beezle had said.

I woke up to Beezle patting my cheek insistently.

"What?" I grumbled, rolling over in bed. "Didn't I earn a day to sleep in?"

"Get *up*," Beezle said. "You've got to come and see this."

The urgency in his voice finally penetrated the fog of sleep. I rolled to my feet, following Beezle into the living room.

Jude, Samiel and Nathaniel stood in front of the TV, their eyes grave. They cleared a space for me so I could see.

At first I wasn't sure what I was looking at. A reporter's voice came intermittently over the images, but the camera kept jiggling everywhere, and it was hard to see exactly what was going on. People were screaming and running, but I couldn't see what they were screaming and running from.

Then the camera finally stabilized, and I realized what I was looking at. It was live footage from Daley Plaza, and the camera was shooting the action just in front of the Picasso statue.

There were vampires everywhere, and the sun blazed down on the plaza.

"Gods above and below," I whispered. "Azazel's formula worked."

What good is an Agent of death when the dead won't leave?

FROM AUTHOR

CHRISTINA HENRY

BLACK HOWL

A BLACK WINGS NOVEL

Something is wrong with the souls of Chicago's dead. Ghosts are walking the streets, and Agent of death Madeline Black's boss wants her to figure out why. And while work is bad enough, Maddy has a plethora of personal problems, too. Now that Gabriel has been assigned as her thrall, their relationship has hit an impasse. At least her sleazy ex-fiancé, Nathaniel, is out of the picture—or so she thinks . . .

"A gutsy heroine."
—Nancy Holzner

M1138T0712

FROM AUTHOR

CHRISTINA HENRY

Madeline Black is an Agent of death, meaning she escorts the souls of people who have died to the afterlife. But lately, some spirits don't feel like crossing over . . .

THE BLACK WINGS NOVELS

BLACK WINGS
BLACK NIGHT
BLACK HOWL
BLACK LAMENT

christinahenry.net
facebook.com/ProjectParanormalBooks
penguin.com

M1139AS0712